PRAISE FOR THE WORK OF ALISA VALDÉS:

Hollow Beasts
Named an Amazon Editor's Choice: Top 10 Thrillers of 2023 and to the *Washington Post*'s 10 Best Mystery Books of 2023

"Packed to bursting with big questions for readers."
—*Kirkus Reviews* on *Hollow Beasts*

"[A] strong action-packed thriller and series launch from bestseller Valdés.... Readers will look forward to seeing a lot more of this tough, smart heroine." —*Publishers Weekly* on *Hollow Beasts*

"With a ripped-from-the-headlines plot, Valdés' novel offers an authentic voice, fine writing and a protagonist with a complicated backstory and one of the most dangerous jobs in American law enforcement: game warden."
—*The Washington Post* on *Hollow Beasts*

"Lots of background enriches the plot ..."
—*Publishers Weekly* on *Blood Mountain*

Praise for *The Dirty Girls Social Club*

"Váldes-Rodriguez's debut novel delivers on the promise of its sexy title …. This is a fun, irresistible debut." —*Publisher's Weekly*

"*Dirty Girls* sets out to prove Latina can mean anything—black, white, rich, poor, Spanish-speaking, not Spanish-speaking. The feel of a night out with the girls … charming … undeniably fun."
—*Miami Herald*

"… the summer's must-have beach book." —*Latina* magazine

"… Valdés-Rodriguez has written an incredible first novel, told in six distinct voices and points of view." —*Library Journal*

"… in the end, it's the complex, finely drawn characters who make the book work." —*Rocky Mountain News*

"… a heartfelt, fast-moving and often funny page-turner."
—*Booklist*

"This season's most scrumptious book … a summer must."
—*Advocate*

"(an) affecting debut that takes a long, hard and funny look at life in the US for Latina women … an upscale *telenovela* with well-drawn, charmingly flawed characters from an author who explodes some myths." —*Kirkus Reviews*

"Valdés-Rodriguez' compelling characters are enhanced by their racial identities but not at all inaccessible to the non-Hispanic … an enjoyable read." —*San Antonio Express-News*

CRY

by *New York Times*, *USA Today* and Amazon bestselling author
Alisa Valdés

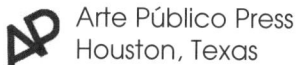

Arte Público Press
Houston, Texas

Cry is funded in part by a grant from the Texas Commission on the Arts. We are grateful for their support.

Recovering the past, creating the future

Piñata Books
An imprint of
Arte Público Press
University of Houston
4902 Gulf Fwy, Bldg 19, Rm 100
Houston, Texas 77204-2004

Photo credit STwul-stock.adobe.com
Cover design by Ryan Hoston

Names: Valdes, Alisa author
Title: Cry / by Alisa Valdés.
Description: Houston, Texas : Arte Público Press, 2025. | Audience: Grades 10-12 | Summary: After being struck by lightning and brought back to life, sixteen-year-old filmmaker Grace can communicate with ghosts and helps a teenage spirit unravel the mystery of his death.
Identifiers: LCCN 2025028002 (print) | LCCN 2025028003 (ebook) | ISBN 9798893750263 trade paperback | ISBN 9781518508844 epub | ISBN 9781518508851 kindle edition | ISBN 9781518508868 pdf
Subjects: CYAC: Ghosts--Fiction | Grief--Fiction | Supernatural--Fiction | LCGFT: Paranormal fiction | Novels | Fiction
Classification: LCC PZ7.V2158 Cr 2025 (print) | LCC PZ7.V2158 (ebook)
LC record available at https://lccn.loc.gov/2025028002
LC ebook record available at https://lccn.loc.gov/2025028003

∞ The paper used in this publication meets the requirements of the American National Standard for Information Sciences—Permanence of Paper for Printed Library Materials, ANSI Z39.48-1984.

Cry © 2025 by Alisa Valdés

Printed in the United States of America
October 2025-November 2025
5 4 3 2 1

"Because to take away a man's freedom of choice, even his freedom to make the wrong choice, is to manipulate him as though he were a puppet and not a person."

—Madeline L'Engle

Chapter One
Then

I was a part-time cashier at a rare-books store when I died, partly because I fancied myself a wordsmith, but mostly to earn money to get things my dad refused to buy me—like piercings, pink hair dye and drugs. As an added bonus, the shop, called Shadowbound Books, specialized in the occult, and as such, it terrified my shiny and hairsprayed new stepmother, a real estate agent named Candi with an i. The bookshop was forgotten, as the best things often are, off a winding brick path behind an abandoned building full of pigeons. Few people ever shopped there, meaning I could write my screenplays and poems behind the checkout counter while getting paid.

Shadowbound Books smelled like dust and camphor, just like its owner, a tiny one-eyed hunchback named Milagros Palladino, who my stepmother thought was a witch because my stepmother belonged in a century where people still got drawn and quartered. Milagros was a self-proclaimed medium (as in clairvoyant, not shirt size—that would be a small) who was at least 80 years old and made her way around the store by thumping a cane hard against the soft wooden floor. She lugged her half-dead pug, Platero, across the shop's small rear courtyard (her tiny, cluttered apartment was on the other side) to work with her every day. The dog was named after the donkey who represents innocence in the famous 1914 prose-poem *Platero and Me*, by Juan Ramón Ramírez. The pug's broken black tongue dragged the floor, collecting lint like a damp rag. You could hear Platero breathing and scratching himself no matter where you were in the little store—a small, soft wheezing, a tinkling of too many metal tags. You could also hear Milagros muttering to the ghosts she claimed she could see escaping from certain books from time to time. She had made it her life's work, she told me, to wrestle them back into their pages where they belonged. I felt relatively normal at that bookstore, like, yes, I was living in a Harmony Korine movie but so was everyone else, like something big and weird was always about to happen. It was also cool that I actually got to hold in my hands a first-edition of Anne Sexton's *The Book of Folly*, from 1973. My mom was a lot like Sexton, in the best and worst ways. Both were prize-winning writers who were terrible at life. For what it's worth, even though I died, as did they, I one-hundred-percent did not *kill* myself like those two flipped-out fleabags. I'd never do that to the people who care about me. There aren't many, but they do exist.

When I wasn't working for an accused witch, I could be found at The Sandra Annette Bullock High School for the Performing & Visual Arts. It sounds like a private school on a Hollywood movie lot, but it's not. It's a public charter school for students interested in all aspects of filmmaking, from screenwriting to directing to acting. Our school was named in honor of perhaps the most famous actor and producer from Austin and occupied an old art deco movie theater building. We had no sports teams and did not miss them. The generation before ours had ungratefully begun to call our school Bird Box High, after Sandra Bullock's worst yet most remembered movie, and, like so many other mean-spirited things in Texas, it stuck.

I was a sophomore at Bird Box when I died, sixteen years old. The school wasn't as great as my dad seemed to think it was, but life had already disappointed him so much that I kept its true mediocrity to myself. We students did a lot of sitting in circles and talking about *feelings*. I sucked at feelings, by choice, because feelings were stupid, so I hardly ever spoke. I was not fond of feeling things, because when I did it never ended well.

My favorite class that semester was 10th-grade Documentary Filmmaking, not because I was all that interested in docu-dramas or, God forbid, TV news, but because the teacher, an old wizard-looking hippie named Mickey who hated big things (big banking, big pharma, big agribusiness, big chain stores, big brother 'in our wombs' despite his being wombless), was always nice to me, even that time I came back from lunch extremely high and told him to eat a giant bag of dicks. When everyone else laughed, Mickey just told me he was holding me in light and peace, with his arthritic hand over his heart. He would probably have hugged me, except it was now against the law to touch students. Small blessings. He told me he was "holding space" for my "trauma." That was the day Mikaela Hoffmaster, my gum-smacking, perfect-haired, Ibiza-going, loudmouthed influencer nemesis convinced everyone to start calling me Therapy Girl. It was not a nickname I enjoyed, but it *was* accurate, so I did not fight it. Since my mom killed herself, it was safe to say I had been getting sent to therapy by every adult in my life—the way other kids got enrolled in music and dance lessons—with the goal of getting me out of the house, in hopes that one day I'd amount to something entertaining rather than depressing.

 Mostly, in the days leading up to my death, I wrote semi-autobiographical fictional short screenplays about numb, re-bellious, tattooed kids with pink hair and dead moms, punching girls like Mikaela Hoffmaster in the throat.

In case you're wondering, my mom, famed Tejana true crime novelist Eva del Río, stopped her own heart when I was fourteen with anti-anxiety pills and a pint of tequila. I was the one who found her. She was 35 years old, face-down in the bath in her wedding dress, with the same Lana del Rey song playing on repeat on her phone in the soap dish. "Hope is a Dangerous Thing for a Woman Like Me to Have," is the song. I stood outside the bathroom door, knocking, for a long time, sweating in my yellow polyester turtleneck and orange corduroy blazer with tweed trousers. I'd dressed up like Carl Sagan for the freshman Halloween Dance at Bird Box High, and I needed a ride. I was knocking because she'd said she was going to take me. I thought maybe she just forgot. Turned out she hadn't forgotten about the dance so much as she'd forgotten that I needed a mom, generally. She hadn't bothered to lock the door, or to leave much of a note. She was literally a *novelist* by profession, specializing in stories about girls who flee repressive cults, and yet her suicide note, which smelled like lavender bubble bath, was only two sentences long: *It's for the best. Let me go.*

You might think there's nothing worse than a parent committing suicide, but there is. A notoriously verbose parent being so lazy and selfish they commit suicide without really bothering to tell you what the "this" is that there was no other way out of. No matter how many different child therapists lean forward in their expensive German chairs, fingers steepled in faux concern as they tell you it wasn't your fault, you never believe it, not if you're a kid when someone leaves you, no matter how they go. They could die, or move away, or never claim you in the first place. Doesn't matter. It's always your fault. You start pushing people away after that, snarling at them before they have a chance to leave you, for the same reasons you might avoid playing in traffic or drinking bleach. It's self-protection. This is why, no matter how many times Candi with an i suggested we go get mani-pedis together, or that I just give the "nice folks" in the youth group at Saint Mary Catholic Cathedral a chance, or whatever else she thought might help us bond, I always pretended not to have heard her, and if she pushed, I stared her straight in her big mascaraed eyes and said, "Nope. Never."

I should mention that I only talked back to my stenchmom when her son, my stepbrother Jacob Garza, wasn't around. Jacob scared me. He was my same age, but the size of your average biker bar bouncer, with the intellect of a beanbag, and fiercely protective of his mother. There was nothing other than our age, ethnicity (another Tejano, like most people in Texas) and the fact that our mismatched parents inexplicably married each other when we were fifteen that was similar about me and Jacob in the least, and we almost never interacted at all. He went to a normal public high school, where he was so terrible at academics he needed a private tutor just to pass algebra, but so excellent at football that all the teachers usually passed him as their patriotic Texan duty, even when he should have failed.

I'd like to note here that there was one boy at my school who got through all my Therapy Girl defenses, and one girl. I had precisely two friends, both of them made during freshman orientation, shortly before that Halloween dance I never went to. They'd waited there for me that night, dressed as Noam Chomsky and Stephen Pinker, respectively. The costume theme we'd chosen was "white male intellectuals who probably smell like mothballs." My boy-space-friend, as opposed to my boyfriend, was Blake Abrams. He was a soft-spoken yet spectacularly witty aspiring cinematographer in my same grade, a self-described "ethnic but not religious Jew" who made me laugh like no one else. He had medium brown hair that he wore long and curly. He had pale skin and healthy pink cheeks and, because of this, his face reminded me of some sort of fecund anime rabbit. Tall for our age, he was narrow as a pencil and fit from running on his own, which he did while listening to political podcasts or vintage punk rock. The three of us shared a passion for the latter, and as freshman we'd begun playing in our own garage band that practiced in the guest house at Blake's place. I played bass, Blake manned the guitar and Lucía Cabra, my girl-space-friend (as opposed to my girlfriend) played drums and sang at the same time, like Karen Carpenter minus the eating disorder.

I should note here, and not that it matters even a little bit, but I have been attracted equally to boys and girls for as long as I can remember. I mention this only because it is one of many things about me that my stenchmother believes is broken and fixable if I'd just get right with the Pope. She is incorrect about this. In kindergarten, which is the first memory I have of ever developing a crush on anyone, I had two simultaneous crushes—one on Christopher, this little boy with a flopping mop of brown hair and sparkling eyes, and another on Claudette, a clever, laughing girl who amazed us all by being able to leap off a swing at its apogee, always landing on her pretty little feet like a cat. That I was, and am, and would always be bisexual did not, does not, and will never mean, however, that I was, am or will be attracted to all boys and all girls equally, as some people seem to think. I'm attracted to some boys and to some girls. I am discerning, like other human beings, in my attractions, and it just so happens that while I was romantically attracted to Blake, I was not romantically attracted to Lucía in that way.

This does not mean that Lucía was not attractive, she was and is movie-star beautiful. It just means that I did not feel that dangerous combustibility with her that I did with him. I am drawn to people who despise themselves, like my mother. Lucía loves herself a lot, like her old school idol, Jennifer Lopez. For what it's worth, the (lack of) feeling with Lucía was and remains entirely mutual, because despite her being a bonafide genius actress—we are talking a young Meryl Streep—Lucía was and is inexplicably most attracted to extremely cis-het boys like my stepbrother, boys who chest-bump each other and fart the alphabet, and do not, therefore, go to our school. None of this is a commentary on gender or sexuality or anything grandly political, and I don't want to be celebrated or canceled on the app formerly known as Twitter for any of this, and I don't want to include a trigger warning on my life because I am triggered by trigger warnings. It's just my own personal heart doing the unfathomable and unpredictable gymnastics hearts tend to do all on their own, without any rhyme or reason to it, and I would appreciate it if we all just left it at that.

Lucía's last name, Cabra, means goat. Our garage band was called GOAT because of this, although we liked to come up with really stupid things it could have been an acronym for, like Geriatric Oddballs Adore Twerking, or Green Oblong Alien Tits. That kind of thing. The official acronym we came up with for the band was Grit Over Authority's Domain, but Grumpy Old Aunt Tilly was a personal favorite among the fakes. It's stupid how much we made ourselves laugh with ridiculous things like that. Anyway, Lucía was very fit and conventionally pretty, with olive skin, a delicate nose, long black hair and large deep brown eyes she emphasized with black winged liner and the occasional false eyelashes. She'd been born in the Philippines but moved to Texas with her mom when she was two and did not know much about her dad. Lucía was a talented aspiring actress who read two or three books a week for fun and also spoke three languages. She was the only one of us who ever had formal music lessons and wrote most of GOAT's songs. When she wasn't taking understated selfies or recording herself performing elegant monologues, Lucía spent most of her time beneath headphones with her eyebrows pinched together in this sort of furious concentration that instantly won my respect. Though she had a significant social following, she was definitely *not* a vapid VSCO girl. More like a younger, half Filipina-American, half-African American version of Aisling Franciosi, intellectual, empathic, and someone who had been unwaveringly supportive and present in my life from the first day I met her.

Blake and Lucía were with me when I died. It happened on a Sunday, the weekend before spring break officially started, which was exactly one week ago today. The three of us went camping together, at McKinney Falls State Park, just southeast of Austin. It's a state park with more than 600 acres of wilderness, and 81 campsites. You can swim there, and hike, and, best of all, get very, very high and commune with nature. We were surprised to find we had the campsite all to ourselves, probably because everyone else had actually checked the weather forecast. I hadn't checked the weather because I'd been too busy sneaking out of the house to go on the trip after my father told me I couldn't. I don't know why Blake and Lucía didn't check the weather. If I had to guess, I'd say it was because Blake was so convinced of his unimportance that he assumed someone else would do it, and Lucía was too busy reciting Georgina's Morning Monologue from "Dream Girl" on a live social media feed. I hated that the last conversation I had with my father before my death was me telling him that the universe screwed up and took the wrong parent. I don't have much to say about that now except that I was terrible, literally a terrible person, and no one should ever say anything like that to their widowed parent, whether they see them again or not.

Anyway. Blake had borrowed his uncle's camper-van. Even though it had a whole tiny kitchen in it, Blake made a fire in the designated pit using dried pine needles for kindling because, he said, we weren't pussies like his uncle, which, now that I say it out loud seems a little ungrateful considering the guy let us use his van. We charred hot dogs on the ends of sticks like cavepeople, then smoked a little weed like cavepeople with cancer. Lucía shared music with us on a speaker. Stravinsky, Sibelius. She taught us about tonics and subtonics in music in her animated and very extra actress way. I stared at the stars that first night, before the storm moved in, and felt small and vast at the same time. She let me put my sleeping bag in the middle of the van mattress that we all shared and had agreed to call The Vatress, her subtle way of encouraging me to act on the secret crush I'd developed on Blake ever since he stopped being awkward and started being graceful. Ever since his braces came off and he wasn't so slobbery. Ever since he stopped toe-walking and grew seven inches taller in one summer. Lucía was the only one who knew about my change of feelings toward him, and she also knew that I was far too much of an insecure dork to ever tell him. As we were falling asleep he pressed his leg against mine. I was pretty sure he did it on purpose. It made me melty and terrified. I held my breath and worried he could hear my heartbeat. For a moment, I remembered what it felt like to be almost happy again. In the morning I woke up big-spooning him. He hadn't moved away yet. I moved myself away from him before he had a chance, and we didn't say anything else about it.

 We got up, and everyone peed in the woods, one at a time, and then we ate shrooms with stale granola bars and maybe that's why we weren't all that concerned by the dark approaching clouds. Even when thunder began to echo low and deep in the canyon we just laughed. When it started to rain, and hard, we ran back to the van. While we sat there on the Vatress watching the storm out the open back door I decided it was important for me to run out into the rain, to wrap my arms around a wet tree trunk, the thickest one I could find, convinced that because of its roots it could never leave me like my mother had.

 "Love me!" I screamed at the sky. "I'm sixteen and never even been kissed!"

Then, just like that, the universe kissed me. No matter how hard you try, you won't be able to understand exactly how hot it was. Even hotter than big-spooning Blake. A lightning bolt is said to have a temperature of 50,000 degrees Fahrenheit. It hit the top of my tree and instantly entered my body. I don't remember much. Only that for an instant every muscle in me fired at exactly the same time, with a stinging, screaming, horrible ferocity. The pain is impossible to describe, even for a budding wordsmith and the daughter of a dead novelist, though others have tried. They've said its like being stung by 10,000 wasps, all at once, or that it's like your body turning to gravy in your clothes. For me it was as though I had suddenly been turned into a cramped fist made entirely of fire, and in the next moment, my heart stopped.

Just like my mom's.

Chapter Two

I didn't realize I was dead until I was already near the top of the bald cypress tree I'd been hugging. The whole forest had gone white and hot, with a loud booming crack, and then I felt myself shoot out of the top of my sizzling head like the thumbed cork of a champagne bottle. Not that I'd know anything about underage drinking, wink wink. Anyway, in an instant all my pain stopped. I was floating, but it didn't feel exactly like floating because I didn't have any sense of gravity or time. I just popped out and then there I was, in the treetops, looking down.

I saw my body, though "see" isn't quite the right verb. I experienced its presence in sharp detail. There was smoke coming out of the sleeves of my green quilted bomber jacket. This was interesting to me rather than horrifying. I felt no attachment to that body at all. It just looked like any other inanimate object. Like a large pot roast someone had stuffed into some Forever 21 wide-legged jeans and capped with a short, jagged black and pink wig. Like a wooden jointed puppet someone had tossed on the ground, with its elbows and knees bent all wrong. A thing. A not-me thing.

Then I noticed two animated objects moving across the landscape. It took me a second to remember who they were. Lucía and Blake. Lucía and Blake were running toward the lifeless body through the rain. Lucía was barefoot in black leggings and a hot-pink sports bra with an open plaid fleece oversized jacket. She was screaming like a weirdo, like full-on, bent-at-the-waist, helpless-horror-movie-chick screaming. She had always been a bit "extra" as a personality, but this took her excesses and innate dramatic nature to the next level. Blake, in gray sweatpants, running shoes and a white T-shirt, was silent as he dropped to his knees next to the body, to check for a pulse that wasn't there, calm and determined as a doctor or a boy scout, one of those. So this, I thought, was death ... and I was still here. Huh.

When my mom was alive, my parents would sometimes take me to the Unitarian Universalist Church of Austin. The ministers at First Unitarian rarely, if ever, used the word "God" at all. Instead, they talked about The Great Mystery or The Magic, and how those puppeteer phrases pertain to things like the anti-war movement and immigrant rights. They honored all the world's faiths, but mostly talked about psychology. The closest they came to asking you to pray was when they directed people to the social justice table in the courtyard after services. Our family walked in the pride parade every year with people from our church, with a banner that for sure said "church" on it, but the organization didn't feel like a church that way most churches in Texas feel like churches. First Unitarian was more like some weird comparative philosophy class for old white people from Vermont who mysteriously got stranded in Austin, polite but dispassionate people who sang hymns about Emma Goldman and the labor movement to break the world's big ideas into bite-sized chunks. All this is to say, I'd never really known anyone who was truly religious in that vindictive-Sky-Daddy, team-sports, school-spirit kind of way most people in Texas seemed to be religious, so I'd never given any afterlife much thought. Even after my mom died, I'd just thought of death as The Big Nothing, like most secular humanists with Buddhist tendencies.

But once I was actually dead, I was stunned to realize I still existed. And it was a remarkable existence. I sensed the rain in new ways. I could taste it, smell it, feel it landing on the earth, all at once, but there were also so many other sensations. I could curl up inside each and every raindrop, fall with each and every drop at once without losing the sense of each drop as distinct. I could understand raindrops at a molecular level, and it was like living inside fractal geometry. The rain was full of colors, too. Colors I'd never experienced before. Colors that sounded like music and felt like vibrations. Everything was a vibration, everything was music. Colors were visible music. I was music. I was everything and everything was me, and I was overwhelmingly at peace, because I understood how all of it worked and fit together like a puzzle.

Something started pulling me away from my body and my friends and the forest then, toward a swirling tunnel in the sky, with a circle of light at the end of it. It wasn't as cheesy as it sounds. It was wild, like a wormhole had opened up in spacetime with my name on it. Then, to my great surprise and delight, there was none other than Mister Carl Sagan standing at the edge of eternity like a Wal-Mart greeter.

As you will recall, I had dressed up as this particular astrophysicist and 1980s PBS icon for Halloween the day my mother killed herself. I knew who Carl Sagan was only because when my equally nerdy friends and I got high, which we did more than we should have, even back then, Blake, Lucía and I liked to watch old *Cosmos* episodes from the 1980s on YouTube. Those old *Cosmos* were *way* trippier than the pompous newer *Cosmos* with Neil deGrasse Tyson. Anyway, point being, I was extremely happy to see that Mister Carl Sagan still had a full forehead combover in the afterlife, because, let's just be real here for a minute, heaven would not have been heaven without it.

"Billions and billions of greetings to *you*, Carl Sagan," I said, delighted and feeling light as air, bowing to the astrophysicist with medieval flair. We communicated telepathically because death was like that.

"Never heard *that* before," he replied with a roll of his big brown Carl Sagan eyes. "Good one."

I floated toward the tunnel like a dead guppy in a fishbowl. The light it held was pure love. I wanted to go to it, but Mister Carl Sagan stopped me with a muppety shrug.

"Sorry, kid," he said, in that embarrassingly earnest Carl Sagan way. "It's not your time."

"Am I dead, though?" I asked. "Pretty sure I just literally got hit by lightning and killed."

"Truc," he said. "You did. But the nature of nature is change, and you won't be dead for much longer."

"But I like it here."

"Everyone has their time. This isn't yours."

"Does that mean everything is predestined?" I asked. "Free will is a myth? Were the determinists right?"

"No. It means your friend Blake down there actually paid attention to the CPR portion of health class. As I recall, you ditched that week."

"To be fair, I ditch health class almost *every* week," I said. "I have overexciteabilities. I am extremely sensitive to smells, especially bad ones, and CPR dummies smell like someone licked the inside of a Barbie's head."

"Blake didn't worry about that, and now he's applying what he learned, to save your life."

"Well, tell him to stop, Carl Sagan!" I said. "I don't want to go back to that shish-ka-body."

"Alas, I cannot," said Carl Sagan. "For Blake's channel is closed."

"I don't know what that *means*," I replied. "But knowing Blake, it wouldn't surprise me. Also, please don't send me back. At least not before giving me a chance to find my mom and ask why that fleabag abandoned me."

"There's still work left for you to do down there," said Carl Sagan.

"Fine. But first, tell me, Carl Sagan. Is this the part of death where people claim they come across religious figures or dead ancestors?"

"Yes," said Carl Sagan.

"So, why am I seeing you? No offense."

"None taken. Everyone sees what they need to see in this way station between realms, in order to feel safe and comfortable and, I might even say, amused."

"So, you're not actually Carl Sagan?" I asked.

"I am, yet I am not."

"That's messed up."

"It is not."

"I expected it would feel different to be dead. I gotta be honest with you. Like, either it would be nothing at all, or it would be sad here. This doesn't feel sad."

"People expect it to be sad here," he said. "Because it's sad for the ones who get left behind. But you'll find the universe has a pretty good sense of humor about everything."

"It's way rad how the universe is just super chill about letting your mom ditch you, dude," I said.

"The universe doesn't like it when you try to use slang," said Carl Sagan. "There aren't many rules here, but that's one of them."

"Me specifically, or 'you' as in everyone?" I asked.

"You specifically, Grace Chantico Martínez. You should stop trying to look cool. It will never work."

"Wow. So apparently even the universe thinks I'm a total loser?"

"No, not totally. The universe has big plans for you. But they'll work best if you don't use slang. Be your authentic self."

"Who is decidedly uncool, is what you're saying?"

"Time for you to go back now."

"Okay, but before I go, could you say billions and billions, just once? For me? Please?"

"No."

"*Please*, Celestial Carl Sagan?"

Mister Carl Sagan frowned.

"Look," he said with an exasperated sigh, like he'd explained this a billion billion times. "What I *said* was that there are maybe 100 billion galaxies and 10 billion trillion stars. It's hard to talk about the cosmos without using big numbers. But I never said 'billions and billions.' For one thing, it's too imprecise."

"Okay. Sorry. Please don't be mad at me now, heavenly Carl Sagan."

"I am not mad at you, Grace. And I won't be, as long as you allow the spirits to guide you to where are you meant to be, once you go back."

"I don't want to go back."

"Just remember, you can find us in your dreams, and coincidences are our way of letting you know you're not alone."

"Who is 'we'? What coincidences?"

"Time's up," said Carl Sagan. "Just remember, your channel is being kept open for the work you need to do. Don't fight the work."

"That sounds kind of anti-union to me. Are you sure you're Carl Sagan? Because I'd imagine he'd be pro-union."

And then Carl Sagan shoved me, somehow. Hard. I plummeted back to earth. The moment before I entered my body again, I heard Blake begging God to save me. Yes, God. That thing he purported to find ridiculous.

"I love her," he said, softly. "Please, G-dash-d, don't let her die. I'll go to temple again. I'll do the summer camp in Israel."
Then, just like that, I was back in my boiled body, and everything hurt. Blake seemed happy to see me again, but I couldn't understand anything he was saying. My muscles were convulsing all on their own. I had a deafeningly loud ringing in my ears, and unfocused eyes that twitched on their own. I heard a distant wailing siren through the screaming noise in my ears. It got louder. Then stopped. Ambulance doors snapped open. Then the voices. Men talking. A radio crackling. I was lifted up and dumped onto a gurney. They carried me off the hill.

Then I was in the ambulance with two paramedics and one gray zombie-looking college-aged guy with a hole blown through his chest. I could see through this, to the wall of the ambulance. Despite this wound, he sat on the floor as though he were sitting at a party talking to someone, with one leg out straight and the other bent so that his arm rested casually on the knee. He saw me see him and sat up straighter in surprise. He stared at me, and I felt a rush of terrible emotions blow through me like wind. I don't know how I knew they were his emotions, but I did. He had regrets of some kind. Loads of guilt.

"Who the hell is that guy?" I yelled, finally able to form words.

The paramedics looked at each other fearfully.

"Why is there a massive-ass hole in his chest?"

The paramedics looked like they wanted to laugh but also did not want to get sued or fired for laughing at an almost-dead patient.

"I want to go back to heaven with Carl Sagan!" I wailed.

They strapped me down and pushed a needle into my arm, assuring me it was all going to be better soon.

Like so many other adults in my life, however, they were lying.

Chapter Three

Salvador Dalí is this surrealist painter from Spain who makes everything look like it's melting under a pale hot sun. He also has the number one worst mustache in the entire history of mustaches, long and waxed into a big smile whose points stab into his own eyes. Just, why? *Why*, Salvador? Interesting painter, but definitely not someone you want to watch eating an ice cream cone, or anything else for that matter. He is the painter who makes me realize you should probably never google actual photos of people whose paintings you admire, because most of the time it could ruin their artwork for you, forever. I wake up inside a 3-D Dalí painting of a hospital room.

"Grace?" I hear the gentle female voice cresting and dipping with what sounds to me like an East Indian accent, all toasted turmeric vowels and rolled Rs. "Grace, can you hear me?"

I nod. This is a mistake, because the physical motion causes razor blades to blossom inside my skull. Right. "Grace." That is me. My name is Grace. Actually, it's Altagracia, which means High Grace in Spanish, but I do not think it was meant to be descriptive of the way in which I am often high. No one calls me Altagracia because they know I'd punch them in the throat if they did.

"Can you look at me?" the voice asks.

I roll my eyes around in their sockets. It feels like there are toothpicks stuck in them, like they're something you might find floating in Joseph Goebbels' martini.

"Where am I?" I croak. My throat feels chapped and peeled, like I tried to swallow a microplane zester. I try to sit up but discover I'm pinned to the bed by a tangled nest of primary-colored wires and hollow clear tubes with some kind of fluid in them.

"Easy there. I'm Doctor Kapoor. You're in the Intensive Care Unit at the Dell Seton Medical Center. I am a pediatric neurologist here. Can you look at me, Grace? Can you focus your eyes and move them toward the sound of my voice?"

I try to figure out which of the faces staring at me from the side of my bed is Doctor Kapoor. There are only two choices. Doctor Kapoor is either the sad, pretty young indigenous American-looking woman with dirty, wet long hair, who is half-transparent, wearing a white dress with a high lace collar and corset and holding two dead babies, or Doctor Kapoor is a solid, cheerful, colorful, healthy-looking young woman in a white doctor's coat, stethoscope and a shiny black ponytail. I put my money on the one who does not appear to be a zombie-ghost hybrid.

"There you are!" the doctor says, with a kind smile, as our eyes connect. Her whole face brightens and her teeth can only be described as dazzling. She seems unaware of the dripping, muddy zombie-ghost hybrid standing next to her.

"Is it normal for me to be seeing fucked-up zombies?" I ask.

The doctor hesitates, blinking rapidly as though distressed by the profanity, then says, "Given what you've been through, I suppose anything is possible. Speaking of which, do you remember what happened to you, that led to you being hospitalized, Grace?"

I consider the question, and it all comes back to me. The tree. The lightning. Carl Sagan and his magnificent combover. Blake, desperately coaxing me back from death. "Was I hit by lightning for four hundred, Alex?" I ask.

She chuckles politely at my lame Jeopardy joke. "You were," she says.

"Some bitches just have all the luck, I guess," I say. It is meant to lighten the mood with self-deprecation, but the doctor just seems surprised and disapproving, the unimaginative type of adult who finds curse words offensive regardless of their context. My dead mother, who had grown up in and escaped from a literal cult that controlled her every move as a kid, had never forbidden me from using curse words. She taught me that all words could be used with good or bad intent, and that it was the discernment of intent that mattered, and gave the example of a cult leader telling people he loved them while doing things that were the opposite of love, and of herself, at sixteen, yelling "hell yes" when she finally got over the fence at the compound the night before she was scheduled to be forced to marry a 64-year-old man, and ran. I didn't have much of a filter before I died, and I am pleased to find that it has only dissolved further with electrocution.

"Bear in mind, too, that you've been in a medically induced coma," says Doctor Kapoor. She enunciates clearly and deliberately, the way you might talk to a small child, or someone with dementia. "You're coming down from some powerful sedatives. So, all of that might be mixing together with the lightning and ... well, the psilocybin you took when it struck you, to produce hallucinations. You can expect to perhaps have some moments of memory loss, or scrambled thoughts, as you recover. We'll be doing a full neurological workup on you before you go home tomorrow. Are you seeing ... zombies, Grace?"

"*Fucked-up* zombies," I correct her. "Well, zombie. One. Three, I guess. If you count the dead toddlers she's dragging clutching to her chest. She looks like she just crawled out of the rubble of an earthquake directly into a deep-fryer."

"You're right," the doctor says to someone behind her with a surprised grin. "Grace certainly *does* have a way with words."

I focus my eyes beyond Doctor Kapoor and see Blake, hunched in a chair in a corner of my room wearing the same clothes he'd had on when he performed CPR on me. His eyes are bloodshot and his hair is greasy. He looks like he hasn't slept or bathed in many days. When our eyes lock, he gives a weak little smile and salutes me by way of an embarrassed greeting. I can't tell if he's embarrassed to *be* here, or if he's embarrassed *for* me, or if he's just embarrassed because that's Blake's emotional due north.

Doctor Kapoor pats me on the arm reassuringly. "I'm sure it's nothing to worry about. Just try to rest and the visions will all sort themselves out, okay?"

"Okay," I say, but I don't quite believe her. I've *had* hallucinations. You don't take shrooms as much as I do and lack familiarity with them. This ghost-zombie thing standing next to her and, as it happens, staring at me with a desperate kind of urgency, is not a hallucination. Or at least she doesn't seem like one. Then again, I have never taken drugs with the addition of lightning.

"It's just ... the thing I'm seeing is pretty upsetting," I say. "It's not exactly easy to ignore."

"I'll ask the nurse to bring you a sedative," says Doctor Kapoor. "Sometimes that can relax the nervous system enough for these visions to fade into the background."

"That would be nice, thank you."

There's a light rapping on the door, and a dark-haired middle-aged woman with a longish face pops her head in, smiling behind her zebra-print eyeglass frames. It takes me a second to remember who she is, because she's so out of context here. She's Dr. Janice Levinson-Abrams, PhD, Blake's mother.

"Okay to come in?" she asks, stepping into the room before anyone answers.

Blake grimaces an apology at me, then salutes his mother in that same embarrassed way.

"Janice?" says Dr. Kapoor. Her face lights up. "Janice *Levinson*?"

"Sati? Oh, my God! Hi!" Blake's mom's face lights up, too, and the women embrace.

"I didn't realize you knew ... the patient," says Dr. Kapoor, as though she's forgotten my name in all the excitement.

Blake's mom talks over her. She talks over Blake's mom. They talk over each other in the excited way of old friends running into each other somewhere unexpectedly do.

"Blake's my son," she says. "They're good friends."

"Ah, of course. Makes sense!"

"And, unfortunately, he's about to make me late for my board meeting," she says.

"Oh! Are you still on the board of the Texas Society of Child and Adolescent Psychiatry?" asks Doctor Kapoor.

"Yes, but this is for a different board." Blake's mom lowers her voice and looks around conspiratorially before saying, "It's for NARAL."

Doctor Kapoor's eyes widen. "Good on you. And brave."

"Well, it's either fight or flee, right?"

"Frankly, we have been looking at Boston," says Doctor Kapoor.

"New York," says Blake's mom, pointing at herself. "Or Seattle. This is untenable, here."

"Mom, you're interrupting Grace's medical care," says Blake.

Blake's mom shoots him a good humored, patient look. "You're right. Sorry. How's she doing?" asks Blake's mom, presumably of me.

"Very well, we're quite pleased with her recovery," says Doctor Kapoor.

"Oh, I am *so* glad to hear that," says Blake's mother. She smiles at me, and I try to smile back but am distracted by, you know, the *zombies no one else can freaking see*.

"Honey?" she says to Blake, tapping her watch. "I've been waiting for you downstairs, but you're not responding to texts."

"No charger," he says. "Dead phone."

"Well, whatever. We need to get going. This meeting is important."

"Just let me say goodbye, in private," says Blake.

His mother holds her hands up like she surrenders, albeit unhappily.

"Grace, I am so pleased to know things are going well," she tells me. I'm not sure that's a good description of "things," but I thank her. "I'm sorry to pull Blakie away."

"Blakie?" I say, grinning at him because I have just gained a new tool in the box of things I use to torment him.

"I'll be down in a minute," says Blake, his cheeks reddening harder than ever.

"I'll wait for you in the main lobby," says his mother. She blows me a kiss and is gone.

"Isn't that something?" says Doctor Kapoor to Blake. "Your mother and I went to medical school together at Yale."

"Small world," says ... *Blakie*, though he does not seem to honestly care.

I remember, then, that Blake's mother is a psychiatrist, and that psychiatrists have medical degrees so they can drug people and take kickbacks from big pharma—or at least that's what my mom used to say.

The doctor's pager crackles to life, and someone on the other end of the radio barks out a bunch of codes. She frowns as she listens, then says, "Grace, I apologize. I need to leave for a moment. I'll be back to check on you in a bit. Until then, if you need anything, just press the nurse call button on the armrest of your bed. It's the large red button, right there."

I look at the button. It is, indeed, red, and big, and has a white cross in the middle of it. More like an X, I suppose, but I prefer to see it as a cross. "Are you sure this won't call forth the Spanish Inquisition?" I ask her.

Blake shakes his head in an approving way, with a half-smile, like he can't believe I'm still a wiseass, but also like he is relieved that I'm still a wiseass.

Doctor Kapoor is already out the door and preoccupied with something else and doesn't answer my question. The wet zombie lady with the toddlers shrugs a sort of incongruous apology at me, as though she feels sorry for me, then follows the doctor out of the room. I am relieved to have them both gone.

"Rude," I say, of Doctor Kapoor. "Guess I'll have to find out for myself, then." I pretend to press the button, except my hand doesn't seem to be listening to my brain very well, and I end up pressing it for real, by mistake. "Oh, God!" I say.

Blake gives me a playful now-you've-really-done-it face and says, "Guess we'll find out if it's a nurse or King Ferdinand who shows up now."

"Nurse, or Inquisition," I say, in my best falsetto Monty Python voice.

"One out of five, terrible drinking game, would not recommend," he says.

He cracks a handsome grin, seems to relax as we fall back into our usual pattern of witty banter, and runs a hand through his hair. When did he sprout dimples?

"Damn, I'm glad you're okay," he says. "It's been a long seven days. Never do that again."

"It's been seven days?"

"Yeah."

"Please don't tell me you've been here the whole time?" I say, just now remembering that he said he loved me when I was dead.

"Okay. I won't tell you that. But I will say that it turns out you actually can live off vending machine Cheez-Its and Mountain Dew for an entire week if you really *need* to."

"You didn't."

"So far, I've only had one heart attack. Good thing this place is filthy with defibrillators."

"Blake! No! Go home. Bathe. Eat a vegetable. Be with family. What's wrong with you?"

He blinks slowly as his cheeks redden yet again, and he looks up at me through his eyelashes, with his head dropped down. "I didn't want you to be all alone if you woke up." He's mumbling, embarrassed.

I feel tears prickle behind my eyes as it hits me, the meaning of what he's just said. *If*. If I woke up. Not *when*. If. He's been here at my side as I was in a coma for a week, unsure of whether I would survive or not. I will not let myself cry. Not in front of him. Not in front of anyone. I am Grace Martínez, and while I do many things, I do not, and never will, cry, because what's the point?

"Your dad's been here, too," he says. "He's a wreck. And your stepmom."

"Stenchmom," I correct him. It is what I call her because her aura stinks, not because she smells particularly bad. She is actually almost annoyingly tidy and clean and wears expensive perfume.

"Right. Her."

"Was she wearing a sensible pantsuit and pearls?" I ask.

"That depends upon whether you believe lime green to be a sensible color choice."

"She calls that color 'zesty burst,' just so you know," I say.

"Senseless waste of the word zesty."

"Did she try to convince the doctor to sell her house?"

Blake laughs. "Holy crap, Grace. Not the doctor, but I actually did see her giving a business card to someone at the nurse's station a couple of days ago, and I heard the words 'cathedral ceilings' floating around her head, while your dad paced the halls looking like he wanted to cry."

"What did I tell you? She's evil."

"She seemed pretty worried about you, to be honest." Blake is usually nicer than I am about my stenchmom. "She's the reason you have so many of those," he says, indicating a pile of gift baskets wrapped in pastel cellophane.

"Great," I say. "I have told her my love language isn't gifts, but demons."

I can tell my jokes at my stenchmom's expense make him uncomfortable, probably because he actually likes his family, and he changes the subject, saying, "Lucía has come as much as she could, too. But it's harder for her to get around."

He doesn't say the implied portion of his statement, which is *because she's poor and lives far away and doesn't have a car and public transit in Texas sucks ass.*

"You could have gone to get her," I say, feeling guilty.

"I didn't want you to be alone, even for a second," he says. "Lucía's really worried about you. I've never seen her this shaken up before."

"Yeah, I know," I say. "I saw her freaking out when I was dead. I had no idea she could scream like Amber Heard. Did you?"

Blake turns even redder and stares at me like he's trying to figure out whether I am joking. "What are you saying?" His forehead knots up the way it does when he disagrees with something one of our teachers has said but isn't courageous enough to confront them. "Are you saying you saw Lucía when you were ..."

A perky blond nurse pokes her head into the room, interrupting. "Hello, hello!" she says with way too much enthusiasm.

She looks like she runs and has girlfriends she goes to trendy microbreweries with karaoke. I would not be caught dead doing karaoke—though I would, apparently, be caught dead by Carl Sagan.

"You rang?"

She can't be much older than we are, and for some reason seeing a young person with a stable job like this makes me feel depressed for being basically directionless still, even though I'm almost a junior in high school.

"Hey, hi," I say. "I pressed the button by mistake. Sorry."

"No worries! I'm Bree. I'm the nurse on the ward for, let's see here ..." she looks at her watch. "For another half hour or so. Then it'll be Tabitha."

"I'm fine, really," I say, embarrassed but also wondering how anyone named after cheese could be that cute.

I notice that Blake is checking out her ass but trying to look like he's not checking out her ass, and this makes me jealous, and the fact that I'm jealous makes me angry at myself.

"Good! I'm glad to hear that. We've all been rooting for you." She looks at some numbers on a white board. "But it also looks like you're due for your meds, so we might as well do a quick check of your vitals and give you your drugs while I'm here."

"See?" I say to Blake. "This is why hospitals are dope. We usually have to drive to the barrio for our drugs."

The chipper young nurse widens her eyes at me in shock, and I can tell she wants to laugh but doesn't. She doesn't know what to say, it seems. I have struck her mute, as they say. Grace, one; pretty nurse, zero. She checks my temperature by running a device across my forehead, then checks my blood pressure. She tells me everything seems "hunky dory" and gives me a couple of tablets of ibuprofen to keep inflammation down, and a vitamin C and vitamin E tablet. She also puts a sedative in my IV line.

"This is Midazolam. It's to help you rest," she says, patting my arm as though I need someone to explain to me what a sedative is.

"I thought it was to enhance the cocaine," I say. "Also, why do all the best pharmaceuticals have names like anime superheroes?"

She ignores me, but blushes almost as hard as Blake.

"You'll probably start to feel pretty woozy pretty quick here," she says. "That's normal. You should just try to sleep. The more you sleep, the faster your brain will heal."

"Thanks," I say.

She leaves. Blake's looking at me like he's very scared, but also like he was trying to hide the fact that he was yawning. He's exhausted and afraid of me, a terrible combination of miserable things that I was pretty sure I usually only inflicted upon my father.

"Go home," I tell him. "Seriously. Please go home? It's stressing me out that your mom has to come hunt you down in my hospital room. Leave. I'm fine."

"You sure?"

"Yes, I'm sure. I need to sleep, and I can't do that if you're here."

"Why not?" he asks. "You've been doing that all week."

"One, a coma is not sleeping. And two, now that I'm conscious and heavily sedated, I am aware that you might bear witness to me farting in my sleep, and I could not live with the shame. Also, because I care about you, I don't want you to have to experience that."

Blake laughs. "Spoiler alert. I kind of already experienced that."

"I was in a coma, it doesn't count."

"No, not here. Well, yes, here. But also at the campground. You forget I slept next to you on the Vatress." He waves his hand in front of his nose to indicate farts.

"Oh, God. No. Really?"

"It was cute. I could almost detect a hint of broccoli from the day before, with a note of matcha."

"I am absolutely one-hundred-percent sure it was *not* cute. Also, maybe I said fard instead of fart."

It's a running joke with me, Blake and Lucía, the fact that there is an actual verb in the actual English language that actually sounds exactly like fart but has a D instead of a T at the end, whose meaning is "to apply makeup." Lucía believes there is no better shorthand for everything wrong with the patriarchy, and I did not disagree.

"Well. You definitely don't fard in your sleep," he says. "Because I am one-hundred-percent sure you are incapable of putting on mascara without opening your mouth into a mirror."

I remember now that I'd done a full smoky eye before running into the storm to get hit by lightning. This makes me wonder just how bad, exactly, I must look right now. And this makes me want to make Blake go away even more.

"Go home," I say as I run my fingertips underneath my eyes, in case I have dark racoon circles underneath them. The words come out slurry, as I feel the meds kick in.

"If you insist. But I'm just a phone call away, except that your phone melted." He gathers himself, gets up and heads toward the door. "There's a landline, or so they tell me. I've never actually seen one. Is this it?" He picks up a box of tissues.

"Dork. Go."

He hesitates to look at me, with a strange mixture of adoration and fear.

"Go," I command him. "Before I lose my composure and tell you something secret that I would for sure regret, like that I love you, too." I absolutely hadn't meant to say this. The truth just came vomiting out of my stupid mouth. I am for sure feeling the wooze now.

He stands in the doorway for a long moment after that, looking at me. When did he start looking more like a man than a boy?

"Sorry," I say. "But just so you know, I already heard you say you loved me first. So it's kind of no big deal now, right?"

"When?" he asks.

His eyes grow wide and his breathing seems shallow. The look of a man coming face-to-face with a hungry tiger. I didn't want to scare him away. I needed to control my mouth. But my personality combined with sedatives made that difficult.

"When you were saving my life with those chest compressions we learned in health class and complained about probably never needing," I say. "Which reminds me, thank you for saving my life."

Blake, who is not usually at a loss for words, seems like he can't find any now. He struggles and finally breaks a few loose, but they only sputter out. "Did ... did someone, who, I ... did someone tell you I did that?"

"No. Did you not do that? Did I imagine it?"

"No, I did it. There's no way you could have known that, though, unless someone told you."

"I watched you do it," I say.

"But you were unconscious."

"I was more than unconscious, Blake. Don't underestimate me, bro. I was dead. I was outside my body and I could see you perfectly."

"That's ... like ... um, that's ... amazing, Grace," he says, but his facial expression is more confused than amazed.

"Thank you for not saying, 'That's Amazing Grace,' without the comma, like everyone else," I say.

He cracks a polite smile, but there's a new depth to the way he looks at me, a fear of the unknown, a bad kind of awe, like a person who has seen a ghost but is too embarrassed to admit it. I can tell that this is freaking him out because as a rule Blake never inserts the word "like" into conversational speech. It's one of his biggest pet peeves. I'm pretty sure he's coming undone because we are talking about the supernatural. Blake has always been clear about being a materialist, about being a cultural but not religious Jew, a proud intellectual. I want to set him at ease, so I try a joke. "I want to thank you, by the way, for not coping a feel when you did the chest compressions."

He laughs out loud. "God, Grace, you're so weird."

"Hey, how are you saying *God* now, but you spelled it out when you were doing CPR on me?"

"You *heard* that?" He looks astonished, and terrified.

"I mean, yes, I *told* you. I saw the whole thing. And heard it. All the senses. I experienced it all."

He just blinks at me as though he has no idea what to think, or say, or do.

"Tell me why you spelled God out."

He looks embarrassed. "I don't know, it's like this Jewish thing. The Torah or whatever, we're not supposed to say his name out loud."

"Like Voldemort?"

He laughs uncomfortably. "I don't know about that," he says, like he's afraid God might smite him for agreeing to the comparison. "You know that old military aphorism, there are no atheists in foxholes?"

"No, I do not," I say. "I try to avoid military aphorisms."

"Well, I think it's true of any crisis. I was so damn scared, Grace, and when you're that scared, I think you just kind of default to faith, whatever faith you were raised with. You just start to really hope there's something bigger than you in charge of things."

"It's weird," I say, trying to defuse the situation because he looks so afraid of me now. "You never think you're going to have to use CPR but it turns out you might. At this rate, we might have to pull out quadratic equations and iambic pentameter in an emergency, too, am I right?" I hold my hand up for a high-five. I am so super tired now, silly and sleepy.

Blake smiles sheepishly and saunters over the bed to meet my demand for a high-five, only he doesn't let go of my hand after clapping his against it. He laces his fingers into mine.

"For what it's worth, it's true," he says, softly. "I do ... love you."

"Can I ask you something?"

"Yeah, go ahead."

"When we were on the vatress, did you intentionally press your leg against mine, or were you just asleep or something? Because I really, really liked it." I sound like a drunk and can barely keep my eyes open.

He just stares into my eyes and comes closer and closer, until he's leaning over the bed, lowering his face to mine. We are both unwashed and our teeth are unbrushed, but I've thought about this moment so much I'm not about to ruin it on a hygiene technicality. I'm so nervous. I freeze as he puts his warm, soft lips against mine and kisses me. It's just a peck, but it's on the lips, okay? The lips. I keep my eyes open like a fool, for my first kiss. His eyes are closed, until he finishes, but he's had exactly two girlfriends, and this is not as brand-new to him as it is to me.

"Does that answer your question, Miss Martínez?" he says, resuming an upright stance. This time it is I who is at a loss for words. He takes this as a good moment to make a dramatic exit, grinning and kissing my hand before placing it gently upon my chest. He backs toward the door, like a used car salesman you've told you're "just browsing" but doesn't want to go too far away in case you change your mind.

"I'll see you soon, Greasy," he says.

"You mean Gracie. And if you ever call me that I will always call you Blakie."

"I mean Greasy. It's your new nickname. You like it?"

"No. I hate it."

Because I clearly have no idea why he's chosen this new and horrible nickname for me, he explains. "You know, 'Greased Lightning.' From *Grease*, the musical."

"Oh, good," I say. "See? Now you've just ruined the moment right after my first kiss."

He smiles as he stands in the doorway, blushing and looking humiliated and terrified and makes flinty eye contact with me. "If you let me, I'd like to keep ruining all the moments after all your firsts."

"I'll think about it," I say, feeling an embarrassing, exhilarating rush of excitement. "Bye."

"Bye, Greasy," he says. "I'm glad you didn't stay dead. Keep doing that, okay?"

"I'll try," I say.

He leaves on that note, and within seconds I feel myself falling into the kind of unsettling sleep that can only occur in a hospital, when you're surrounded by zombies.

Chapter Four

It's dark when I open my eyes again, or as dark as it gets in a room in the Intensive Care Unit of a hospital. There's a square window in the door, and the light from the hallway floods in, casting an eerie blue hue that somehow feels even worse than complete darkness. I've just been jolted awake by the terror of a recurring nightmare. I've had this same frightening dream for the past two years, at least once a month, since my mom died. Sometimes, I dread going to sleep because I worry I'm going to *have this dream*. In it, I'm in a river, and I can't swim. Someone is pulling me under, clawing at my ankles. I try to get away, but the current is strong and the hands just keep grabbing me and pulling me down. Once I'm yanked down under the water, I can see the blurry shape of a woman in a flowing white dress, with long black hair. She's the one trying to drown me. She's crying, and she's coming for me. My therapists (yes, I have had more than one) all have said it is just a dream related to finding my dead mom in her bathtub, but it feels like something else. Like she's someone else.

I glance around the room with my pulse still thundering from the dream. With a shock, I notice there's someone standing in the darkest part of the room, in the shadows, watching me. I can't tell who, or what, it is, only that it is human in shape, a shadow only slightly darker than the one in which it has hidden itself.

"Who's there?" I ask, my voice barely above a whisper. The shadow ripples and moves forward, toward me. I grope for the nurse call button but can't find the remote.

"Easy now," says a man's voice, with a slight bouncy accent. Irish? Scottish? "I didn't mean to frighten you. I was trying to stay quiet so as not to wake you."

I'm about to scream when the shadow steps into the light from the window and I see that it's just a man, and he's dressed in nurse's scrubs. The demon from my nightmares turns out to be nothing but a male nurse with a messy bun on the top of his head. He's holding what's left of a Three Musketeers bar that he's scarfing down like a man who's not eaten in months.

"Do you work here?" I croak.

"Hello, Grace," he says, the back of his candy bar hand over his full mouth. "Sorry. Please don't fret. My name is Kilian, and I am a nurse on duty this evening. I was taking a quiet moment to fortify myself before checking your vitals, hiding out in your room."

"Is everyone who works in this hospital from somewhere else?" I ask. I have no idea why this is my first question to him.

"Sometimes it seems like it." He pops the remainder of the candy into his mouth and smiles with his eyes so pale and bright the blue of them shines through even in the dark.

"I shouldn't have said that," I say. "It was uncharacteristically xenophobic. I'm on drugs."

"Oh, don't I know it. Who do you think gives 'em to ya? Might want to cover your eyes," he says before he flips on the lights. "This is gonna hurt." The buzzing brightness is loud and comes fast, like a knife to the brain.

"Jesus, ugh," I say, squinting. "You didn't even give me a chance to cover them."

"Time is of the essence in the ICU, I'm afraid," he says as he hurries over to adjust the machine to make it stop beeping. "If I didn't stop that infernal beeping, my manager would have come in, and she'd have smelled the chocolate on my breath. She doesn't like us eating if we're not on break, but I was starving."

"Do you people always use the coma victim's rooms for secret snacking?" I ask, and he ignores my question. I probably would too, if I were him.

"I just have to get a better look at these wires. Make sure you didn't yank the IV out or anything." He runs a hand over the cords with the same expertise as a piano tuner with strings. "Nope, it all looks good."

He dims the lights after that and answers my question about his origins. "Dear girl, your country has a health care crisis, in case you didn't know. Not enough nurses, especially. Or doctors. Seems like everyone in America is too busy trying to be a real housewife of something-or-other, or an influencer of other influencers, and not enough of you are going to medical school or doing any kind of reading other than tweets."

"I think we're supposed to call those 'posts' now that it's X," I say. "Other than that, I actually do not disagree with your analysis. Where are you from? Ireland or Scotland, right?"

"Irish. I'm from Dungarvan, originally. I'm truly sorry for waking you. You were sleeping so peacefully. But you're scheduled for a couple of medications right now, and I'll just administer them and be on my way."

As he connects a syringe to my IV port, I try to ignore the gray zombie-like people who have decided to come seeping into the room, now that I'm waking up more. Time for hallucinations, I guess. There are so many of them this time. More than there were earlier. The lady with the dead toddlers is back, shuffling around the room like she's lost something. And there's a new guy, headless and holding a motorcycle helmet, standing in the corner. No, wait. His head is inside the helmet, and the eyes are blinking sarcastically at me, as though in protest of useless helmet laws. Great. Just great. I *realize* these are hallucinations, but it doesn't make them any less terrifying. If I look directly at any of these things—and they are like half-ghost, half-zombie—I can feel their emotions and their physical pain. Why is my brain doing this to me? Why can't I have hallucinations of me winning the lottery and sailing around the world in a yacht with a young Henry Rollins instead? I feel my chest tighten with what can only be a heart attack when I look at an older balding man peering curiously in through the door. I feel a pain in my lower belly, and lower back, when I focus on a new woman who seems to be holding an umbilical cord in her hands. Yep, she's dragging a fetus around like a dog on a leash and seems very interested in whatever the nurse is doing. She comes up very close to him, the way a drunk lady-for-hire might sidle up to a cowboy in a saloon in a Hollywood western from the 1960s, grinning in a manipulative flirty way, and reaches her free hand out as though to touch my arm at the IV port.

"Falbh a nis," scolds Killian, in some language other than English, with the same tone of voice you might use on a dog you've told to shoo. At first I think he's scolding me, but he's looking directly at the gray woman in a stern way that stops her in her stupid creepy tracks. She flinches and slouches away like he's hurt her feelings.

"Can you *see* them?" I ask, dumbfounded.

He unzips the velcro of the blood pressure cuff around my upper arm and avoids eye contact with me. "Blood pressure's a little high. Try to just relax."

"Are they zombies?" I demand. "Because zombies aren't *real*. I mean, are they? They're more like ghosts, right?"

A little wet boy with a missing front tooth crawls out from under my bed and steps between me and Kilian to stare right at me, with all the hate in the world. I feel his struggle to breathe, the lack of air, and I know, somehow, that he drowned and that he thinks it's, what, my fault? Seriously? I see Kilian look at the boy and shake his head in the same "tsk tsk" way a teacher might if they caught a kid about to poke another kid with a pencil in class. The boy looks back at him in abject disappointment.

"Fág í ar lár," the nurse says to the boy.

"You're looking right at him! He drowned, didn't he?"

Kilian takes a medical gown out of a cabinet, snaps it open the way a scullery maid might snap open a sheet in a fancy manor, and uses a couple of thumbtacks he finds in a drawer to fasten the gown over the window. He clears his throat before turning toward me and all the other things in the room, affecting a grand stance with his arms outstretched as though he were a smarmy stadium preacher addressing a large crowd.

"Ye, spiorads who linger near," he says, with great Celtic flourish that sounds almost fake, like a Circle K cashier who dresses up and pretends to be a medieval wizard on the weekends. "Ye, with great unfinished business here, I promise I will hear thine cries, if now my circle, ye uncompromise."

With the last of his strange Harry-Potter-ish words, whose grammar frankly didn't even sound correct to me, the gray people begin to literally fade, the way water soaks into the ground, only they're being absorbed by the air and walls and furniture.

"You *do* see them, then."

"That I do." He winks at me as though seeing horrifying zombie things were no big deal and maybe even fun. "It's the real reason I came to see you, Grace. I noticed them sniffing around your room earlier, all agitated and excited. I mean, I was hungry, too. That wasn't a lie. But mostly I was waiting for them to show up so I could give them a piece of my mind. They sniff around like that when they realize someone can see them and, trust me, they can become insufferable in their incessant need for attention."

"So, are they dead people?"

"Yes."

"Like real dead people?"

"Yes."

"Should I be afraid?"

"No," he says, tucking his chin into his neck as though surprised I'd even ask such a thing. "Well. Not of *them*, anyway. They can't hurt you. Not directly."

A chill trickles down my spine. "Not directly? That implies that they can hurt me, indirectly."

He shrugs and wobbles his head side to side in the world's weakest gesture of "maybe."

"So they can?"

"Sometimes, I s'pose. But they usually won't."

"'Usually' is not comforting. People don't usually get hit by lightning, and yet …" I gesture to myself, in a bed in the ICU.

"Okay. Mostly."

"That is not comforting, either. Okay? None of this is comforting." I'm starting to panic.

"Grace, your chart says you might have been clinically dead at that campsite for a bit. Do you have any memory of it?"

I tell him about when I died, seeing Carl Sagan and the tunnel.

"Did this 'Carl Sagan' say or do anything?" He makes air quotes when he says "Carl Sagan," which offends me.

"I'm telling you, it was *him*. I would recognize that combover anywhere."

"That's what they wanted you to think," he says.

"Who?"

"Your guide."

"What guide?"

"Some people call them guardian angels. They're these higher beings that watch over us our whole lives, and when our moment comes, they help us to cross over."

"Why would my guardian angel manifest as Carl freakin' Sagan? Unless my guardian angel actually is Carl Sagan, which would be cool as hell."

"They show up the way they need to show up to make the person dying feel safe. So what did this 'Carl Sagan' fellow say?"

I tell him about Carl Sagan shoving me back to earth. "He said it wasn't my time. He said coincidences aren't coincidences but God's way of letting us know we're not alone, and we're on the right path."

"Classic," he says with a gentle roll of his eyes. "Almost to the point of cliché. And also not something the real Carl Sagan would likely have said, I s'ppose."

He strokes his chin for a moment, nodding thoughtfully, then launches into his story as though I'd asked him to, which I didn't. "Well Grace, I'll tell ya, when I was a wee lad of eight years old, I fell off a horse back home in Dungarvan," he says. "Well, outside Dungarvan, in Ballykilmurray, the town I'm from back in Ireland, but no one's ever heard of. So, anyway ... everyone says I lost me consciousness, but I know I must have straight-up died. I remember the tunnel, the family members, it was a lot like what happened to you. Ever since then, I've been able to sense spirits. I call them spiorads, it's an old Gaelic word my grandmother used for them. They're souls that are stuck between this world and the next. You will know they're around when you feel strange and see a little smoke or something. Sometimes, like in a mirror, they look almost like people for a second, and then they're gone."

"Um. No. They look almost like real people to me, all the time. Like whole, like they're actually in the room. They're grayish, though. Like zombies, sort of. They fade in and out, from almost solid to transparent."

"Oh, wow." His brows shoot up in surprise. "And you see spiorads, like, constantly?"

I nod.

He lowers his voice. "You probably shouldn't tell too many people about this. Most people won't believe you. People like to attack what they can't understand. Trust me. The only person I ever told about it who believed me was me grandmother, before she passed away, God rest her soul. She had also had a gift of sight, in a way, and was able to communicate with the dead. A medium, she was. She could see them the way you do. She called their world the Orbus Alias. She said it was Latin for 'otherworld,' and told me there was a long tradition in Ireland of people communicating with spiorads stuck in Orbus Alias. I don't know why they pick some of us and ignore others. I come across lots of people, because of this line of work, who've been resuscitated after dying, but until I saw the spiorads congregating at your door, I hadn't run into anyone else who can see them."

"Why me?"

"I don't know. It's so remarkable you can actually see them like real people. A rare gift."

"It doesn't feel like a gift, unless by gift you mean repulsive and scary."

"Yeah. I know. I'm sorry. I used to feel the same way. They don't bother me that much anymore."

"Yeah, because you're able to make them go away."

"For a while. But they always come back."

"I want them gone forever."

"That's what I wanted to talk to you about right now," he says. "I don't have a lot of time. I'm on the clock and I can't stay in one room too long. But I wanted to do a thing, I guess you'd call it a spell, to protect you while you're here, so they won't bother you. My grandmother, she taught me this, and it works for a while. With your permission."

"Please, God, yes. Just do it."

"Okay. Do you think you can get up and walk a little bit?"

"Maybe. I can try."

"Not far. Just around the room here. I think you'll be okay."

I lower my feet in their hospital socks to the floor and do my best to keep the awkward gown wrapped around me, while also holding the IV rack and moving it with me. I follow Kilian as he walks to one corner of the room.

"I need you to do as I do, and repeat after me," he says. "Not too loud, we don't need nosey people coming in and asking what's going on, right?"

"No, for sure."

"Okay. First, the east corner." He lifts his arms. "I call to the east, raise my arms, hear my voice, that your winds will blow forever through me."

I raise my arms as he does, and repeat, "I call to the east, raise my arms, hear my voice, that your winds will blow forever through me." I feel completely stupid.

Kilian moves to the next corner. "I call to the south, raise my arms, hear my voice, that your fires will burn forever in me."

I do as he's done, feeling really weird about the whole thing. It makes zero sense.

On to the next corner. "I call to the west, raise my arms, hear my voice, that your waters will flow forever through me."

Again, I copy him.

Finally, the last corner comes. "I call to the north, raise my arms, hear my voice, that your earth will forever ground for me."

I repeat it.

"There," he said, when I had finished. "That should hold them off for a while."

"What's a while?"

"Usually a day or two."

"So … I'm going to have to do this crazy spell crap every couple of days for the rest of my life if I don't want to go insane?" I asked.

"Hey, it could be worse."

"How? How could it possibly be worse?"

"If there weren't any spells at all."

"I guess. But how were you able to make them go away with a much shorter phrase than the one you want me to use? Seems sadistic."

"Ah, that. I was wondering if you'd ask about it. Grace, the spell I'm giving you is for the novice spiorad seer, sort of an extra-strength Lorica."

"Lorica?"

"Spell. I'm an old hat at it, and I've studied with some of the best elders in the world. You can learn techniques, over time, and you can get more powers. But for now, this is the best spell for your particular circumstances."

"Oh." The disappointment drips off my voice.

"Just remember, they're people," he says, with a comforting sympathetic tilt of his head. "Like me and you. They're not demons or monsters or anything weird like that. Just people who had a bad thing happen, or a surprising thing happen, and they haven't figured out what to do about it yet. Many people accept death and move on to whatever comes next for them. But others are completely surprised by it and don't know how to accept it, or they have unfinished business here that they think they can attend to, but they usually need our help. The help of a medium."

"How is that my problem? I mean, what can I do about their problems?"

"Honestly, a lot. Like, if you really listen to them and get a feeling for what they want done, a lot of times you can help them. If you want to. Okay, like this one lady .... She was hanging around because she needed her husband to know that she had a life insurance policy she never told him about. She was really adamant about it. She wanted him to have a good retirement and asked me to make sure he was taken care of. So I figured out who he was and told him what I knew."

"Was there a policy?"

"Of course. Guy got like almost two million bucks."

"That's crazy."

"Yeah. Spouses really need to work on their communication sometimes."

"Maybe she thought he'd kill her if he knew about it?" I suggest.

"That actually makes sense, now that I think about it. Because I told him the truth, about me seeing her spirit. He didn't believe me. Bloke thought I was having an affair with his wife before she died or something. It was pretty screwed up. It's how I got this." He points to a scar on his forehead.

"What? I thought you said spiorads can't hurt us!"

"They can't. The living can, though. The husband came at me with an empty wine bottle, hit me, pow, right on the noggin."

"Whoa."

"Yeah."

Kilian takes a piece of folded paper out of his pocket and puts it in my hand. "This is the spell we just did. I wrote step-by-step instructions for you while I was standing there in the dark corner eating chocolate. I also included my cell number and my email address, in case you need to ask me anything else about this, once you go home."

"Thanks."

"But I have to ask you to keep this all in strictest confidentiality. I'm sure your parents wouldn't be thrilled to know a grown man from the hospital was giving you his contact information, and I could lose my job for this. It's important you don't tell people about it."

I resist the urge to tell him Candi with an i is not my mother and just nod to let him know I understand. I look around the room, relieved for a moment that it is empty of the gray people, but then I see, with a terrible shock, that there's one left, under the desk portion of the long counter along one wall, crouched behind a rolling stool, emanating a stubborn sorrow.

"Um, are they all supposed to be gone now?" I ask.

"Yes. Why?"

I point at the one remaining spiorad. She's a little girl, maybe four years old, with half her face missing, cowering under the desk built into the wall.

Kilian looks to where I'm pointing, but he shakes his head and shrugs as though he doesn't see her. "Are you seeing something there, Grace?"

"A little girl with half her face missing. I think her name might be Olive"

"How do you know her name?"

"I don't know. I got the taste of green olives in my mouth for a second when I first looked at her."

"Ah. They do that." He looks grave. "They can plant ideas and feelings in us. Olive, you say?" He seemed to remember then. "Could it be Olivia, perhaps? Olivia Chávez?"

"Yes." I have no idea how I know this, only that it sounds right.

"The kid mutilated by the meth heads?"

"Yeah." This also sounds right.

"She's still *here*?"

"What do you mean 'still'?"

"Well, she died in this room about ten years back. One of the worst cases I've ever had to attend to. Grace, look. You should know that when a spiorad is very strong, very determined, they can get through the spells, for the strongest of seers. It has never happened to me that I know of, but you are more sensitive than I am. Ask her what she wants."

"No, thanks." I am full-on terrified now. I do not like it that some "stronger" spiorads can hang around no matter what you do. I do not like it that I'm seeing her and he's not. None of this is cool with me.

"Well, it might seem counterintuitive, but the best way to get rid of her for good is to confront her now, to see what we need to do."

"So we can get rid of her?"

"Yes. With some work."

"Ugh," I say.

"And I prefer to think of it as helping them along, rather than getting rid of them. They're poor lost souls. Find out what she wants. See if you can feel it."

I look at her and feel horrible again. All her emotions come blowing through me like a strong gust of frozen wind. One of them stands out, for its familiarity.

"She wants her idiot mom," I say.

"Well, yes. Naturally. Can you see anyone else? A woman, perhaps?"

"No. Her mom's still alive, pretty sure," I say, though I'm not sure why I know this.

The weight of wanting from the child is so heavy it feels violent.

"Dude, she wants her mom. That's all I'm getting. She was raped and murdered while the mom watched, and it's like she can't understand how her mommy let it happen to her, but instead of being mad about it, she wants her mommy even more. It's twisted."

"No, it's not. That's how children think. In all my years on this job, with all the cases of child abuse I've seen here, I have yet to find a child who doesn't love their parents unconditionally. People are programmed that way, wired to love our mom and dad no matter what they do to us. I had a kid whose mom broke his arm once, and as we were trying to take him from her so we could patch him up, he was clinging to her with his good arm. That's what children do."

"You shouldn't want your mom," I tell her. "She's a worthless junkie."

The ghost girl's face knots up the way children's faces do before they're about to pitch a massive tantrum. A weight of anger fills the room like dark lead. Suddenly, the box of tissues Blake had pretended was a land-line phone goes flying on the counter and slams to the floor next to my feet. Needless to say, this is absolutely terrifying.

"Nope," I say, grabbing Kilian's arm out of instinct. "Just, nope. No. I am not doing this."

"Poltergeist." He says this with interest but doesn't seem particularly fearful.

"Holy crap. I hate this. Make her go away."

Olivia is staring me down, kicking her feet.

"I can't. She can't see me. You'll have to do it," Kilian says.

The lights in the room flicker.

"Whoa," says Kilian. "That's not good. Try to calm her down."

"How?"

"Lie to her."

"Lie to a little kid?"

"Oh, like people never do that? C'mon. They aren't the most rational creatures on the planet."

"You have a point. It just feels worse lying to, you know, a *murdered* kid."

"Tell her you'll help her get what she wants."

"Her mommy?"

"Yes."

I take a deep breath and steel myself, summoning whatever courage I have left, and I talk directly to the furious little ghost. "Olivia? Olivia? Can I get you to calm down for a second please?"

The lights flicker again and go out. The machines I'm hooked up to also go out.

"I can't do this," I say. "I need to get the hell out of here."

"I need you to do this. For her sake, and for yours. The IV drip is on a machine. This is endangering your health now."

"Oh, my God. I can't do this!" I'm in a full panic. The lights in the hallway are still working and some illumination comes in through Olivia's gown, but not much.

"Grace, do it before she causes any more havoc."

"Fine." I take a deep breath and try to find the courage. I look at her again. "Olivia. I can get you to your mommy, but you have to listen to me."

"Be kind to her. Be like a mommy."

I laugh, because Kilian clearly doesn't know everything about mommies, at least not the two I have been saddled with. But this isn't really the time or place to talk about that.

I take a fake sweet tone of voice, channeling my stenchmother. "Olivia? Sweetie? I want you to do what I say, so you can be warm and you won't be alone, okay?"

The tiny ghost stares at me with her one eye.

"Ask her if she can see a light," Kilian suggests in a whisper.

"Olivia. Do you see a tunnel and a light, anything like that?"

She ignores me for a second, the way tantruming kids do, so I repeat the question. Five times. Finally, she points toward the ceiling above my bed.

"Tell her to go to the light," Kilian says.

And so I do. She shakes her head, stubborn little brat.

"Please, you need to do this."

Now, the stool moves a couple of inches, when she kicks it. Exasperated, I look at Kilian and shake my head. "I can't do this. Please, just you do it. She's not listening. I don't think she knows what's going on. She's out of control."

"You can do it. Try again."

"No. I can't stand this. I'm not the right person to be doing this."

"Sometimes you have to be persistent," Kilian says. "You have to outsmart them, and you have to convey confidence to them. I know it doesn't seem like it, because they can be scary, but spiorads are actually very gullible and vulnerable. They are lost souls, and so they will follow anyone who shows them any sort of confidence and conviction. They are hurting and clueless, and if you step up and act like you can help them, they will follow you almost blindly."

"Okay, so how do I do that?"

"Right. So you should probably tell her you found her mommy and that she's in the tunnel in the light waiting for her."

"That's not very nice."

"No, but at least she'll be at peace on the other side, and from what I've felt of it, when little kids are murdered like that, there are lots of loving spirits waiting on the other side to take care of them and heal them. It's torture for her to stay here, because they are stuck in that pain and betrayal, and she doesn't have the maturity to even understand what happened to her. She needs to go there. It's for her own good. People lie to children for their own good all the time."

"Okay." I look at Olivia again. She's trying to suck her thumb with half a mouth and my heart breaks. "Olivia, honey? I found your mommy."

Her tantrum subsides instantly, and she seems to perk up, at least as much as a torture victim missing half her face *can* perk up.

"She's in the tunnel waiting for you. She told me to tell you to go in the tunnel and go to the bright light. That's where she is. She's waiting for you."

I feel like such a massive piece of trash. But it works. I can't believe it's that easy. Olivia crawls out from under the chair and turns her mutilated face toward the ceiling. She floats up and starts to dissolve, right above my bed, and I literally see two beautiful and weirdly tall—like eight feet—angelic women in flowing white robes materialize on each side of my bed, and they reach out and take the child into their long, willowy arms. When they do this, her face heals and she is instantly whole. They kiss her on the top of her head, and then, in a flash of bright light, she is gone.

The lights in the room came back on as though nothing were amiss. All that's left to hint at what just happened is a faint scent of something similar to creosote after the rain. Kilian is beaming at me when I turn my eyes toward him again.

"See? You did it, lassie," he says. "You set that child free."

"Damn," I say.

"Or whatever the opposite of damned is, frankly," he says. "That's what my grandmother told me. The full seers, they're selected for the gift so they can help lost souls find their way home."

"I can't help anyone," I say.

It's a reflex, putting myself down like this. Like, if I can get to insulting myself first, no one else will bother and life will hurt less.

"I beg to differ, Grace. You just did. You have the gift."

"I hope it's a card with money inside."

He grins. "It's better than that. It's the gift of saving lost souls. And even if you don't realize it yet, I believe with all my heart this calling is why you were sent back to life."

Chapter Five

Because all the clothes I was wearing when I was hit by lightning burned or melted, my father arrives to take me home the next day, bearing my favorite flannel pajama pants, a faded vintage Sid + Nancy sleep T-shirt, fuzzy slippers and a pair of underwear. He has also brought me a bra, which is weird because only serial killers wear bras with pajamas. Whenever he makes mistakes like this—and he does it a lot—I miss my mother more than I thought was possible. He also forgot deodorant but brought the bottle of Tokyo Milk perfume I wear only sometimes, which I only purchased because it has a gun on the label, which I think is hilarious and very American in the worst possible way. Oh, and I should mention he's brought me a brand-new cell phone, because mine ... um ... melted. I'm grateful for the phone, but I honestly would have been okay without it, because I am not exactly what you'd call a phone girl. There are lots of phone girls in this world, and I strive not to be one of them, in part because my employer, Milagros, is always going on and on about how much better the world used to be before everyone was staring at their phones. I use mine so rarely I am actually somewhat famous in my small circle of acquaintances for leaving it at home as an oversight. It just doesn't matter that much to me.

Happily for me, my stenchmother couldn't come. Her aggressive optimism and veneered white teeth might be a bit too much for me right now. I need quiet. She's off trying to sell ginormous houses to extremely wealthy people from her church, so it's just me and my dad. When it's just the two of us, he almost seems like the semi-cool parent he'd been before he met her and politely began adopting many of her most milquetoast qualities. Also happily, Kilian's little spell seems to still be holding, and I don't see any of the gray zombie-ghost hybrids—okay, *spiorads*. Fine, I'll call them that because I don't have any other word for them. I guess I could call them ghosts. That's what they are. Whatever. I'm just super glad they're gone.

What I don't expect, and what is almost as terrible as seeing stranded dead people, is the mopey news reporter slouching toward us as soon as my dad wheels me out of the elevator in the hospital lobby. (The nurses insisted on a wheelchair, but I am pretty sure I could have walked.) She's probably fresh out of journalism school, doesn't look much older than I am, and I only know she's a reporter instead of, say, a substitute schoolteacher who hates her life, because she tells me.

"Excuse me, are you Grace Martínez?" she asks, running a nervous hand through her stringy, oily hair. Her glasses are smudgy.

"Yeah?"

She takes a rumpled pad of paper and a capless ballpoint pen out of her jeans pocket and frowns intensely. "I'm Tish Adoeoye," she says. "From the *Austin Alternative Times*? I was hoping to ask you a few questions about the lightning strike. It's good to see you survived."

"No," says my dad to the reporter. "Absolutely not. We are not speaking to reporters."

He shoves my wheelchair past her angrily, toward the automated sliding door leading to the parking garage. Tish

Adoeoye of the *Austin Alternative Times* slouches after us like a shadow.

"How are you feeling, Grace?" she calls out, in the echoing parking garage.

"Don't answer that … *b-word*," says my dad.

"Language!" I say, sarcastically, because my father, ever since marrying Candi with an i, has been big on not cursing, like he forgot everything my mom ever taught me and expects me to forget, too.

"I feel like I got hit by lightning, Tish Adoeoye of the *Austin Alternative Times*!" I yell, my voice reverberating through the cavernous parking structure. And it's true. I feel stiff, like crispy bacon trying in vain to get bendy again.

"I'd love to hear more," says the reporter.

"Hey, back off," yells my dad. He stops pushing the wheelchair and steps between Tish and me. He's usually very slow to anger, but this broad is trying his patience. "Have some respect, will ya? She's just a kid. She's been through a lot."

"Is it true your daughter was using illegal drugs when it happened?" Now Tish holds her phone up as though taking a video of me.

"Turn that thing off. She's not going to answer anymore of your questions," says my dad. "I understand, you're just doing your job here. But Grace is a minor, and we are on hospital property. What you're doing is likely in direct violation of hospital policy and is definitely a violation of the federal Health Insurance Portability and Accountability Act. I'll ask nicely, one more time, that you leave us alone. If you persist, I *will* contact your employer about a lawsuit."

"I get it," she says. "You're an attorney. I know all about that. Which is why I'm surprised you don't realize that if the private health information is revealed to a journalist such as myself by the *institution*, that's a HIPAA violation," says Tish.

"But I'm not asking the hospital. I'm asking Grace. And if the patient herself, a mature minor of sixteen who understands the consequences of speaking to the press, opts to speak to me about her condition, that's perfectly legal."

"No wonder your profession's dying," says my dad. "The only people who can stomach what you do are sociopaths."

"Perhaps it would be better if I were an attorney for an unethical multinational tech company," says Tish.

This makes my father so angry he tells her to go "eff" herself. He resumes pushing me toward our car, and Tish hangs back a little, but still slinks after us once we're in my dad's new gunmetal gray Tesla. He attempts to rev the engine, forgetting, it seems, that electric engines don't rev in what seems to be an attempt to frighten the reporter away from the back of the car. He rolls down the window.

"Unethical, my ass," he mutters. "Hypocrite much?"

He backs the car up fast now, like a bowling ball racing down the lane toward the last pin. Tish jumps out of the way, and we speed through the garage to the exit.

I should note here that my father, after my mother's suicide, stopped being a low-paid public defender and went to work in something extremely boring called "contract law" for a big Austin-based tech company called NexaWave Communications. At NexaWave he has steadily risen in status to the point that he now attends things like the Super Bowl with his boss, the world-famous Smitty, a guy who is on par with other mega-rich evil techbros like Elon Musk and Jeff Bezos.

Shortly before my death, my dad bribed me into applying for a summer internship at NexaWave, in their relatively new "narrative design incubator" department, which, he said, trains and employs talented screenwriters to write scripts for AI, interactive storytelling and chatbots. "It could help with your film school applications," he told me, referring to my goal of one day attending NYU or USC to study screenwriting formally. I told my father that I'm a real filmmaker, and I'd rather die than write scripts for AI. But now that, you know, I've actually *died for realsies*, I can honestly say I would *much* rather write scripts for chatbots than get hit by lightning again. No contest. But I probably won't get the internship because, while I did fill out the application, I filled it out as badly as I possibly could in hopes of being rejected.

Anyway. I don't know whether what my dad does at NexaWave is ethical, but I do know it is mind-numbingly dull. I also know that doing boring work means he has much nicer clothes now, too, and this car, and a perky, pretty new wife to whom nice clothes and fancy cars matter a lot. The one time I asked him about his weird about-face in values, he told me that "in a hellscape like Texas, being altruistic doesn't pay the bills and only makes you depressed, 'and I'm tired, Grace, so very tired, of depressing things.'"

I took that to mean *if you can't beat 'em, join 'em.*

The drive from the Dell Seton Hospital to our *very* new house in East Austin normally would take about 10 minutes, but it takes us longer because my dad, who is driving faster and more aggressively than I've ever seen him drive, keeps intentionally taking wrong turns at the last second. It's like he thinks he's some kind of international spy with this crazed look in his eyes, zooming around weird neighborhoods full of porch refrigerators. I assume he's trying to lose the reporter, though I don't see much evidence that she's following us. Also, I believe it would be easy enough to look up our address.

I spend most of this extra drive time texting with Blake and Lucía on my new phone. I'm still a bit uncomfortable about what happened between me and Blake, so I text him and Lucía both privately, off our group chat, in case he wants to bring up The Kiss—which he doesn't. I'm not sure where Blake and I stand,

and I'm too worried about rejection to ask him. Is he my boyfriend now? I've never had a boyfriend and wouldn't even know how to ask him a thing like that. So I play it cool and just text things like *yo whaddup homie i'm out the joint bro*. He texts back politely and cheerfully that he's glad I'm going home and asks how I'm feeling. He doesn't bring up the kiss, either. I'm not going to be the one to do it, in case he's changed his mind. You know what they say about that box with the cat in it (as opposed to the Bird Box that is our school): Keep it closed, Mr. Schrodinger, keep it closed. Closed, the cat might always be alive.

Lucía tells me her mother suggested it might be nice for Lucía to stay with us for a few days, if I need company. For what it's worth, I kind of wonder whether this is just an excuse for Lucía's mother to have the house to herself. I don't often agree with Candi with an i on much, but when she once suggested that my friend Lucía might be "feral and neglected at home," I did not argue.

Me: I'll see how I feel.
Lucía: I prefer living with you.
Me: Fine. Starting tomorrow?

She texts back a mushroom and a lightning bolt and the words OK corpse. For some stupid reason, I can't stop laughing after I read her text.

"Glad to see you're feeling better," says my dad. He loosens his grip on the steering wheel, and sighs, relaxing back into his seat. "I think we finally lost Tish. Welcome home."

When I look up, I see that we've somehow ended up in our new neighborhood, a place of quiet, tree-lined streets, historical homes and bungalows, community parks and jogging trails. We've only lived in East Austin for about a year, which is plenty of time for me to have stopped referring to Holly as "our new neighborhood," but the last house we lived in was the only other house I've ever lived in. It was the same house my parents lived in when I was born, the house in which my mother died. I'm sure it makes no sense to most people that I feel like I left my mom in the old house, like I abandoned her somehow by moving to this much nicer new place my dad bought with his new wife. The old house wasn't a terrible house, although it was extremely modest compared to where we live now. It was a simple rented craftsman in the Rosedale neighborhood, with two bedrooms and one bathroom, close to the university where my mom taught creative writing. Sometimes, I drive out to the old house and park across the street to watch the windows, hoping to see some sign of her. I wonder what would happen if I did that now, with my new ability to see dead people. I'd have so many questions for her. However, Doctor Kapoor gave my dad explicit instructions to not allow me to drive until she clears me to do so, hopefully that's after my next neurology appointment with her in two weeks.

Our new house is on Jesse E. Segovia Street, near Chicano Park and Lady Bird Lake. This used to be a working-class Mexican barrio, and you can still find some traces of that in the *taquerías* and colorful murals. Like so many other neighborhoods that exist near a beautiful waterfront, rich white people decided it was much too nice for all those poor people and immigrants and moved in and pushed everyone else out. Now, our neighborhood is one of the trendiest, fanciest places you can live in Austin, a place where far too many people wear "stylish" eyeglasses, even though they can see perfectly well without them.

Our house is literally new, as in brand-new. It's a sleek and very beautiful three-story glass, iron and stone contemporary, all right angles and windows, with views of the lake from the top two floors. The house has five bedrooms and four bathrooms, and a kitchen that is probably almost as big as our entire last house. I'm able to tell you more about the Segovia house than I should be able to, because my stenchmother, as I am sure I've mentioned, is an exuberant and aggressive real estate agent, one of the most successful in our city, if not the entire state. She talks nonstop about real estate day and night. She went on and on about how she got a great deal on the "creepy little shack" that used to be on the lot where our house is now, how she jumped at the opportunity to buy it when no one else would, "seeing its potential," which means anticipating the gentrification. She had the former house bulldozed to make room for her dream home. Even though she acts like the destroyed home was nothing important, there are little handprints and footprints in the cement pad in the backyard where a shed used to be, with dates etched in by someone who lived there and cared about their kids. I've been forced to hear my stenchmom tell that same story at least four hundred times, at various dinner parties. I dislike many, perhaps even most, things about Candi with an i, but the house on Segovia is not one of them. It is a stunning house. The kind of house you see in architecture magazines. She has good taste, or at least she had the good sense to hire an architect and interior designers who have good taste. I still don't quite believe I live here. It feels like someone else's house, and I've never felt like I deserve it.

As my dad eases the Tesla into the long driveway—our garage doors are on the back side of the house for aesthetic reasons—he says that if any reporters show up, he won't hesitate to exercise his second-amendment rights, or his "God-given right" to stand his ground.

"As if *you* have a gun or believe in God," I say.

"There's a lot you don't know about your dad," he says, speaking of himself in the third person for reasons only he understands.

"You never said things like that until you married Candi," I say.

"Yeah, well, maybe your stepmother has helped me to get more realistic about life." He doesn't say "than your mother did," but I feel the weight of it there, hanging in the air.

I get it. My mom was a liberal dreamer. Candi with an i is a conservative doer. My mom would have looked at an old shack in a dying neighborhood and would have wanted to write a poem about how heartless the system is; whereas, Candi with an i sees a thing like that and thinks about how she, personally, can profit and benefit from the misfortune of others, which she can only see as "neighborhood improvement." I should mention here, too, that my mother would never accuse me of stealing money from her, but my stenchmother has done so exactly twice, shoving printouts from her credit card app in my face and demanding to know whether I have been using her cards to pay for mysterious charges to an app-hosting company in Bangladesh and upgraded cloud storage from a different company in Canada. It didn't matter that I had zero interest in her, her money and tech, generally, beyond filmmaking, and, in fact, hardly ever used the new iMac desktop computer my dad got me. Candi with an i did not trust me, because I had lots of piercings and worked for a witch, and she, therefore, assumed whomever had hacked her cards in Bangladesh was, you know, me.

Dad presses the button on the screen to activate the garage door and pilots the car into the now-open three-car garage of our 4200-square-foot house. I catch a glimpse of a gray three-dimensional shadow, human-sized, slinking along the back wall, directly in front of us, past the shelves with all their neatly labeled plastic storage bins. It's indistinct, maybe even a little blurry, compared to the ones I'd seen in the hospital, but I can still tell it's one of them. A spiorad. Maybe because we've just been talking about her, I get the strangest hopeful feeling that maybe this spirit is my mother. Maybe she came with us when we moved and isn't condemned to haunting the bathroom in our old house forever. When this spiorad swivels its head as if to look at me, I get a blast of emotion from it, as though it were silently screaming the feelings into my awareness, and the main feeling coming through is a slow-simmering, controlled fury. It feels as though I've been slapped.

"This is so messed up," I say with a shiver.

"Yeah, well, maybe you're too hard on her sometimes, Grace," says my father as he cuts the engine.

It takes me a second to realize he thought I was referring to Candi when I said things were messed up.

"Candi might be as pretty and polished as a debutante, but I'll tell you what, she's a wise woman, your stepmom. You could learn a lot about life from her if you'd just listen to her once in a while."

"Uh huh," I say, absently, still watching the pale spiorad move like liquid spiders across the garage. I haven't told my dad about them and don't want to. With his ever-changing belief systems, I'm not sure how he'd take it. And if he told Candi, with her upbeat megachurch mindset, there's no telling how that would end up. The spiorad, still radiating anger, seeps itself into the door that leads from the garage into the mudroom. Great. Just great. It's in the house now, which means I do not want to go in there.

My dad gets out of the car and jogs around the front, coming to open my door for me.

"Can you walk?" he asks me.

"Yeah. I got this." I stare at his outstretched hand for a moment, afraid to take it.

"You okay?" he asks. "You look a little freaked out."

"It's fine. Sorry. Just a little spacy." I take his hand, and stand up. I tell him I'm dizzy, but that's a lie.

"Understandable. Let's just get you inside so you can rest. Candi stocked up on all your favorite snacks."

As I walk carefully across the spotless beige epoxy floor toward the door to the mudroom, I feel a cold wind of despair rip through me. This is not metaphorical. I actually feel despair the way I feel wind, only it doesn't stop at my skin the way wind does. It burrows deep through my tissues and bones, then blasts out the other side of me. I can almost hear a mournful cry in how cold it feels, how hollow and lonely and terrible. Though I feel this despair I know it isn't my despair. As sad and hopeless as I've felt in my life, I have never, ever felt as bad as this cruel invisible wind of sorrow. I don't know whose it is.

"I don't want this," I mumble.

The despair circles back and claps through me again. It flows through the room like a large eel, in graceful dreadful arcs that remind me of those large dragon puppets at the Chinese New Year parade. It has an energy field so powerful I feel like I can't breathe through it.

"Sweetheart, do you need to sit down?" asks my father. "What's going on?"

"No, I just need to be somewhere else," I say.

My dad looks confused, because anyone would. I'm not making sense. But true to form, he swallows his feelings and tries to be supportive. "Of course. One step at a time, kiddo. Take some nice, deep breaths."

I'm trembling. I'm glad I have the "hit by lightning" thing to fall back on, because I'm a mess right now. I don't think of myself as a person who spooks very easily, but I'm straight-up terrified out of my mind. The weight of the suffering in this room makes it feel like I'm walking through jelly. Or maybe it's the lightning? The meds? Maybe it's all hallucinations and none of it has been real, not spiorads, not the emotions, not the Irish nurse with his spells. I don't know what's real and what isn't.

"It's so heavy," I say.

I don't realize I've spoken until the words have escaped my mouth. My father guides me, ready to catch me if I fall. He's been like this, overly protective, since my mother died, not so much a helicopter parent as a whole squadron of Black Hawks parent, and I feel his fear now, too. Though he smiles and tries to put me at ease, I understand, for the first time, that he's deathly afraid to lose me, the way he lost my mother. His fear, plus the despair of this room, is overwhelming. I feel like misery lives here, this frozen snaking scream, this forever desperation, like it belongs to this garage. To the ground beneath our feet. How did I never notice it before? I don't know how I know this, but I know this floating agony is older than anything I've ever known, and deep, and empty, and cold, and alone. The best way I can describe it is the way a person might feel if they've fallen into a well in the middle of nowhere, and they know they will never escape no matter how long they tread water, but they keep treading anyway, trying to keep the worst outcome at bay but unable to think of anything but the nightmare that comes next.

I don't know what happened here, but it must have been horrific.

I brace myself for whatever is coming next, and head inside.

Chapter Six

I avoid looking around too much and hurry, to the extent I'm able to hurry on my crispy bacon legs, through the bright and airy gourmet kitchen with its bouquet of get-well roses on the big white island, across the chic, modern living room with its pale leather sectional and massive black and white photos of highland and longhorn cows, up the pale bamboo wooden stairs and down the long second-floor hallway, to my wing of the house. I'm happy to find the sleek black doors to both my bedroom and my music-slash-media room are closed. My stenchmom has a thing about teenagers keeping their doors open. She makes her son Jacob keep his rooms open at the other end of the hall when she's home, and it's the only thing about Jacob that makes me feel sorry for him. I'm happy to see my sweet golden retriever Charlie waiting for me outside my bedroom, until I remember that Charlie died last year. Then I notice that *this* version of Charlie is gray, like a dog from a black-and-white movie, and slightly transparent.

"Charlie?" I immediately look around in hopes that Jacob isn't here to witness me conversing with a dead dog. Then I remember my stenchbrother is with his dad in West Lake Hills until after school tomorrow, when he comes back for a week. The dog's floofy eyebrows twitch at my dumb question. Who else would he be but Charlie? He has somehow found his way home after Candi with an i had him "put to sleep" at the vet's after doggie chemotherapy failed to stop his cancer last year. I hear the garage door motor and then what can only be the distinct tinkle of Candi's keys as she enters the kitchen. Whenever I hear her or Jacob coming home, I always run to hide in my room as fast as I can. The walls and floors are thick in this house, but somehow I can always hear her keys, just like I can always smell her Jo Malone perfume everywhere in the house other than my room. She and my dad are talking in low voices down there, probably about me. I listen harder and hear her say, "Ben, I'm sure these unauthorized charges are coming from her. She does it to torment me. I'll just run up and ask her."

No. Please, no. I don't want to deal with her coming up here to accuse me, again, of using her stupid credit cards. I would never do that and I hate her for thinking I would.

"Come on, hurry," I whisper to the dog. I open my bedroom door and motion Charlie to go through. He politely does as commanded, but I realize from his pitying gaze that he could probably have just gone through the door or the wall if he wanted to, like the garage spiorad did earlier. Was it Charlie who I'd seen down there? No. Absolutely not. That thing had non-canine energy. Charlie is pure happiness and that thing, whatever it was, is the opposite.

Charlie sits on the rug in the center of my spacious room, waiting, it seems, for me to give more orders. I realize dogs are as polite in death as they are in life. When he was alive, Charlie had been unbelievably thoughtful. Candi used to try to force him to eat carrots and celery while she took a video of it, because she had seen a dog on social media that liked those things. Charlie would give the trash vegetables a cursory lick to be nice but never actually eat them. He'd just done something like that now, with the door.

I step into my room and lock the door behind us. I immediately text my dad to tell him I'm going to take a nap and don't want to be bothered, asking him to please stop Candi before she disturbs me. Charlie comes to my side, smiling up at me. I have zero fear of him. I *love* seeing him again. I bend down and try to pet him. My hand, naturally, goes right through him. But it isn't like I don't feel anything at all. I feel something, like a tingling and an almost imperceptible warmth. Nothing like the cold residue of despair in the garage. Charlie looks at me as though he knows I had been hoping to be able to fully feel him, and I swear it's like he feels sorry for me. Dogs really hate disappointing you. Dogs will do anything to make you happy. My mom should have studied dogs instead of writing a PhD thesis entitled, "The Poetics of Confession: Exploring Anne Sexton's Transformative Narrative in 20th-Century American Poetry."

I sit cross-legged on the carpet. It smells freshly shampooed. Candi had been nagging me to let the housekeeper in to clean my carpets, and I kept telling her to go screw herself because I didn't want anyone in my room. She seems to have used the opportunity of my hospitalization to override my express wishes for privacy. Anyway, Charlie hops into my lap, to whatever degree he can. It feels like I'm suddenly sitting in a beam of sunshine. I begin to cry. This surprises me. It just happens. I'm so tired, and so tired of being in pain, and so tired of being afraid and confused. He wants to lick my tears away but can't. He tries anyway. His failure seems to make him suspect he is being a bad dog, which he absolutely is not. For Charlie's sake, I need to pull myself together.

Suddenly, Charlie's attention is directed to the wall whose window looks out at the front yard. I feel a rumbling beneath us, and for a moment I think it's just the garage door opening or closing again. It is not. It's something that makes the floor feel ice cold. Charlie climbs out of my lap with a worried expression in his eyes and starts pawing at the floor underneath the window. A sort of silvery steam is oozing through the floor, going through his paws, snaking through the air and slowly taking shape. He can't bark but totally has angry-bark energy going. Like he's sensed danger and is ready to attack to protect me. I freeze, helpless to do anything, just completely terrified and exhausted.

The snake of smoke twists and knots itself around and around and finally settles into the vague shape of a person. It continues to solidify before my eyes, until I see it is a guy about my same age. He stands on my floor with a noose around his neck. The rope is draped down over one of his shoulders, with the free end dragging behind him. His neck is grotesquely stretched out as he glares at me with his bugged-out eyes. The pressure from the noose seems to have pushed them halfway out of their sockets. It's almost as disturbing as his outfit. He's wearing high-waisted acid-washed jeans, belted, with the cuffs rolled up to show off his white Reebok high-tops. He has a matching jean jacket, with a "Beastie Boys Licensed to Ill 1987" concert tour T-shirt tucked into his pants. He's also wearing an elastic terry cloth headband around his forehead, with matching ones on his wrists, and none of what he's wearing looks ironic enough to be retro. He has a curly feathered mullet hairstyle, dark brown. This guy is straight up from the actual 1980s. He grins hello, cocky, like "aren't you glad I'm here," and winks at me like he thinks he's smooth.

I can't speak. I can't do anything. I'm not even breathing. I need to breathe. I force myself to breath and immediately notice the room smells like my dad's nostalgia cologne, Polo by Ralph Lauren, and I only know this because I went with my mom to buy it for him one Valentine's Day when she put together a whole package of corny old things that were in style when they first met in high school. Charlie keeps charging the hanged guy, nipping at his heels. The guy totally ignores him and instead saunters with his floppy giraffe neck over to the wall by my bed, where he rolls his bug-eyes over my mattress in an unclean way, then leans back with a degree of comfort that tells me this isn't his first time doing so. Has this creep been watching me sleep … and whatever else I do in here when I think I'm alone? He looks me up and down and nods his approval, as if it were something I wanted. He gives me a thumb's up.

I find my voice at last. It comes out in a hoarse whisper. "What do you want?"

He just stares at me. I want to scream. To run. I remember Kilian's advice, to try to look as confident as I can, to get these things—these spiorads—out of my space.

"So what the hell happened to you, anyway?" I ask him.

He directs his bulging gaze to the rope hanging from his neck, then back at me like, "Duh."

"Well, yes. Okay. I get that. You were hanged. What I mean is, did you kill yourself, or did someone else hang you?"

He is upon me in an instant, flying across the room with alarming speed, and absorbing himself into me in a cold and gooey, horrible way. I did not know they could do this. I'm helpless to resist and have never been so afraid in my life. I'm paralyzed. He is literally inhabiting me, uninvited. Soon enough I understood why. He's almost, like, hijacking my mind, to show me things.

The scenes all flood into my mind at once, with no explanation. They're disjointed in the way of memories, as if you were watching someone else flipping through their memories in a dream. A refugee camp somewhere dry and depressing, overcrowded, lots of crying. A woman being beaten and murdered while the viewer—I am assuming it was this hanged boy—screams in a language I don't understand. Jostling, fast, backwards motion, as though the viewer is very small and being held by someone who is running, somewhere in the night, with gunfire all around. Sitting across from a weeping man and a toddler girl on an overcrowded boat in the inky black sea. A street, clean and shiny, somewhere in Europe, being spit on by white men speaking …. What language is this now? French? Definitely French. Being bullied by stupid kids in a school somewhere in America, in English, for his accent, for being Muslim, for the rice dish with meat and raisins that he has in his lunchbox, for his long tunics, turban and embroidered jackets, for being an immigrant, for having a dead mom, for every stupid thing bullies bully people for. Then also being yelled at, at home, by a man, possibly a father, who seems almost as bad at handling life problems as my mother. A brutal father who took it all out on this kid. Christ. The feeling of despair. Loss. Hopelessness. More than anything, the sense of being completely, utterly alone. I see the shoreline of Lady Bird Lake. Walking along it, then turning toward home, which is a small shack-like house, on an oversized lot with little handprints in the cement by the shed in the backyard. This lot.

He lived here.

That cold despair in the garage is his.

I feel him goop his way back out of me. He zips back to the corner where he had been before, leans against the wall again, casual as a summer afternoon, like he's waiting for the dead-guy bus. I feel nauseated and have a terrible headache now. He looks at me with a hint of vulnerability now, and I notice that his eyes have somehow gone back into their sockets. It seems like sharing his memories, his story, has healed him, at least a little. This is interesting.

"It wasn't your fault," I tell him. "Why would you hurt yourself if you didn't do anything wrong? If it was everyone else being clueless idiots?"

He lifts his brows at me as if to say, "Like you're any different than me?" and gestures toward my nightstand. The one on the right, where I keep the hammered tin box I call my "escape hash," as in escape hatch, only it's not just hash in there. It's weed, shrooms, a few pills and a serrated steak knife that I use to cut my arms when those other things don't work.

"You really shouldn't watch girls in their rooms without their permission, even if you're dead."

He looks amused.

"Okay, fine. Maybe you're right. Maybe I'm not that much better than you. Or no better than you. I get it. I'm a lot like you. Or, I was, before the lightning. I got hit by lightning a week ago. I don't feel that way anymore."

I ask him where he's originally from, and he answers me by looking at the little globe on my desk. It was a gift from my mother. I walk on very unsteady legs to the desk and pick it up. "This?"

He nods.

I begin to point to different continents, and narrow it down based on his head shakes or nods, to one part of the world: The Middle East. I point out Saudi Arabia. He shakes his head no. Yemen? Nope. Oman? Nope. Iraq? Nope. Syria? Nope. Afghanistan? He doesn't say no. He doesn't say yes, either, but he looks entirely too sad to do anything but frown.

"So, Afghanistan," I state.

He nods.

I call up Google maps on my phone and close in on Afghanistan. I zoom in to a bunch of different places, until I'm able to narrow down that he came from the city of Kabul. Armed with this new information, I google "muslim student" and "Afghanistan," "Afghan refugee," "Austin," "hanged" and "suicide." Nothing comes up. I go to Google Scholar and continue searching. Nothing. Then I use my school login to access the Lexis-Nexis newspaper database and try again. A couple of short local news stories from 1987 pop up. There's a grainy newspaper photo, and it's this same boy, and a name. Mohammad Ahmadi. He was sixteen years old when he died. If he had lived, he'd be 54 years old right now. The article quotes his father as saying his only son ended his own life because of bullying at Johnston High School, which I've never heard of. When I read this part out loud, Mohammad shakes his head vehemently.

"What?" I ask him. "Is bullying not why you ended your life? Was it something else."

He looks very frustrated, as though he would be taking a deep breath to calm himself down if, you know, he were still a breathing kind of guy.

"Are you saying you didn't kill yourself?" I ask.

His eyes light up, he nods and points at me as if to say, "You figured it out."

"Who killed you?"

Now he looks like he'd be sighing if he could sigh. Like the answer to my question is way too complicated for him to get into right now. He shakes his head no in a hopeless sort of way that tells me he himself might not even know who killed him.

"Well, let's figure it out," I say.

His eyes are grateful but pitying, the way you might look at a tiny kitten that just told you it intends to kill a massive moose for you.

I google the school name and find out it used to be the public high school for my current neighborhood until it closed down in 2008 and was later repurposed as Eastside Memorial High School, the school my stepbrother Jacob attends.

"You died in 1987, at sixteen," I say. "So that makes you the class of, what, 1989, if you'd lived?"

He nods.

Cry 73

I google online yearbooks. I find a bunch of them for the 1980s, for Johnston High School, and what I see makes my skin crawl. The 1980 yearbook leads with a page talking about how the teachers and students had to contend with desegregation from 1979 and how uncomfortable it all was for them. The school mascot was The Confederate, as in, I assume, confederate soldiers. I'm only able to see a couple of pages before a new popup window appears asking me to pay to see the rest. I search a bit more and see that I can look at free copies of the Confederate yearbooks at the Austin Public Library downtown. I'll have to do this another time. But one thing is certain: This is no hallucination. Mohammad is not a hallucination. There is no way in hell I could have known any of this. Mohammad is very real, and so is Charlie, and so are the spiorads I saw in the hospital. Whatever is happening to me as the result of the lightning strike and my near-death experience with Carl Sagan is not just a problem with the electrical circuitry in my brain, or the drugs I took.

"I wish this world weren't so stupid," I tell him.

I begin to cry, quietly, for him, for me, for Charlie, for my mom, for everyone who was a victim of idiocy, racism, ethnocentrism, nationalism, war and violence. Charlie tries to comfort me, within his limitations.

Incredibly, as I speak kindly to Mohammad, his wound closes up. His neck just sort of knits itself back together again and shortens to a normal length. Aha! I can help these spiorads just by listening and caring? Damn.

Mohammad notices my relief and looks at me with gratitude.

"You seem like a really nice guy, when you're not invading a girls' privacy," I say in a joking tone.

He smiles, and then the rope disappears from around his neck. He notices and seems surprised, just as surprised as I am. All he's ever needed, it seems, was one real friend. Just one.

How many people, I suddenly wonder, don't even have one friend? I've seen them, lurking alone on the playground when I was younger, or in the proverbial "eating by themselves" scene mined for every cheesy teen movie ever written by some fifty-year-old guy. And I've never bothered to hang out with them. Never even crossed my mind. It's such a simple thing to do, to say hello and just sit with a person. Just ask someone how their day is going. To listen to them. I'd been the worst.

"Why are you still here? Still in this house? Can you see a white light?"

He points at me.

"What? Me? I'm the white light?"

He just stares at me some more.

"I'm the reason you stay?"

He keeps staring.

"I don't know what any of this means. I don't know if I should be scared or flattered. But you don't need to stay for me."

Mohammad is next to me in an instant again, with that "I wanna goop you" look in his eyes, only this time he seems to await my permission.

"No," I say. "It made me feel sick. I don't like it. I can't, not right now. This is all too much."

He seems to beg me, with his eyes, to let him infiltrate.

"No means no," I say, only half joking. "Or were you born before that was a well-known thing?"

He backs off. Sort of.

He's still in the room. Watching me. I am so, so tired.

"You need to go to the light, Mohammad. It's really nice there. I promise."

He shrugs to let me know he doesn't care how nice it is, he isn't going anywhere.

"Seriously. It's so nice. You will like it. I promise you."

He seems to remain unconvinced, maybe even bored. He yawns dramatically.

I've had enough of this, and I want him to go away. I can't deal with his kind and his pain, not right now, not anymore.

I remember then, the spell in my bag from the hospital. I can get rid of Mohammad right now if I want to, and that gives me comfort. I hurry to the bed where I'd thrown the clear plastic bag with my stuff from the hospital and fish the spell out. I read the instructions and do exactly as they say. I clear my mind and try to think of a happy time. I note that Mohammad watches me with great amusement and interest, and patience, and confidence. I don't like this attitude in him right now. I want him to take a damn hint and ooze back down to the garage or wherever.

He looks a little bit worried when I start to recite the words.

"I'm sorry," I say, interrupting myself. "I get it, you're lonely. And I totally think under different circumstances we could have hung out for real. I just ... I need to rest. I can't do this right now."

I close my eyes against him and begin again. I complete the spell and brace myself for it not to work, just because sometimes it's good to hope for the best but prepare for the worst. When I open my eyes, I can still see Mohammad, but not for long. He's dissipating, like actual smoke, fading, and he doesn't like it, not one bit, because I can feel his anger. When he's finally gone, I sigh, relieved. I look down to where Charlie had been, to share this triumphant moment with him, but he's gone, too.

Right.

With sadness, I realize the spell works on all spirits, both good and bad. Not that Mohammad is bad. He's just a *lot*. But I want my dog.

I feel this intense and crushing melancholy, for the world, for the way people treat other people when they don't understand them. Humanity has this incredible spectrum, from being hugely compassionate and creative to being absolutely stupid and evil.

Sometimes evil is just stupidity, like the careless act of ignoring a kid who is right there in front of you and needs a friend but is too afraid of rejection to ask, like refusing to welcome a person to your community who has gone through utter hell to be there, who wants more than anything to be American, too. It's all too much. Why do the best people seem to be the ones who always get hurt the most?

My mother, too insightful and fragile for this world. Anne Sexton.

Mohammad Ahmadi.

Why is it that the Elon Musks of the world, the ones who pretend to care but are too selfish to even know what that means, always seem to be the most successful?

Not knowing what the hell else to do with myself and this new messed up life, I flop down onto my bed and try very, very hard not to cry. I find my phone and stalk Blake's social. He doesn't post much, and when he does, it's usually clips of our band rehearsing or stupid pranks he and his younger sisters play on their parents. He's so hot. I can't believe he hasn't said anything about the kiss or how we've said we love each other. The whole thing just sucks. I am tempted to send him a text just asking him where we're at with each other, what we are to each other now, how I'm supposed to think of him and our friend group. But that's much too risky for me.

I decide to text Lucía and tell her what happened with me and Blake, but when I do, she doesn't respond. Is she busy? Ignoring me? Does she hate me now because she also has a secret crush on Blake, and I've betrayed her? That last one is doubtful, because Lucía's most recent secret crush is on my horrible stepbrother, Jacob. More likely than not, she isn't answering me because her mom discovered the cheating asshole app and has confiscated her phone altogether. I need her right now. I need Blake. I don't know what's going on anymore. I only know that I live in a haunted freaking house, in a haunted freaking world, and nothing makes sense anymore.

    I stare at the ceiling for a long time and try to remember nothing. I try just to focus on the ceiling itself. But the memories come. My mother in the tub. Olivia under the desk. The spiorads in the hospital. Mohammad's memories of war and bullying and abuse. I can't take it. I just can't. After a while, and more out of habit than anything else, I open the drawer in my nightstand to look for the escape hash. It's gone, probably taken when stenchmom Candi with an i came snooping around and cleaning the carpets as I lay in a coma. I'm not as upset about the missing drugs as I am about the missing knife. I could really use it right now, to make me stop feeling all those horrible emotions, or the crushing weight of the dead and their tragedies.

    I grab my earpods and phone and fire up the Spotify app, the next best means of escape, after drugs and cutting. To my astonishment, the app begins to play on its own, a song I would never have chosen, one that absolutely does not appear on any playlist of mine. The song is "Hey Ladies," by Beastie Boys.

    "Mohammad, you little shit," I whisper.

    I've never heard this song, and for the hell of it, I let it play. It's bad. In fact, it's completely terrible. I have no idea how anyone ever listened to this song sober without wanting to stab their own eardrums with knitting needles.

    "If you're going to keep haunting me," I tell the ghost in my room, "at least have the decency to update your fucking playlist."

Chapter Seven

There is less than one minute till the first bell rings for schoolwide assembly the next morning. Everyone in the entire school seems to already be seated in the auditorium, staring at me as though I'm a celebrity they all love to hate, as I limp down the center aisle of Bird Box High's Performing Arts Center to join my advisory class in the third row.

My dad and stenchmom have assured me I don't need to go back to school right away if I feel I need more time to rest, but I don't exactly want to hang around the house, in a room above the Garage of Doom, performing Lorica spells to keep hangboy Mohammad away. He was waiting at the foot of my bed when I woke up this morning, by the way. With Charlie. I immediately banished them because I wanted my life back to its previous level of bad instead of this new elevated level of bad. I also wanted to get out of that house. So I put on my high-waisted faux-leather black leggings, purple chunky platform boots, distressed vintage Ramones T-shirt, gunmetal choker, stacked rings and skull earrings. Then I headed down to the garage. I have a car. Not sure if I mentioned that yet or not. My dad got it for me when I turned 16 a few months ago, a new black Ford Mustang GT that he let me pick out myself. But the car's off limits until I'm no longer super-charged by lightning. My dad drove me to school, and because we were once again trailed by that journalist, Tish Adoeoye, he again acted like he was in a Jason Bourne movie. We got to school late.

And here I am.

Some genius starts playing the "Chariots of Fire" theme song on their phone as a soundtrack for my faltering gait, to mock me in my pain, because people suck. Hilarious. I have a suspicion it is Mikaela Hoffmaster. More than a suspicion. A conviction. There is no one other than Mikaela, my apparent rival and self-appointed nemesis, who is mean enough or ignorant enough to do something like this. She'd done something similar once before, when I threw up on a field trip in ninth grade and she pretended her phone "accidentally" played a Beck song called "Steve Threw Up." No one seems to find her latest antics funny, not even her minion, Lexi Vaughn. Strangely, I don't feel angry about it, as I would have before. I feel … sad. For Mikaela. It hits me like a ton of fossilized cow crap that in order for a person to become so terrible, that person usually has to have gone through something equally and possibly more terrible themselves. I have a deep intuitive feeling that Mikaela's home life is worse than mine. I glance at her and wave a little. She responds by dropping her jaw as though I've just burped up a leprechaun, then laughs at me. Incredibly, I'm still not angry. Just annoyed.

I ignore the whispers and stares of pity and go directly to the seat Blake and Lucía are saving for me. Lucía looks as happy to see me as usual, and Blake seems a tiny bit embarrassed, awkward as usual, but also sort of happy, I think. They both seem surprised I've come to school and get up to help me, which is good, with pitying looks on their faces, which is bad. I do not wish to be pitied, ever. I've had enough of that as the daughter of the suicide lady to last a lifetime.

"Hey," says Blake, all worry and relief. "How are you feeling? Are you okay?"

"Please stop treating me like a thing made of fragile glass," I say.

No sooner do my friends help me into a seat than our school's director, an eccentric named Doctor Andrea Ramsey, spots me from the stage and lights up with excitement. She clomps down the steps in her weird clogs and up the aisle to the row in front of ours and squeezes herself in the empty seat directly in front of me to face me with her lunatic smile. She wears a kimono-like dress today, and her hair springs out in cheerful short dreadlocks that she's stabbed at some point with four chopsticks. I can smell the patchouli oil from here.

"*Miz* Martínez," she says in breathy fascination, emphasizing all the Zs as though she were auditioning for the part of a bumble bee.

"Um. Good morning?" I say, not sure what response she wants after just saying my name at me with grand intensity.

"My *God*. How *are* you?" she asks. "We've all been so *worried* about you."

"No need," I say. "I am just fine."

"Especially for someone who was struck by lightning *and* cupid," adds Lucía for some reason.

I look at her and have a very hard time reading her facial expression. Is she mad? Joking? Bitter? Is this really how she's going to acknowledge the text she left on read?

"*Yes*. My my my. Yes. Struck by *lightning*, by lightning, Lord!" repeats Doctor Ramsey, shaking her head in amazement and totally missing the cupid part. "My God. Of all the *things*. My *God*. What are the *odds*?"

"About one in one-point-five-million over any given year, but one in fifty-three-thousand over the course of a lifetime, in Texas," says Blake, rattling off facts as he often does when he's nervous or wants to shut people down, and totally missing the point that Doctor Ramsey had asked the question rhetorically.

"Fun fact. The odds of being struck by lightning are actually higher in Texas than in any other state. People here have a better chance of being struck by lightning than of winning the lottery, being eaten by a shark or getting crushed by a vending machine. Our state scores highest among all the states for lightning strikes per capita. We had forty-two-thousand of them last year."

We all stare at him, and Lucía tells Doctor Ramsey, "This is why I call him Mister Roboto, by the way."

For some reason, this entire exchange makes me feel like our friend group is still solid, like things might be okay.

"Fascinating, as always, Mr. Abrams," says Doctor Ramsey, trying to quickly move on.

"I mean, I thought so," says Blake.

"You know," Doctor Ramsey muses, interrupting him as though he weren't there, staring off into the distance with a dramatic expression on her face as though she is being interviewed for a Ken Burns documentary about her life's philosophies. "As an administrator of a high school for gifted young artists, you're prepared for any number of tragedies to befall your students. Car crashes. Rudimentary sets catching fire. Alcohol poisoning at the senior project wrap parties. Accidental peanut contact when filming a pro-bono video for the zoo foundation with a baby elephant. Mistakenly leaving a student behind, in the airport, on the class trip to Amsterdam."

"You *left* a kid in *Amsterdam*?" asks Blake. "Sorry, *what?*"

Doctor Ramsey waves the memory away as though she regrets having mentioned it. "Yes, but it all turned out for the best in the end. The student used the opportunity to run away with the circus, and the family decided not to sue. Win, win."

I avoid looking at my friends because I know I'll lose my cool if I do.

"Oh, don't make that face, dear hearts," says Doctor Ramsey. "It wasn't like you think. It wasn't a three-ring circus with lion-tamers and heroin-addicted clowns. Not *that* sort of circus. She ran away with Circusstad Rotterdam."

She pauses here to beam at us, as though we should know what on earth Circusstad Rotterdam is, like we should be impressed with her foresight in accidentally abandoning a student in a foreign country.

"C'mon you guys! I thought we were artists here. It's a world-famous Fresh Street Art Circus. They bring circuses to the streets of Europe."

"So she joined a socialist street circus?" asks Lucía.

"I hadn't looked at it that way. But now that you mention it, all the performances are given away for free. She became a top aerialist and tightrope walker."

"Dope," says Lucía.

"So, wait," says Blake. "They just set up a circus in the middle of the street and start doing tricks?"

"Equitable redistribution of circuses," I say.

"Art, Mister Abrams," says Doctor Ramsey. "Art. Not tricks. Sustainable, accessible, contemporary circus and outdoor art. She would never have done that had we not accidentally abandoned her in Amsterdam. Point is, we're so glad you're back, safe and sound, Grace."

"Yeah," I say. I'm not quite ready to give up the circus topic yet. "But what if, like, you hate the circus and you're just out walking around Rotterdam, trying to find some nice Dutch street food, but you can't, because you're stuck behind some free street art circus you did not consent to having to watch?"

"Oh, I saw a show about that," says Lucía.

"Dutch street circus as tyranny?" I ask.

"No, Dutch street food. I remember it because it almost made me throw up. They eat french fries slathered in mayonnaise, like drowning in it, with raw onions on top. So, also tyranny."

"Way to ruin any food, Dutch people," says Blake.

"Yeah," says Lucía. "They interviewed a guy who had just eaten this horrible thing, and he had," she has to stop to dry heave at the memory. "He had," she dry heaves again. "Oh my God. He had mayo," dry heave, "in the corners of his mouth as he talked."

Doctor Ramsey seems at a loss for words.

"I think someone should introduce a bill making non-consensual circus a crime," I say to my friends.

"It has my vote," says Blake.

"So, Grace, not to change the conversation, but I wanted to ask you," says Doctor Ramsey. "Is your experience with lightning something you'd like to get up and tell your fellow student about, or …"

"No," I interrupt, but she keeps talking as though I hadn't said anything.

"I think that your fellow students …"

I interrupt her louder to nip this in the bud. "No. Nope. Not even a little."

"So you just want to …"

"Get on with school like it never happened?" I ask. "Yes. Exactly."

"Okay," she says, disappointed. "But I know a lot of students have been talking about it, it's been all over the news. In fact, just this morning my office received a call from a Tish Adoeoye from one of the city's alternative newspapers, asking me for a comment about you. And I've found in these things that sometimes it's better to just be open with people instead of leaving it to the rumor mill. You know what I mean?"

"I think," I say, diplomatically, "it would be best to treat me like a forgettable student in an Amsterdam airport, at least for today. Do not talk to that reporter, or anybody else. For my healing."

Doctor Ramsey sighs and shrugs, giving up and returns to the stage to get on with her life. She taps the mic, then speaks into it.

"Good morning, artists!" she booms, pronouncing it arTEESTS. "Nice to see so many smiling faces. First order of business, Lingqun Li has had his short film, *West of Eden*, accepted in the youth filmmaker contest at the Austin Film Festival, and ..."

Here she is interrupted by everyone in the ninth grade cheering for Lingqun, who is only a freshman but is already on course to kick all of our asses.

"Pipe down," says Doctor Ramsey. "Not to diminish Mister Li's accomplishment, but he has asked that we help him find a replacement for his shift next Thursday afternoon working at the Making Sandwiches Cafe. He needs to be in a planning meeting with the festival committee and can't make the shift. If you can cover it, please visit the school website and sign up."

The Making Sandwiches Cafe is a real cafe owned by our school. It's attached to the real art deco theater in downtown Austin where our school is housed and named for one of Sandra Bullock's least well-known films, an arthouse short called "Making Sandwiches," that she directed, wrote and produced. (Classes are held in another adjacent building that used to be a bank.) Students can take shifts at the cafe for college work-study credits and earn money, though many of us take shifts there just to hang out because famous film stars and directors who come to town are now in the habit of stopping in to give us an autographed photo for the Wall of Fame.

"Second item of business," says Doctor Ramsey. "I would like to remind all you sophomores that your tenth-grade documentary topic is due to your advisor by the end of the school day this Friday. That's two days from now." She holds up two fingers in case we've forgotten how to count to two. "I think about half of you have already turned in your topics, but the rest of you? It's time to get your focus on. If you can't think of something on your own, we have a basket of assignments that you can use, on the desk in my office. These are real prompts and loglines from people we know in the industry. Let's be honest here .... If you want to work in the film business, lots of your paid work is going to consist of realizing someone else's idea to the best of your ability. If that's not your cup of tea, then we are eager and waiting to see what topic you've decided to chase all on your own. If you need an extension, talk to your advisor. But extensions are only being given in truly unusual, extenuating and possibly surreal circumstances."

    At this she takes a break to look at me, because of course she does. I am now the Bird Box High poster girl for extenuating circumstances, apparently. I feel everyone looking at me and try to pretend they aren't by keeping my eyes on the stage instead. I pretend there is something interesting in the shadows toward the back of the stage, except it turns out that there actually is something interesting in the shadows toward the back of the stage.

    "Everyone else," says Doctor Ramsey, "will need to get those sophomore film projects done and screened. This year, we have a panel of well-known Hollywood directors, actors, producers and writers judging our sophomore films at the Sandra Annette Bullock High School for the Performing & Visual Arts Film Festival, or as we like to call it, Sab-*hiss*-pah-vaf-*ff*, so please do your best. Those students with the top three films will earn college scholarship money and a trip to Los Angeles, where their films will be shown at the top agencies, to actual agents. Don't slack off on this."

    I see the little dead boy standing upstage right, watching the rest of us. He looks like he's maybe in first or second grade, with the kind of slicked-back short hair I associate with racist football coaches from the 1950s. He wears jeans and a striped button-down shirt, a jacket and shiny black shoes. He looks proper and formal as children from that time period seem to, at least in movies. His eyes rove over the crowd of students, and when he sees that I can see him, his unnerving stare settles on me. I avert my gaze then and instinctively grab Blake's arm.

"Crap, crap, crap," I say under my breath. I realize I left the Lorica spell paper on my desk at home and do not have it memorized yet.

"What's wrong?" he asks in a whisper.

"Nothing. Something. I don't know."

"Is she okay?" Lucía asks Blake.

"Yes," I answer for him.

Onstage, Doctor Ramsey is still talking. I try to pay attention as she says, "Fourth item of business, I would like to share the wonderful news with all of you that one of our own students, Mikaela Hoffmaster, has been selected as this year's recipient for the New Mexico Film Office's 'George R. R. Martin Most Promising Youth Screenwriter Grant' in the amount of five-thousand dollars!"

The students all clap tepidly, and so I let go of Blake's hand and pretend to clap, too. I waggle my hands as though both wrists are broken. Mikaela makes the most of her moment, oblivious to how much most of us dislike her, standing up and waving with the polish of a politician. Mikaela is always winning minor awards in other states for her mediocre horror and fantasy projects. It doesn't hurt that her family is one of the wealthiest and most politically connected in the nation, and that she has better equipment at home than we even have here at Bird Box High. It's well-known that her dad hires actual SAG actors for her projects, and union crew members, and professional screenwriters to give her scripts "a polish," and that the family knows several rich and famous people and leverages those relationships on Mikaela's behalf.

"Mother-fracker," says Lucía, who had done a Kickstarter to raise money so she could also enter that contest. Did I mention it costs money to enter the contests that give aspiring filmmakers money? Yeah.

"Like she *needs* a grant," mutters Blake.

"Exactly," I say, though in all honesty, none of the three of us are from impoverished families like some of the other kids at school.

"Come on up, honey," says Doctor Ramsey.

Mikaela does a coy "who me" gesture with her long, manicured fingertips to her collarbone and pretends to be embarrassed. She leaves her row and starts up the steps to the stage, presumably to stand there in her designer clothes and talk about her experience with the contest she's won. It wouldn't have been the first time she stands there flipping her perfect shiny hair and saying she's "humbled" when, in fact, she's the exact opposite of humble from the moment she was born.

The little dead boy has other plans for her, however.

With a mischievous grin, he runs to the apron of the stage and waits for Mikaela to arrive. I can see now that he is a little chubster with a pot belly. He is cute and evil, a kid who embodies the word menace, the kind who might put a firecracker in a frog's butt. As Mikaela starts to walk across the apron toward the podium, the little imp sticks out one of his dead feet, right in her path. She is busy looking out at her friends and smiling at them as though they were fans, waving like a damn beauty pageant queen. When her foot passes over the spot where the ghost boy's foot is, she loses her balance, trips and, arms windmilling like a cartoon character's, falls.

Flat on her face.

And when her phone flies out of her hands and skids across the floor, it begins playing the theme to *Chariots of Fire*. Mystery solved.

The little dead kid finds this hilarious. He pantomimes laughing and points at her as if he were saying "Oooh, burn! In your face, Mikaela Hoffmaster!" He is all about the physical comedy, a real mini Charlie Chaplin this one.

The crowd gives off a collective gasp, then is silent. Mikaela does what all people who aren't disabled or killed by their falls tend to do. She tries to laugh it off.

"I'm okay, I'm okay," she says, over and over, as she stands up. She gets the phone and turns the song off. "I meant to do that," she jokes. "Ta-da!"

She has no idea that the dead boy is dancing all around her now, making faces at her.

I kind of love him for it.

I try to control myself, but watching him strut around and hold his fat little belly while he ho-ho-hoes at Mikaela Hoffmaster like a little Buster Keaton, I can't help myself. She has been nothing but awful to me since we both started the ninth grade, almost like she's been trying to live up to the "mean girl" stereotype.

I start to laugh too. At him, mind you. Not at her. But no one else seems able to see him, and no one else is making a sound, so everyone most definitely must assume I'm just being a raging witch toward Mikaela Hoffmaster. Except the dead boy. He looks over at me and gloats at me, pleased that I'm a fan of his work.

"I'm so sorry, everyone," I say, unable to stop all my pent-up giggles now. I get up to limp as fast as I can out of the theater before I laugh so hard I piss myself or something. "The doctors said I might laugh at weird times," I call out, lying. "It's the lightning."

The lie seems to do the trick, as they all nod in relieved understanding. I have to be careful not to use it too much as a crutch, because I can probably get away with almost anything now.

Blake and Lucía, being the most loyal friends even with everything weird going on, get up to help me escape.

"Congratulations, Mikaela!" I call out as I limp, leaning on my friends, toward the exit. "Sorry, oh God." I start laughing again.

"This is the best moment of my life, I think," says Lucía under her breath.

"It's kind of amazing," agrees Blake.

Then, like floodgates that can't contain the weight of water, Blake and Lucía burst out laughing, too. This leads to a few other students laughing, which, because laughing is contagious, leads to the entire auditorium laughing, except for Doctor Ramsey and Mikaela Hoffmaster.

"Hey, let's hear it for Amazing Grace Martínez," sneers Mikaela into the microphone. She takes it out of the mic stand and clutches it in her fist so she can run to the edge of the stage to get closer to me as she yells about me into it.

She knows I hate when people call me Amazing Grace. She is doing it on purpose.

"Come on, you guys! Show her some love. The lightning made her do it! Bless her heart. Amazing Grace, ladies and gentlemen! Amazing Grace, how sweet the light-ning."

Her "kindness" is all for show. Two weeks ago, she cornered me in the girls' bathroom and told me she was "going to wipe the school's ass" with my "blood" by beating me in every competition and contest possible. I told her to work on her metaphors and imagery because they were mixed at best. Although I thought maybe death made me nicer, because of being able to feel the pain of Olivia and Mohammad, I find that, yep, I still greatly dislike Mikaela.

As Blake opens the side exit door for me, all my fellow students burst into applause. I turn back to see they are giving me a standing ovation. For laughing at the mean and powerful girl most of us probably secretly resent.

My friends and I sit down on one of the antique carved wooden benches in the lobby.

"I mean, I kind of feel bad for her, but ..." says Blake.

The little menace has followed us out of the theater. He wanders over to the antique popcorn machine in the corner and hangs out there, watching me with a playfully threatening grin, the way someone might look at you if they wanted to throw you fully clothed into a swimming pool for fun. He's rubbing his hands together like a black-and-white silent film villain. When he sees me looking at him, he starts to do a little tap dance with jazz hands, as though trying to make me laugh.

"Why?" says Lucía to Blake. "She's literally in there right now insulting Grace, who is apparently your girlfriend now."

Lucía seems to notice that I'm distracted and says, "Hello, woo-hoo, anybody home?" while waving her hand in front of my face.

"Yeah. Hi. Sorry."

Only now do I realize she's said something about me being Blake's girlfriend. This statement hangs in the air for a minute.

"So, yes, I got your texts about 'the kiss,'" Lucía tells me. "I just wasn't sure what to say about it, so I didn't respond. But I feel like someone has to acknowledge it because you're both acting weird now."

"I mean, there are many reasons I'm acting weird right now, because, *lightning*," I say. Most of which, I think but do not say, I cannot tell them.

"And you?" says Lucía, to Blake. "What's your excuse?"

He looks more embarrassed than usual. "Yeah, I don't know," says Blake, and my heart sinks.

"Oh," says Lucía to Blake. Surprised. "It's just, Grace said …"

I am shaking my head at her to get her to please for the love of God shut up. I shouldn't have told her about the kiss. Why the hell did I do that?

"Right. Okay. Never mind," she says, holding her hands up like someone trying to show the police they aren't holding any weapons. "Just ignore me."

"I-I need to use the restroom," I say.

It's a lie. I mean, I could pee, I guess. But it's not urgent. What *is* urgent is getting away from Blake, now that it seems like I've read everything all wrong and made things extremely weird with our friend group.

"Do you want me to come with?" asks Lucía.

"No. And I don't want you to come either, buddy," I tell Blake, hoping to lighten the mood. Buddy? Jesus H Christ. Why did I say that?

"Got it, pal," he says, seeming hurt by this, and he salutes me.

I hobble to the old theater bathroom that is now the girls' john, lock myself in a stall, take my phone out of my backpack and take it off airplane mode before doing a Google search for "ghost," "Starlight Harrison Cinema," which is the old name for the theater that became our school, and "Austin."

Sure enough, a couple of articles pop up, but so does a text from Blake. I'm about to read it when the latch clicks and the stall door pops open. I'm not using the toilet, so I'm not worried about that, but I am worried about the fact that the little naughty spiorad boy is standing nearby, laughing and pointing to the door to let me know he was responsible for this. I remember now that students are always reporting problems with this bathroom—the sinks leak and the toilets flush themselves before you're finished, or the door latches seem weak, or the hand dryers come on at weird times all by themselves.

"Who are you?" I ask the spiorad. "What do you want?"

His contented expression shocks me. He appears to want nothing. He has everything he wants. I don't get any of the usual dread and sorrow from this spiorad that I've gotten from the others. This dead kid is perfectly happy just the way he is, stuck in our school's performance center.

"I don't suppose I could interest you in going into the light?" I ask him, feeling weirdly like a Jehovah's Witness trying to convert someone outside a supermarket.

The little boy clutches his belly and silently "ho ho hos," then scampers through the main door, back out into the lobby.

"What the actual …?" I mutter to myself. I lock the stall again and call up Blake's text.

Blake: R we cool?

Me: Define cool.

He texts back a screenshot from an online dictionary for the word cool. I need to just face this head-on, because Blake is even worse at being vulnerable than I am.

Me: What are we to each other now?

Blake: Will U B my GF, Greasy?

Relief washes over me. "Yes!" I say out loud. I am not proud to admit I even add a fist pump. I'm glad no one is here to see that.

Me: Only if you stop calling me Greasy.

Blake: OK. Stop hiding from your feelings by pretending to poop and come back now?

After I read through the articles I'd found and learn about the origins of this little obnoxious spiorad, I return to my friends in the lobby. There's the little ghost now attempting to do blowfish on the window of the old ticket box while also making the armpit fart gesture so popular with fifth graders. When he sees me noticing him, he grins and flies up to the very high ceiling and comes to rest on the massive old deco chandelier. He waves down at me, and I try to ignore him.

Lucía smiles when she sees me and immediately says, "Relax, girl. He told me. You're a thing. 'Grake' is a thing. Yay."

"I don't like 'Grake,'" says Blake. "Sounds too much like Drake."

"Fine. How about Glake?" says Lucía.

"Sounds like a fake glock," I say.

"Which, it should be noted, is still enough to get you shot by Austin police," says Blake.

"Blace, then," says Lucía.

"No," I say. "Please stop."

"Whatever. You two dumbbells are a thing, and I'm cool with it. Other than you sticking your tongues down each other's throats and me always feeling like the third wheel on a bicycle, I'm going to assume nothing else about us changes."

"Wouldn't that just be a tricycle?" says Blake. "And as such imminently more stable than a bicycle."

"Shut up, Mister Roboto, I'm trying to feel sorry for myself."

"Thank you for understanding," I say. Lucía and I embrace. "Nothing changes. We still love you."

"Just not like we love each other," says Blake, and Lucía pretends to stick her finger down her throat.

"Why do you think I put Grace in the middle on the Vatress, fools?" she asks. "I *made* this happen, as far as I'm concerned. I should be a matchmaker, I swear to God. And, speaking of which, if you are so inclined to return the favor, Grace, set me up with your stepbrother."

"Gross," I say. "Jacob is about as smart as a sack of hammers."

"Exactly how I like them now," says Lucía. "Strong and silent. Give me all the talkin' space."

Blake pats Lucía on the back. "Well done, you."

I sneak a look up at the boy ghost and see that he has begun to swing on the light fixture as though he were on a playground. Again, he grins and waves, like he's trying to make me laugh. The kid seems like he was born to be an entertainer.

"You guys," I say, trying to change the subject and also putting out feelers to see if they're open to hearing about spiorads and my newfound abilities. "Listen to this article I found. 'The Performing Arts Center at the Sandra Annette Bullock High School for the Performing and Visual Arts, formerly known as the Starlight Harrison Theater, is not only an art deco gem in the city of Austin, it is home to two of the city's most notorious ghosts."

"Ugh. Why did that reporter write the phrase 'the city' twice in one sentence," says Blake.

"Is that a local paper?" asks Lucía.

"One of the alternative weeklies," I say.

"They need better editors," says Lucía.

"Please shut up for two seconds and let me finish reading it to you," I say.

"You're pretty mean, for a corpse," says Lucía.

"Shut up, assholes," I say. "Listen. 'One of these ghosts is little Bobby Castro, who was killed in the theater lobby in 1951, when he was just nine years old. The youngster, who friends and family said loved going to the movies and dreamed of being a comedian, was in the balcony with his older brothers, when they decided to send little Bobby down to the lobby for some popcorn. Little did they know that they were sending the chubby youngster down to his doom."

"Holy crud, that's mean," says Blake. "The kid is dead, and they're calling him a chubby youngster?"

"Fat-shaming a dead kid is pretty low," I say.

I notice that the prankster spiorad in question has crept closer and appears to be eavesdropping on me reading the article about him. He seems flattered and greatly interested.

"Hey, someone had to come in last in journalism school," says Lucía. "Pretty sure all of them work at alternative weeklies in Texas."

"Shut it!" I say. "I'm almost done. Listen. 'As he stood waiting for his order to be filled, Bobby was engulfed in the fiery flames of a freak unexpected explosion of the boiler in the basement just below the concession stand.'"

I glance at the spiorad and he nods to affirm this is indeed what happened, as though he can hear our conversation, from way up there. His demeanor seems to have changed a bit now, with a hint of a scowl crinkling his forehead, and he starts to pump his legs harder. The chandelier actually starts to pendulum, and it makes me queasy. It doesn't look stable.

"Are there any other kinds of flames except fiery?" asks Blake.

I place a finger over his lips. He kisses my finger and then wraps my hand in his hands.

I keep reading without missing a beat even though the very boyfriend-like gesture sends a whole flock of butterflies through my ribcage. "No one else was harmed in the incident. Performers over the years have reported being pranked by the little pint-sized ghost, and it has been a longstanding tradition at the theater to leave a box of donuts out for the tiny portly specter, as these were said to be his favorite food."

"Again," says Blake. "There was no need to say 'little' and 'pint-sized,' then 'tiny,' all in the same sentence. We get it, he was young. And fat."

The little spiorad glances down at his belly, and the scowl deepens angrily. When he looks at me, he has the same determined expression little Olivia Chavez got right before she started poltergeisting.

"Guys, maybe be a little less harsh when you talk about him," I suggest.

"Since when are you Miss Sensitive?" asks Blake, laughing at me.

Bobby is making the chandelier spin on its axis now, and I have a feeling this isn't going to turn out well.

"I think we should move," I say, but Lucía talks over me, louder, and my friends don't seem to hear me.

"That's a very sad, very poorly written story, Grace," says Lucía. "Thank you for sharing it. Why are you sharing it, by the way? Please don't share it again."

"No reason," I say. "I just thought it was interesting that there's supposed to be a ghost here." I have to come up with a quick lie. "I was thinking of doing my sophomore documentary on him."

They both look politely unimpressed. I stand up and gather my things. I suggest we go somewhere else, but again, I get talked over, this time by Blake. When our friend group starts riffing, we tend to talk over each other in our verbal jousting for the Most Clever remark.

"I mean, it's an idea," says Blake, with a shrug.

"It is for sure an idea," says Lucía. "She could also do a short film in which we watch tea steep for twenty straight minutes."

"Or you could document having a tooth filled," says Blake.

"Oh, c'mon," I say. "Why don't you like ghost stories?"

"Because they're ridiculous," says Blake.

"That's not true," says Lucía. "Some of them are good. I happen to like *good* ghost stories."

"But?" I ask.

"But a ghost story about your own school, about a little kid ghost with one of those names, you know? I don't know." She shrugs awkwardly.

"What do you mean 'one of those names'?" I ask.

"You know. Those diminutive names they gave boys in the last century. Old pedophile names. Bobby, Jimmy, Billy. I feel like ghosts with those kinds of names are just played out. You know?"

"That's mean," I say, hoping to calm Bobby down. "Also, I think we should go back in the auditorium."

"Why do you keep looking up at the ceiling?" asks Lucía.

"It's nothing. But let's get back to class."

"Um, no," says Blake. "You getting hit by lightning is going to get us out of a lot of B.S. classes for the next few weeks, and I, for one, am here for it. Morning assembly is a total waste of time."

Lucía immediately changes the subject, turning to Blake. "Hey," she says. "Did you actually pick your documentary topic already?"

He pushes his lips together in a tight, uncomfortable smile, the way he does whenever he braces for being accused of being too focused on being the perfect student. Lucía tends to take his and everyone else's successes as little more than proof of her own inadequacies.

"You did!" she cries, pretend-slapping him. "I hate you! Which idea did you pick?"

"Come on, you guys. Let's go walk around or something."

Lucía holds a hand up to me in a gesture of "hold on a second."

"I decided on the half-hour documentary about finding the best authentic latkes, matzah ball soup and pastrami on rye sandwich in all of Austin," says Blake, proudly. "But they'll all have to pass the Grandma Epstein taste test."

"I volunteer as tribute," says Lucía, holding up a hand. "You'll need additional tasters, just to be sure."

Bobby Castro starts punching lightbulbs.

"Cut it out," I call out to him.

"Huh?" asks Lucía. "What are you looking at?"

"Let's go. Now."

They ignore me. I am forced to grasp each of my friends firmly by their wrists. I drag them a few feet away, just before the chain connecting the chandelier to the ceiling breaks, and the entire massive candelabra comes crashing down near the bench where we were sitting. The noise is deafening and the impact so jarring we all fall to the carpeted floor.

"What the actual frack!" cries Lucía.

"I tried to warn you guys!"

"How did you know that would happen?" Blake asks me.

I sit up, trembling, as Mister Sanchez, the ancient security guard, comes shuffling over. Doctor Ramsey bursts out of the performance center doors and looks at the three of us on the floor near the shattered chandelier with alarm. A tsunami of students builds behind her.

"There's something I need to tell you guys," I say. "But not here. And you have to promise not to think I'm crazy."

Chapter Eight

Because Doctor Ramsey is so occupied with maintaining order at a school full of rebellious creatives eager to ogle a shattered fallen light fixture and perhaps make a TikTok about it, I am able to get her to quickly and easily agree to let Blake and Lucía "take me home." I, The Poor Girl Who Was Struck By Lightning Dear God, am not feeling as well as I'd thought I was and, because my dad and stepmother are at work and my stepbrother is at his school, I really need my friends to accompany me for physical and emotional support.

"Yes, Grace, of course," she says, half-distracted with directing student foot traffic around the broken glass in the lobby of the performance center. "You kids just need to stop at the nurse's office and have Nurse Rosa call your parents to make sure the absences are excused and they know where you are."

Bobby the poltergeist is standing in the corner by the popcorn machine. He looks ashamed of his destructive works, like he didn't think it would be that bad. He looks like he needs a hug and reassurance, and this reminds me of how Mohammad also looks like he needs hugs and reassurance. Honestly, I can't get out of there fast enough. Since when is it my job to reassure ghosts? I did not sign up for that.

We stop at the nurse's office and tell Nurse Rosa that Dr. Ramsey thinks we should take the rest of the day off. It's the same lie we tell our parents, who, after checking in with each other, agree that it's probably okay, given what we've all been through. Well, mine and Blake's; Lucía's mom can't be found, but that's nothing new.

My friends and I bolt from the theater's front doors into the warm sunshine. We walk to the student parking lot, where there was for sure a deadly shooting a few years back, but I don't see any more spiorads. The seconds I stand still, though, they start creeping out from behind dumpsters and underneath cars. Huh. Weird. As long as I'm moving, it seems like the spiorads sort of leave me alone. It seems like it's only when I'm still in one place for a while that they sense I can see them and make themselves known to me. I have no idea how any of this works, but I'm starting to see patterns and rules emerge. This motion thing makes me feel like the bus in the second-worst movie ever made by our school's namesake, *Speed*. (You will recall the bus has been rigged with a bomb and will explode if its velocity drops below 50 miles per hour.)

We pile into Blake's silver Jeep Wrangler with all the punk band stickers all over it. No one says much of anything too heavy as he drives us from our school's parking lot all the way to Rosen's Bagels in Republic Square. Part of our collective politeness is that we're probably all still freaked out about what just happened at school to get into anything too deep, but also because Blake wants us to listen to a new punk band out of DC that he can't stop raving about. I like the songs. All the talk of Jewish food for Blake's documentary project has Lucía craving Rosen's, the place we usually go between school and band practice on our way to Blake's house on Friday afternoons. She swears she won't let us rest until we go there now, on a Monday. Sounds good to me.

Rosen's is a walk-up bagel shop in a public green space in downtown Austin, with picnic tables set up under the trees. If you want to know exactly how Mexican Austin's default frame of reference for everything is, you don't have to look much further than, well, me, but also the Rosen's Bagels menu, which lists items with names such as, "Not a Taco." To underscore this point, I get a toasted jalapeño cheddar bagel with a lime roasted poblano scallion schmear, and an iced coffee. Blake gets two everything bagels, toasted with smoked lox schmears and hot coffee. Lucía gets an iced coffee as well as a toasted cinnamon raisin bagel with double peanut butter, which Blake tells her is a crime against bagels. She replies by telling him to eat a dick.

We sit at one of the picnic tables and after we've had a bite or two, Lucía tells me to spit it out.

"Not your food," she clarifies. "Swallow *that*. Please."

"That's what *she* said," says Blake and no one laughs.

"That doesn't even make sense, Mister Roboto," Lucía tells him. "Contrary to misinformation shared among incels, girls don't *ejaculate*."

"Can we please talk about something—anything—else?" I ask.

Blake seems about to protest or argue, but Lucía stops him by showing him the palm of her hand. She turns her attention back to me to say, "Spit out the thing you had to tell us but couldn't tell us at school. My breath, Grace? It's baited."

I inhale and summon my courage. There's no time like the present, right? And there's no easy way to say a thing like, "Ever since I did drugs and got hit by lightning and died and was revived by the guy I guess I'm seeing now I've been able to also see dead people, though not in the same way I'm seeing Blake." That is exactly what I say, in exactly that way.

Predictably, Lucía and Blake do not immediately respond. They just chew their food thoughtfully and exchange glances with each other and with me, as though they're trying to figure out whether I'm joking or not.

"You guess?" says Blake.

"Way to miss the most important point," I say.

"Oh. I thought you were joking about the ghost thing," he says.

"I am not joking," I say, helpfully. "And, yes, I know how idiotic it sounds." I tell them about Carl Sagan, and Olivia, and all the other dreadful hospital spiorads, and Kilian the male nurse with the man bun.

"That's sexist," says Lucía.

"What is?"

"The way you described Kilian. He's a nurse, with a bun. You don't have to specify his sex or gender, because doing so implies those things are only the domain of women."

"Seriously, shut up," says Blake to Lucía. "Let her talk."

"No, Lucía's right. My bad," I say, and I continue with my story. I tell them about how I wasn't sure the visions were real because Doctor Kapoor had told me it was likely just me hallucinating, but how seeing Mohammad and the noose, and looking him up and finding out he actually did exist, convinced me this stuff was real. "He is pretty insistent about me helping figure out what happened to him. I can even feel it, like, right now. His urgency."

Then I tell them about how the whole time they were riffing and talking trash about the Bobby Castro article, I could literally see whatever is left of Bobby getting more and more upset, swinging on the light. Finally, I talk about the Lorica spell, and how I accidentally left it at home.

"This is all completely amazing," says Lucía, her eyes wide and sincere. "I have an aunt in the Philippines who sees spirits. She can also sense cancer, but only in dogs."

"Fun party trick," says Blake. He looks at us both like we're mentally unwell.

"What is wrong with you?" she asks him. "This is obviously not a time for quips. Quit quipping!"

"I'm not sure what to say if I'm not quipping," says Blake.

"How about something supportive?" she says.

"We're here to support you as you're going through this," says Blake, awkwardly. "Whatever it is."

"So, you just all of a sudden don't believe me," I say. "You should just say that instead of trying to sound sensitive."

"Ignore Mister Robot. *I* believe you and that's all that matters," says Lucía. "I hundred-percent believe you!" She shoots Blake the side eye and tells him to stop being an ass-hat.

"I believe you *feel* this is real," Blake says to me. His clear, kind eyes tell me he has no idea how insulting that is. "And I don't want to invalidate that."

"Except you just did," I say.

I turn my eyes from him to my bagel because it suddenly holds a lot more appeal than my supposed boyfriend. I think I already want to break up. Then again, I can't blame him, really. I'm not sure I'd believe him if all of this had happened to him instead of to me, and if he was the one sitting here in a public park talking about things none of us believed in nine days ago.

"Dude, she literally *knew* the chandelier was going to fall on our fracking heads and saved our lives, and you're doubting her?"

"Maybe she saw it breaking? And she says she saw that kid, but she showed us an article about him. Maybe she was already researching him for her sophomore documentary. It's a chicken-egg thing for me. Getting hit by that much electricity is bound to make the brain work a little differently. So I am sure it's affecting what she's experiencing."

"*She* is right here," I say. "You don't have to talk about *her* in the third person. And I can't believe you're implying this is just my imagination. It's not. I thought it was, but there's no way I could have known about that Mohammad kid. I promise I'm not making this up. It took a lot of courage for me to even tell you *any* of this."

"I'm sorry," says Blake. "I just … I don't know what to say."

"How about nothing?" suggests Lucía. "You could always just say nothing, Robot."

"You know I saw you when I was dead," I remind him.

I tell Lucía about how I could see and hear everything when I was out of my body. "I heard the things you said. And you confirmed you said them."

"Your brain could still have been taking in information, because of the chest compressions. You could still have been conscious somewhere."

"I can't believe you're just changing your mind like this!"

"I'm not changing anything," says Blake.

"Then why is it that at the hospital you said you believed me? You said you felt me die."

"Yes, I know I said that," he says. "But your heart actually stopping is a little different than suddenly seeing 'spiorads' everywhere. That's not even a word."

"I *was* a spiorad, that's the whole point. You said you felt my spirit whoosh out of my body."

"I say a lot of weird things when I'm scared and tired and high," he says. "I hadn't slept in nearly a week when we had that conversation, and I'd been worried you'd never come back."

I balk and scoff. He's literally calling the entire idea of my death and spirit stupid, and I don't know what to make of that. I suddenly want to be as far from Blake as possible.

"I'm just going to need some time to absorb everything you're saying," says Blake.

I can tell from the look in his eyes that he's afraid of me, and not because he thinks I see ghosts but rather because he thinks I've lost my mind.

"I still love you. You're amazing. But you're a very different person than you were two weeks ago, and it's going to take some getting used to. It's a little bit jarring."

"Maybe you should have just left me dead then," I say.

"What? No! Why would you even say that?"

I've lost my appetite, and all I want is to run away. I look for the Uber app on my phone, and I'm relieved to see that my dad connected it to his credit card, something that was set up on my phone that melted, in case I ever found myself lost without transportation and needed to find my way home when my dad or stenchmom weren't available.

"My mistake. Okay? I shouldn't have told you guys," I say as I walk away. "Kilian warned me not to tell anyone. I should have listened."

My legs feel shaky and tired. I realize I'm overdoing things. Even though I could have easily walked to the big public library downtown from here before I was charred by lightning, I opt for the Uber.

"Hey! Don't lump me in with that dork," calls Lucía, chasing after me. "I told you I believe you."

"Grace, c'mon," yells Blake, but he doesn't follow us. "Don't do this."

I lift one hand and flip him off, over my head, as I walk away.

"Hey. Hold on. Where are you going?" asks Lucía as she jogs up to me. She walks with me and puts a gentle hand on my shoulder. "Are you okay, Grace? You've been through a lot. How can I help?"

"I'm going to the library," I say. "I have to do some research."

"Okay?" she says uncertainly.

I look at the screen of my phone. "My Uber driver, Carlos, is one minute away."

"Good. The library is good. Can I come with you?" she asks. "I need to work on my documentary topic anyway."

"Yeah," I say. Her eyes are so kind, and her posture so accepting, that I collapse into her arms, sobbing. It happens before I realize it. Maybe I am losing my mind. She has never seen me cry before. Lucía just holds me and tells me everything is going to be fine. I tell her that I feel like I'm supposed to help Mohammad figure out who killed him, and that the weight of this task feels more important than school, or anything else.

"He needs me," I tell her.

"Of course, he does," she says, trying her best, but I see her wince as she says it. She's worried I'm going nuts, too. "We all do. Is Carlos in a Silver Elantra, by chance?"

"Yes."

"Good, because this dude is cruising by really slow and he's either an Uber driver or a super perv."

I laugh, and Lucía's face brightens.

As we walk toward the car, I glance back at the picnic table.

"Don't," Lucía says and turns my head with a tender hand to my jaw. "Give him space. He sucks at feeling complicated things even more than you do. Robots have a very hard time with woo-woo things."

It should be noted here that Blake doesn't even try to stop us from leaving, nor does he try to join us.

The boy who worked his ass off to bring me back from the dead, the boy who used to kind of dig it that I worked at an occult bookstore, that boy? He's now just sitting there finishing his snack with his back to me, because even though I'm alive again, as far as he seems to be concerned, I am totally invisible.

Chapter Nine

The Uber driver seems disappointed our trip to the Austin Public Library is so short. I'm pretty sure this is not just because he won't make much money off it. I think he's pissed he doesn't have more time to be a creepy old leech hitting on teen girls in the back of his Hyundai that smells like cheap aftershave trying to wrestle a used diaper into submission. I've never seen anyone wink and waggle their eyebrows so much in a rearview mirror. It honestly makes me consider reporting him to someone, though I have no idea who would care. Grown men do this kind of crap to teen girls all the damn time, and I think the best solution is just to start taking advantage of the open carry machine gun law in my state and show up everywhere with an AK-47 draped across me like a beauty queen's sash. Like, bro, all right, you wanna leer, come at me, dude. *Let's do this.*

I slam the door when I get out, hoping to shatter all his windows. It doesn't work. Onward.

The downtown library is one of those beautiful modern Austin buildings that looks like a big origami box that a giant just unfolded, made of oxidized copper, greenish glass, butterscotch-colored bricks and cement, sort of like my new house. It's six stories tall, modern, airy and sculptural. And, as it turns out, completely the wrong effing place.

Because of course it is.

Even though Google told me there would be a collection of the city's high school yearbooks here, it turns out those things are actually kept at something called the Austin History Center. The librarian is a old white woman who wears her hair in two braids, one on each side, probably because she thinks it makes her look like a Native American. It makes her look immature. She tells us we need to go somewhere else, noting that the Austin History Center is also part of the public library system, and also downtown, but in a whole other building. She shows us a map, and I am crestfallen to see it's on the opposite side of Rosen's Bagels. We will have to cross the bagel meridian again.

I don't want to use Uber again so soon, in case the luck of the draw gifts us with pervy Carlos again. So we wander around the library a bit, then sit outside on its rooftop cafe patio with the panoramic view of our city. Here, I also see the most boring ghost I think could possibly exist. He's a middle-aged man who gives off middle-management vibes. He's of middle height, with a middle amount of hair left, and he's wearing a cardigan, slacks and loafers, like Mister Rogers. He sits with one leg crossed over the other. There's a medium hunch to his not-broad shoulders that makes me think he spent his life curled over an adding machine. Bookkeeper? Auditor? Actuary? All the dull things. He glances at me, but all I feel off him is tired. He's tired. When he gets up to move to a seat closer to us, without breaking eye contact, I feel the stroke that possibly took him out. He's the kind of quiet, boring guy who'd ignore a piercing headache for weeks because his entire mid-sized life was a headache. He wants something, probably something found in the middle of a bunch of boring things, and I'm not in the mood.

I tell Lucía about him and suggest we keep moving. To her credit, Lucía does not keep asking me if I'm okay, even though I can tell from her eyes that she wants to. She's folded her arms across herself as though she's cold and looks around like she's trying to see spiorads, or like she thinks they're going to attack her like Bobby did. She couldn't look more worried if she saw someone feeding chipmunks to a woodchipper.

"Most of them aren't like Bobby, or ghosts in movies," I tell her. "In the movies ghosts only show up in old buildings in the dark and they're always from 1874 and they always have high lace collars. In real life they're shuffling around the brand-new library rooftop cafe in the middle of the day looking for numbers to add together, being boring."

"It's still creepy," says Lucía.

"Let's walk," I say. "To the other building. It'll be nice. I've been bed bound and sitting way too much." I grab my backpack and head toward the door.

"But I thought your feet were melted."

"They're sore. Maybe melted. My nerves everywhere feel like someone took a microscopic vegetable peeler to them. But Doctor Kapoor said that the more I move around the better things will get. Plus, I don't really see spiorads when I'm moving. It's nice."

The Austin History Center is 12 blocks from the library, and the walk is mostly okay, other than the groan that comes from the center of my broken soul when I see that someone has decided to actually name their taco restaurant "Taquero Mucho." I do not want or need to be reminded of "I love you" in any form right now. Effing Blake. I flip the restaurant off, if for no other reason than my general loathing of puns as the lowest form of comedy. We keep moving. I walk faster, and Lucía struggles to keep up.

The Austin History Center, as a building, is night to the main library's day. It's one of those old, important-looking grand buildings that I know is Italian Renaissance mixed, weirdly, with Art Deco in style, thanks to the way my stenchmother is constantly pointing out architectural details to everyone who has the misfortune of riding in a car with her. It has a grand, wide outdoor staircase that leads to an equally grand entrance consisting of three tall arches behind which are three large double wooden doors. Inside, it's quiet and musty, and feels like a fancy old bank from a 1940s movie about the wild west in the 1890s—all marble and dark wood, with gold-leaf stenciled lettering on the glass set into office doors. The corridors are long and our steps echo in them. A balding old male librarian looks up from whatever yellowed book he's squinting at behind the desk and seems so astonished to see us that he quickly places a pair of glasses onto his pinched nose as though to make sure he hasn't imagined us. It's the same look the ministers at the Unitarian church get when young people attend services without being dragged there by their parents. I am guessing this reaction is because we are the youngest people in this building by at least 100 years, at the moment. Combined, Lucía and I probably have ten times more piercings than all the people here put together, too. I suspect the Austin History Center is not generally a place one finds goth teen girls in the middle of a school day.

"Are you girls lost?" he asks. "We don't keep any money up here. And the bathrooms are for patrons." His hand hovers over his old-fashioned desk phone as though the twitching fingers are trying to decide whether or not to call the police.

I tell him what I'm looking for, and his eyes narrow in suspicion.

"It's for a school project," I lie. I shoot Lucía my *go along with my story* face and say, "Give him the note from our history teacher."

Lucía is a good actress and only hesitates briefly before rummaging through her backpack and then declaring with absolute realism that she misplaced it in the bathroom when she had to use the tampon machine. The librarian holds both hands up to stop her from going into any further detail.

"Come this way," he says, still seeming nervous. He leads us to a grand reading room with long wooden tables that have old-fashioned green glass lamps growing out of the middle of them like little trees. He sits us at a table far from everyone else, as though we might have come to pick people's pockets.

"What years did you say you needed?" he asks, producing a pad of paper and a pen from a pocket somewhere.

"Like, 1985 to 1988?" I say.

"Is that a question?" he asks.

"No."

He mutters and shakes his head, as though he is disgusted with young people for the way they phrase their statements like questions, and shuffles away, leaving us to sit in the papery quiet with the floating dust motes. I look around the room. There are six other people here, four men and two women, and everyone is concentrating very hard on whatever they're reading. One woman has before her a massive, yellowed book bound in yellow, with a corroded spine, and as she flips through its pages I can see diaphanous ghost-smoke curling up from its pages, seeping into the air above the table. So it's true! I think of my boss, Milagros, at the bookshop, and how she's always muttering about having to fight the ghosts back into the books where they belong.

"Holy crap," I say.

"Another dead accountant trying to bore you to death?" asks Lucía.

As the smoke solidifies into the figure of a person, I whisper a description of what I'm seeing. It's in the shape of a person who looks to me like maybe they were an enslaved African child. I avert my eyes. I don't want the spiorad from the book to know I can see her. Lucía's still staring in the woman's direction, and I tell her to stop. The longer we sit, waiting for the librarian to return, the more spiorads I see. They're pouring out of the books people are reading, but also just wandering around, sitting at the tables with each other. The room has the same sort of atmosphere as the lunchroom at a school, with spiorads who appear to be dressed from the same era sitting in clumps. So the dead are cliquish too? There is no hope for humanity. I keep my eyes cast down at the tabletop and kick myself mentally, again, for leaving the Lorica spell at home. As soon as I get my next paycheck I'm going to get that thing tattooed to my forearm so I'm never without it again.

"Here you go." There's a loud thump as the librarian, who has appeared seemingly out of nowhere, dumps a stack of four high school yearbooks on the table in front of us. "Treat these with care, please. Are your hands clean?"

"Seriously?" Lucía asks him. "Wow."

"Thanks," I say. I stop myself from suggesting that dropping them loudly on the table is breaking his own rule. The old Grace would absolutely have done that. But I am less interested in fighting with people now.

"Let me know if I may be of further assistance." He bows a little, and slinks away.

I divide the yearbooks so we each have two. "We're looking for a kid named Mohammad Ahmadi," I remind her.

"Ew," she says, pointing to the cover. "They actually called it 'The Confederate'?"

"I know. Gross. It wasn't even that long ago. Like, if he hadn't died, Mohammad would still be alive."

I open the 1985 yearbook and start searching through the freshman class photos.

"Just go to the index of names in the back," Lucía says.

"Right. Duh. I guess I don't know how to use a yearbook. Like, can you imagine paying a ton of money for one of these things? Everything is online now. If anything, there are way too many photos of everyone at school floating around."

Lucía seems too engrossed in her research to respond. I flip to the index and find no Mohammad Ahmadi.

"Ahmadi, Mohammad," whispers Lucía. "Found him."

I scoot my chair closer to hers as she points to his name in the index.

"What year is that one?" I ask.

"1986."

The index says there are four photos of Mohammad Ahmadi in this yearbook, and lists the page numbers. Lucía flips to the first on the list. It's a photo at the start of the book, on a page with a bunch of other "snapshots" of school clubs. We have to search closely, because the print in the captions is so small, but we find him in a blurry black-and-white chess club photo with four other nerds and one smiling teacher who looks to be about a million years old. Mohammad's seated at a table with a chess board in front of him, and he's wearing a turtleneck and argyle sweater vest, with his hair shortish but sort of wild and curly.

"Is that him? Aww. Look how cute he is," says Lucía, meaning cute the way puppies are cute and not cute the way hot guys are cute.

"He is kind of cute. But why is he dressed like Carl Sagan? In my house he's dressed like a Beastie Boy."

"We all evolve in our high school careers," says Lucía. "Need I remind you of the outfit you wore to freshman orientation?"

"Please don't."

The caption indicates that Mohammad was a freshman that year. I pull the book closer and search his face. I'm surprised to see how confident and happy he looks. I'm also surprised to see that one of the other kids, a white boy with blond hair, in a button-down and tie, has his arm draped across Mohammad's shoulders. Their heads lean ever so slightly toward one another, the way you do when you're good friends. Like they trust each other implicitly. I'd expected to find a depressed-looking, friendless kid, given his present condition. I run a finger over his face and feel a sickening weight of sorrow.

"Stephen Smith," I read in a whisper. "So Mohammad had a friend. Also a freshman." I take a photo of the photo with my phone. "Next page number?"

Lucía tells me and I flip to that page. This is the main profile portrait section for the freshman class. Here, Mohammad is also smiling like the happiest kid in the world. He's wearing a white Oxford-type shirt with a black blazer and a green and pink striped tie. His eyes project a fierce optimism and intelligence that crushes me, knowing that two years later he'd be dead.

"Who is that?" asks Lucía. She points to a girl whose photo appears just to the right of Mohommad's. The difference between their moods is jarring, but they otherwise look a great deal alike. Same eyes. Same nose. She's frowning, so I can't really tell about the mouth. She wears a white head covering that drapes across her shoulders and completely covers her torso. Muslim women's wear.

"Safia Ahmadi," I read.

"Think they're related?" asks Lucía.

"I mean, it would be weird if they weren't. Right? They look alike."

"That's racist," says Lucía.

"You're an idiot."

"I'm kidding. They look exactly alike. Did he say anything about a twin sister?"

"He didn't say anything about anything, because I don't think spiorads can talk. They communicate in feelings. Or they try to. He also did this thing where he took over my mind for a minute, to show me his memories. But they were disjointed. I never want him to do that again, by the way."

"He took over your mind? What?"

"I know. To his credit, when I asked him not to do it again, he didn't."

I snap a photo of this page, too.

"Think Safia's still alive?"

"Maybe. We should see if we can find her."

Lucía has beaten me to it. She's already googling.

"This her?" Lucía shows me the LinkedIn page she's found for a Safia Ahmadi, in Austin, who looks like she's in her 50s. It is almost the exact same photo as the yearbook picture, just of an older, fatter woman in a black head covering. It says she's a social worker, employed with something called Unity Haven.

"Time is cruel," I say.

"Yeah." Lucía is googling again. "Unity Haven Refugee Rights Coalition," she says. "Is dedicated to championing the rights and dignity of refugees in Austin, Texas. 'We strive to create a welcoming and inclusive community, advocating for policy change and providing vital support services to empower refugees as they rebuild their lives.'"

"Bookmark it," I say.

"Done. I like this. It's like a scavenger hunt, only for people."

"Let's keep looking," I say.

We find the next photo of Mohammad as a member of something called the Amateur Radio Club. Unsurprisingly, all the members are boys, and by all, I mean three. Here, Mohammad wears a polo shirt with a sweater tied around his shoulders. The same kid from the chess club is here, too, Stephen Smith, along with another boy named Malcolm Jefferson. They stand in front of a table with a bunch of old dissected electronic devices and wires on it, grinning like they've just found a trunk full of gold. The same teacher from the chess club stands nearby beaming at them. Mrs. Lupinski.

"You could not have been a bigger nerd, Mo," I say as I snap a pic.

"No wonder he likes Beastie Boys," says Lucía. "They should have called that club the 'Boys with No Game Club.'"

The final photo proves Lucía wrong, however, as it is of the Freshman Winter Ball, and our nerdy Mohammad is shown slow-dancing with a pretty dark-eyed beauty who is identified in the caption as Rosa Morales. She definitely looks like she thinks he has game, even though she towers over him by at least two inches.

"Damn, Mohammad," I say. "Git it."

"That girl thirsty as frack," says Lucía.

"And he's super chill about it."

"Did not expect *that*," says Lucía.

Mohammad only appears in one more yearbook, the one from 1987. He only had two years of high school and then his life ended. I feel that familiar wave of nauseating sorrow ripple through me.

"I'd say he swanned summer between 9th and 10th grades," says Lucía as we take in the photos of him we find. "Swanning" is our verb for when someone goes from dork to hot almost overnight, like the ugly duckling. He was still in the Amateur Radio Club, whatever the hell that was, but he's about six inches taller as a sophomore, with a faint mustache and big-ass dark glasses like a superstar. There are a couple of new kids in the club, but that same kid Stephen Smith is still there and has not swanned at all; if anything, he's gotten worse—pimplier, skinnier, worse-dressed, although I'm not exactly great at judging fashion choices from the 1980s because they all seem terrible to me.

In the radio club pic, Mohammad is wearing a boxy white T-shirt with that same acid-washed jean jacket he appeared in at my house. In his main portrait he wears another Oxford shirt, but this time it's got the top couple of buttons undone to reveal the concert T-shirt beneath it, and the collar flipped up. The biggest change is in the look in his eyes and the set of his jaw, which has hardened and gotten more square. He looks cocky and self-assured, grinning and almost side-eyeing the camera, smart and, weirdly, actually extremely hot.

He was also still in the chess club, and the photo for that group shows Mohammad playing chess against Malcolm Jefferson, who wears a bow tie with suspenders and therefore deserves to lose. Mohammad holds the queen an inch above the board as though about to make a devastating move and has the unmistakable gloating grin of someone about to win, whereas Malcolm looks like he has suddenly gotten a bitter stomach ache. Stephen Smith stands beside Mohammad and appears to be preparing to do a fist pump, a supportive friend. The last photo isn't of a dance, this time; it's Mohammad standing at the end of a line of other students who have made the National Honors Society. He's taller than most of the other boys and looks like a member of that old movie, *The Breakfast Club*. Is that a leather jacket? Really, Mohammad? The accompanying text, more of a short article than a caption, quotes him as saying he hopes to one day study engineering at M.I.T., to research something called "signal processing."

"Wow," I say.

"Right?" says Lucía. "I'd totally do him, if I'd lived back then."

"No, you horny idiot. I'm saying that because it sucks that he had his life cut short. He seems like he was really smart and happy, a huge-ass dork, but still ..."

"Yeah. It's awful."

My phone vibrates with an incoming call. The caller I.D. tells me it's Shadowbound Books calling. In other words, it's Milagros Palladino, my boss at the bookstore.

"Ugh," I say. I remember I have a job. I mean, I kind of knew that, but I'd assumed my dad had taken care of calling her. I don't know why I think this.

"What?" asks Lucía.

"Work." I'm not supposed to take the call in the library, according to all the signs posted with a graphic of a very out-of-date cell phone with a red circle around it and line through it. But if Milagros is calling, it's important, and I don't have time to find my way out. Because of her advanced age, Milagros doesn't have a cell phone. She's calling from the shop's landline, meaning I can't text her. So I take the call as discreetly as I can. I whisper into the phone, and she keeps yelling that she can't hear me, getting louder each time as though that's going to help. Frustrated, I speak in a normal tone of voice, and this inspires several of the other readers to shush me. Milagros asks me why I've been missing for more than a week and reminds me that I am on the schedule to work today.

"Do you still even want this job?" she asks.

I'd totally forgotten. She doesn't seem to know I was hit by lightning, or at least doesn't say anything about it, probably because she doesn't follow current events or news and prefers to limit her life to the bookstore and her little apartment behind it. I never try to explain anything complicated to Milagros on the phone because she's hard of hearing.

"Sorry. Yes. I still want this job. I'll be there as soon as I can," I say, just as the librarian reaches us. He tells us we are going to have to go outside if we want to talk on the phone.

"That's fine," I say, ending the call. "We were headed out, anyway."

Lucía insists on accompanying me to work, to make sure I get there safely, she says. She also says she doesn't want to go home because there's nothing to eat there. We slip into a new Uber, which, happily, is driven by a woman this time.

Halfway to the bookshop, my father texts to ask if everything's all right, because he's noticed I'm taking Ubers all over town, even though he thought he had given me permission to leave school to go home. I tell him the truth. We wanted bagels, then Lucía and I did some research at the library, and now she's going with me to work. He'd told me to call in sick to Milagros last night, but I forgot, so of course he jumps on my case about it. I remind him that lighting causes short-term memory loss, and he says he knows and he's glad Lucía's with me.

He then tells me he and Candi with an i have to attend some fundraiser for some pro-life charity her business sponsors, because of course it does, and promises they'll send my stepbrother Jacob to pick me up at 8 p.m., which is the usual time I get off work.

I don't respond beyond a lame-ass thumbs-up emoji, because I don't have anything nice to say. I can't believe he's going to anything that organization would sponsor, because as far as I'm concerned, they see me and Lucía and every other young woman in Texas as nothing but pods to incubate fetuses. Also, my dad has never sent my stenchbrother to pick me up before, and I doubt he's smart enough to figure out where he's going, even with GPS. I'm also quite sure he'll use the opportunity of my incapacity and inability to safely drive a car as a chance to lord it over me somehow.

I will handle it all peacefully, because that's who I am now. I think.

See? I'm improving as a person. Keeping quiet is an improvement, right? Not much of one. But I suppose every bit counts.

Chapter Ten

It is almost 4 p.m. when Lucía and I arrive at the Shadowbound Bookshop. There's no one in the store except for my boss and Platero, but that doesn't stop Milagros from waiting by the door so she can chew me out for shirking my duties the exact second I arrive. For what it's worth, the shop doesn't get a ton of traffic, even on its busiest days.

"You're lucky I like you," she says, with her thick Spanish accent, shoving a can of furniture polish and a dust rag into my hands as soon as I come through the front door. She then points a bony finger at me and scowls harder. "You'd be fired many times by now if I didn't think there was something special about you."

I'm prepared to let these comments go, but Lucía, true to form as my greatest defender in this life, isn't.

"Mrs. Palladino, you *do* realize Grace was hit by lightning a little more than a week ago, right? Like, she shouldn't even be here at all, probably. Maybe cut her a little slack."

"Lucía, no," I whisper.

Milagros was probably the only person in Austin who hadn't yet heard about my accident, and I wanted to keep it that way for a minute, to enjoy feeling at least a little bit normal again.

Milagros, who had begun hobbling toward the back office, stops in her tracks and pivots around her cane so that she's facing Lucía. She tilts her head like a curious bird. "*Lightning*, you say?"

"Yes, ma'am," says Lucía.

"Who are you?"

"I'm Lucía. Grace's best friend. You've met me like four other times."

Milagros shifts her gaze to me behind the cash register now. "What's this about lightning, child?"

I tell Milagros what happened. Lucía fills in the blanks. As we talk, Milagros thumps her cane closer and closer, until she's standing feebly in front of me, leaning on the counter, staring intently into my eyes with her own milky gray orbs. Milagros asks questions about the spiorads in a respectful, trusting way. I'm not sure why, but I tell her everything, including the way I saw spiorads steaming out of the books at the Austin History Center. It's a relief to talk about seeing dead people with someone who doesn't think I've gone insane because of it.

"Well, why didn't you tell me all of this sooner?" asks Milagros. She points to Lucía. "You, turn the Open sign over in the front window." She thrusts the ring of keys at me across the countertop. "Lock up, Grace. Deadbolts, too."

"What? Why?"

"I'll just go check the yellow pages and write down the directions, and get my tools, then we'll go. Use the side door. Meet me at the hearse. And tell your little friend it's Ms. Palladino, not Mrs. I was never married because I am not a masochist."

With that, Milagros dodders away again, through the stacks of books, wiith a great thumping of her cane, dragging the wheezing Platero behind her.

"What, even, is *happening* right now?" Lucía asks me.

"I don't know. I think she's closing the store."

"Did she say 'meet me at the hearse'?"

"She did."

"What hearse?"

"Oh. Didn't you know? Milagros drives a vintage Cadillac hearse. It's her everyday car."

"Of course, it is," says Lucía. "Why would she close the shop? She was so pissed off you weren't here five seconds ago, and now she's shutting up shop?"

I shrug but do as I've been instructed.

The hearse, which is parked in the driveway along the side of the shop, is sparkly and gold, with the Shadowbound logo on the sides and the hood ornament—of a gargoyle reading a Harry Potter book.

"I'm not going inside that thing," says Lucía.

But she, like I, does end up going inside that thing. Both of us are practically shoved into the vehicle by my boss, who assures us that it's never actually held a corpse and that the errand we must all run together is extremely important. When we try to protest, Milagros reminds me that I'm still on the clock and must do as I'm instructed. It smells strongly of formaldehyde and roses, and I take it from this that my boss has lied to us about there having never been bodies inside.

Milagros drives without telling us where we're going or why we're going there, other than to laugh to herself and say, "You'll be pleased, don't worry."

She's sitting on an old-fashioned paper phone book so that she can see over the dashboard, and I'm mashed in the middle of the front bench seat, with Lucía hunching miserably against the weird golden-padded velvet of the passenger's side door. The vehicle has four doors, with the back two open to the coffin-size space in the back, and there's a divider up between the front seat and this back space. Not that we could have sat back there even if we wanted to, because looking through the window in the divider, I can see that it is crammed with books and old newspapers. For what it's worth, my boss is a terrible driver. I am sure this surprises no one. She goes far too slow, and her parkinsonian steering is what you might call unsteady. She has the reflex speed of a dragonfly trapped in amber.

After an excruciating 47 minutes of this, we arrive at a nondescript strip mall on the North Loop. Like most strip malls in Austin, it's home to a used record store and a microbrewery, as well as a few other businesses and at least two empty storefronts with "For Lease" signs in the front windows—one looks like it used to be a tattoo parlor. Everyone day-drinking on the patio of the pub watches in amused and maybe horrified fascination as Milagros pilots the sparkly hearse into a couple of parking spaces in front of one of the businesses. Her parking is worse than her driving.

"There," she says, pointing to one of the shops.

A sign in the front window reads Unity Haven: Refugee Rights Coalition. This is the nonprofit for which the woman we have assumed is Mohammad's twin sister supposedly now works.

"Come on, girls," she says. "Let's go see what she can tell us."

"Why are you doing this?" I ask her.

"Because from what you've told me of Mohammad, he's not going to give you a moment of rest unless you figure out what happened to him."

"But I have the Lorica," I say. "I can just keep sending him away, right?"

Milagros chuckles. "I would not be surprised if that determined boy finds a way around that little spell in the next few days. And then what will you do?"

"I don't know," I say. "Move away?"

"Come on," she repeats. "Trust me when I tell you, there's nowhere you can move to where you'll be free of spiorads. Better to learn now how to help them."

She opens her door and with great difficulty extracts herself from the hearse.

"I don't understand why we couldn't just call," says Lucía as we walk across the parking lot.

"There is no substitute for looking a person in the eye when you ask them important questions," says Milagros. "Young people today are suffering because none of you interact with each other in real life anymore. It's all through telephone calls and emails."

"You want to be the one to tell her?" Lucía asks me.

"Sure," I say. "Actually, most of us never make or accept phone calls, Milagros. And we don't use email, like, ever. We text now, or DM."

"Even worse," says Milagros. "No wonder you're all lonely."

We've arrived at the front door of Unity Haven, and my boss waves her hand in an impatient gesture I take to mean she wants us to open it for her. Like we should have known this. Like we are inconsiderate girls for hesitating to open the door for her.

"Your majesty," says Lucía, opening the door for Milagros.

"*Grosera*," mutters Milagros.

Inside, the nonprofit might as well be a Supercuts, except that instead of haircutting stations, there are little drab desks between fraying partitions where people sit on uncomfortable chairs talking to people on slightly less uncomfortable chairs behind cheap desks and old computers. No one looks happy to be here. There's a little waiting area full of people who, with their turbans and *huipils* and *lederhosen* and a wide variety of skin tones appear to be from all over the world—families, mostly. There are lots of worried-looking little kids sucking their thumbs. A very weary young woman sits behind a small reception counter. She thrusts a clipboard at us and tells us to take a number with the same enthusiasm you might find in a fast-food worker with Covid who, because they lack sick leave, are being forced to flip their ten-thousandth burger of the day.

"Hello and good afternoon. We are here to see Safia Ahmadi," says Milagros. The tilt of her head and the sniffing tone of her attitude feel regal and important.

"You got an appointment?" asks the receptionist in a combative way that conveys she knows we don't have an appointment.

"We do not, but we are not here on business. We are here to talk about her twin brother."

The receptionist seems perplexed. "I do not think Ms. Ahmadi has any siblings."

"Her brother is dead. Tell her we have a message for her from Mohammad," says Milagros. "Her brother, not the prophet."

"You have a message from her *dead* brother?"

"Naturally. That's what I said."

"Who do I tell her is asking about her?" The boredom on the receptionist's face rearranges itself into something like curiosity and wariness.

"It doesn't matter who we are."

The receptionist says, "Wait here," and gets up.

She walks to one of the furthest partitioned areas, where she leans in and whispers with someone we can't see from where we are. After a moment, she returns with the woman from the LinkedIn photo, true to form in a head covering and a long tunic over loose leggings. Her face is as scowly now as it was in both of the pictures of her I'd seen before, and I get a terrible feeling about her. Very negative energy.

"It's them there," says the receptionist, pointing to us.

"Hello," Safia says to Milagros in a pleasant and professional manner that seems a bit curious but a lot wary. "How may I help you?"

"I'd prefer we speak somewhere private, if you don't mind," says Milagros.

"May I ask what this is about?" asks Safia.

"It's a personal family matter," says Milagros.

Safia's expression seems to indicate she knows this is about her brother, because the receptionist likely told her, and she doesn't seem very happy about it. She looks a bit scared, if I'm being honest.

"Have we met before?" asks Safia. "I'm sorry, but I don't recall that we know one another."

"We have not," says Milagros. "I know this is an unusual request. If we can just speak somewhere out of earshot, I think it will make sense. Discretion is warranted."

"Yes, I'm sure it is," says Safia, politely. "I apologize, Miss ...?"

"Call me Milagros."

"Miss Milagros. I am very sorry, but the thing is, I'm very busy. As you can see, we're all very busy here today. Perhaps if you call, we can set something up for a more convenient time."

Safia produces a business card and hands this to Milagros, who plucks it and stuffs it into her sweater's pocket. Milagros eyes the crowded waiting room, sighs and gestures toward the front door.

"I'm afraid this is urgent. It will only take a minute of your time, and then we'll be on our way. We can speak outside. Please. It's important. About Mohammad."

Safia takes a deep breath and as she sighs it out, she casts a glance at the receptionist and tilts her head toward the door. The receptionist nods in an "I got your back" kind of way, and we all step outside. Milagros does most of the talking, while Safia listens politely and professionally. Milagros recounts as much of my story as she remembers, which, to my surprise, is most of it. The longer she talks, the more nervously Safia wrings her hands.

"So, as you see," concludes Milagros, "my young friend here has reason to believe your brother's spirit is still lingering on the earth, trying to tell her something, perhaps something important about the nature of his death, which it appears might not be what the officials thought it was. We were hoping that you might be able to provide us with any information that might help us help him."

Safia stands there blinking for a minute as though we've just told her we are from Mars and have landed on the planet to kidnap all the cows.

"Thank you for coming to see me," she says, carefully, crossing her arms over her chest protectively. "Unfortunately, I'm afraid I don't have any information to give you. Mohammad's suicide occurred a very long time ago, as I'm sure you're aware, and I was just a child myself. Everything I knew I told the police and the coroner at that time. Perhaps you could check with them if any new information has surfaced?"

"Is there anything at all, as you think back on it, that might point to someone who would have wanted to kill your brother?" I blurt. "I am almost one-hundred-percent sure he didn't end his own life."

"Listen to me, very carefully," says Safia after a long pause during which she seems to be struggling to compose herself. She narrows her eyes at me and says, "I don't know who you people are, and I don't know what you're up to. My twin brother committed a grave sin by ending his own life. And, yes, he ended his own life. He hanged himself in our garage, and I'm the one who found him."

"I'm so sorry," I say. "I had something similar happen with my mother and me."

Safia looks at me with more softness in her eyes now, and says, "I'm sorry. No one should ever have to find something like that. Especially not a child."

"I know, right?" I say.

"The act of suicide is one of the greatest affronts to Allah that a person can make," Safia says.

There's something secretive about her eyes, and I sense that she is not entirely convinced he killed himself. "You know something, don't you?"

Her eyes flicker across mine for a moment before looking down. "There are some things it's best not to know," she says.

"What does that mean?"

"It means it's best to let things be, not go digging up old bones."

"I got the sense your brother might have been bullied when you guys were students at Johnston High. For ... well, for being Muslim. I saw ... he showed me something about that. Do you remember anything like that?"

"He 'showed' you?" Safia looks spooked.

"It's hard to explain. I experienced it almost as a memory he lent me."

Safia squeezes her eyebrows together sternly as she searches my face. She seems afraid, but also like she believes me. She sighs. "Yes. We were both bullied a bit. Texas was Texas then, just as it is now, and we were Afghani refugees and Muslim. It's not that far-fetched to imagine we'd be bullied."

"Do you remember the names of any of the people who bullied you?" I ask.

"If my brother had been faithful to Allah," she says, sorrowfully but perhaps also angrily, "like the rest of our family, he would have let Him handle the bullies. Their names are irrelevant for us, and on Allah's list. That is the path I chose. Instead, Mohammad took matters into his own hands, which is an insult to Allah. There is no greater insult."

"We understand," says Milagros. She shoots me a look that seems to communicate she wants me to stop talking now. "And I couldn't agree with you more. But on the off chance that your brother *didn't* harm himself, could there have been any particular bullies at the school who might have disliked him enough to wish him physical harm?"

"Are you suggesting someone hanged my brother in our own garage and staged it to look like a suicide?"

"Yes," I blurt again.

Safia scowls. "The garage was locked and barricaded from the inside, and my brother was the only one in it. So, the police would say your theory is unlikely. In fact, they did."

"Wait. Who gave the police the theory that someone killed Mohammad?" asks Lucía, and I see something in Safia's eyes that makes me believe she was the person who thought it was murder.

"Did you initially think he ended his own life?" I ask.

She draws a deep breath and seems to hold it as she weighs her options. Then she speaks. "Mohammad picked a strange time to kill himself," she says, slowly. "He was about to participate in a national science, technology and engineering fair, up in Dallas. He'd raised all the money he needed for that trip by selling candy bars door-to-door, which, for an introvert like him, was hard to do. He was very proud of his science fair project. An invention, I don't remember what. He was always inventing things. I will also tell you, as I told the police, that there was a high window at the rear of the garage, it was a detached garage, and a crank window. It was unlocked and the crank had been removed, meaning it would have been easy to open and close, if someone knew about it and wanted to."

"So, someone could have staged it?" I ask.

"The police did not think that was possible, and my father made it clear to me that now that we were in America it was very important for us to respect state authority in this and all other matters. I respect my father's wishes. As an unmarried daughter, I still live in his home with him, and I will not speak ill of him or challenge him."

"But there *was* someone," I push. "Someone who really had it in for Mohammad, right? Maybe a ringleader?"

Safia flattens her mouth to a tight line, then frowns. She inhales sharply through her nose, then drops her hands to her sides, seeming to relax slightly as she exhales. "There was one particular boy Mohammad had a lot of trouble with," she says. "A football player. The police didn't even question him. I mentioned him, and so did Mohammad's friends. The police didn't care."

"Do you remember his name?" asks Lucía, finally inserting herself into the conversation.

Safia scoffs. "How could I forget it? That boy caused our family a great deal of pain and shame."

We all wait for her to share the name, and it seems like she is weighing whether or not to do so as her eyes stare off across the parking lot. More than anything, she looks scared.

"We won't tell him we spoke to you," I say.

Safia lifts one eyebrow at me as though I were very naïve. "I would suggest you don't talk to him at all."

I'm about to say something else when Milgros gestures subtly at me to keep quiet. So I do, and we wait. After another long moment, Safia sighs loudly again, and shakes her head. "I shouldn't do this." Safia looks at me, specifically, lowers her voice, leans in and says, "His name is Warwick Blackwater."

"Warwick Blackwater," I repeat, mostly because I have a habit of repeating things I want to make sure I'll remember.

The name is unusual. I know I've heard that name somewhere before. That, or it sounds like a name that I might have heard. Safia seems nervous, like she doesn't want me to say the name too loud. Whatever Warwick Blackwater did to her and her family, she's still afraid of him, almost forty years later.

"Thank you, dear one," says Milagros. She touches Safia's arm and Safia recoils as though she's been burned. "We are very sorry to have interrupted your day and taken so much of your time. We'll be discreet. You will not face further dangers on our account."

Safia's eyes glisten with unshed tears as she says softly, "You know, my father and I made the choice after my brother's death to carry on as though he never existed, because what he did—or what they say he did—it brings shame upon our entire family, and there's no room for questioning any of it now. It's too late. My father would be very angry with me if he knew I spoke to you about this, if I even admitted to having any tiny bit of doubt about how my brother died. We do not believe in ghosts, and we respect the authorities in this country. If you decide to confront my father as you have confronted me, please don't mention having spoken to me, okay?"

"Of course," I say.

"My best advice, though, is that you do not contact him at all. He's a very old man now, and not well. He will not be open to any of what you're saying. He's … he can be a difficult man even under the best of circumstances. I fear that a conversation such as the one we've had here today could be harmful to his delicate health."

"Understood," says Milagros. "Thank you for your openness with us. May we be in touch again if we have further questions?"

"I would really prefer that you do not contact me again. It's nothing personal. It's just, this is a very difficult subject for me. I prefer to keep it out of my mind. I moved on long ago and made a good life for myself. I'd like to keep that box closed. It has not been easy for me, living here, and I prefer to keep to myself and rock as few boats as possible. I hope you understand."

"Yes, of course," says Milagros. "Thank you again. Have a wonderful rest of your day."

Safia scoffs as though having a wonderful day now will be impossible. "Sure. Goodbye," she says.

Milagros watches Safia go back into her office and waits for the hydraulic slow-closing door to shut completely before grabbing my hands in hers.

"That boy in your house was up against a lot of intolerance," she says. "Not just from the bullies at his school but in his own family."

"Yes, I see that."

"You might not get the answers you seek from the world of the living," she says. "I think what you need is an ancestor spirit."

"A what, now?"

"A spirit guide, someone on the other side who, because they are related to you, can help to guide you by communicating somewhat more directly with you than a random spiorad."

"Could she use her mom?" asks Lucía.

I feel sick and afraid and maybe even hopeful, the usual mix of things my mother incites in me. Milagros seems to read the emotions on my face and squeezes my hand supportively.

"I'll tell you what we'll do, girls. First, we'll get some ice cream, to center our souls and clear them of negative energies. I know a great authentic Italian gelato place near here."

"I did not know ice cream could center souls," says Lucía.

"It can, but only if coffee-flavored, with chocolate mini-kisses," says Milagros.

I can't tell whether she's joking or not.

"And after that, at dusk, we'll head back to the shop and go to the courtyard. I'll conduct an Ancestor's Embrace Gathering ceremony for you, and we'll see who shows up for you, Grace."

"What do you mean, we'll see who shows up?" I ask.

"Well, just like we don't get to pick our parents, we don't get to pick our spirit guides, either. They choose us. It's often someone in our family tree who has passed on."

"Then it will totally be Grace's mom, right?" asks Lucía. She looks at me excitedly. "You can finally ask her all the things."

"Not so fast," says Milagros as she opens the passenger door to the hearse and gestures for us to climb in. She goes around and gets into the driver's seat and looks at us kindly. "A person's Ancestor Mentor—sometimes also called a Guardian Angel and a million other names—can be anyone, at any point in the past. I've had clients end up with their own parents, though it isn't common, and I've also had clients end up with their 36th-great-grandparents. There's really no way to know who's been watching over you until you do the ceremony. But it's usually someone who has been with you over your entire life, meaning that unless your parent died during childbirth with you or, in the case of a father, before you were born, it is unlikely your Ancestor Mentor, or A. C. as I like to call them, is going to be your mother."

This news feels like a gut punch. I was hoping to see her. Milagros pats my shoulder before firing up the engine.

"Don't worry," she says, "I'm sure at some point you and your mother will make contact again. And you can ask her 'all the things.'"

"Hang on," says Lucía. "Are you saying the A.C. is someone we all have, who watches over us all the time?"

"That's right."

"Do I have one?" asks Lucía.

"Of course, you do."

"So why do you have to do a ceremony to find them if they're always around?" I ask.

"The ceremony isn't to find them," says Milagros. "It's to ask them to please make themselves manifest to the person they watch over. Most people aren't ready for that, so I don't encourage it for everyone. I do think that Grace is ready, given what she's going through, and that a direct and open line of communication with the dead will be of great help to her moving forward."

Chapter Eleven

Dusk arrives. The sun sinks below the horizon, briefly painting the small garden courtyard behind Shadowbound Books in hues of crimson and gold that soon give way to undulating dark gray and black shadows. The cooling air of night mixes with the warmer air from the day, and the tree branches arch overhead like a ceiling. They start to move like the arms of dancing women with the arrival of darkness. The savory scent of someone's backyard barbecue mixes with the delicate floral perfume from the Crepe Myrtle trees and wildflowers, with a faint but unwelcome undertone of the many turds Platero has left here over the years, long since collected by his industrious owner but having left an invisible and perhaps permanent residue on the pavers, nonetheless. Lucía and I stand near the back door of the shop and watch as Milagros bustles about with a sense of purpose, her eyes alight with a mysterious gleam. She's in her element now. I grab Lucía's hand for comfort, and she squeezes back and gives me a look that I think is meant to comfort me but only betrays her own mixed emotions.

"Come, *niñas*," Milagros beckons us closer to the little fire pit where she's stacked cedar logs and has just ignited with a long lighter. Her voice is a low, melodious hum that sounds quite different from its usual high-pitched tones. "Don't be scared. It is time."

With a wave of her hand, she motions for me to take a seat on the weathered wooden bench beneath a gnarled olive tree. Platero settles in a fat lump of fur at my feet, his snoring a soothing backdrop to the gathering darkness. Lucía joins me, her expression a mix of curiosity and skepticism.

Milagros, who usually limps heavily through life, now moves gracefully through the courtyard, light on her feet, as though this task has peeled back years of her life, lighting candles and incense with practiced precision. The flickering flames cast an otherworldly glow over the gathering, and it feels holy and enormous in a way that terrifies me.

"Listen closely, girls," Milagros says, her voice barely more than a whisper. "I will be speaking in Italian at first, because that's the language my own guide, Aradia, most readily responds to. Once she's arrived, I'll switch to English so you understand what's being said. When you hear me speak, it might be me, or it might be her. She speaks with a strong Italian accent, whereas I, as you know, speak with a Mexican accent. I will ask her to call upon the spirits of Grace's ancestors to join us in this sacred space. And we'll see what happens."

"Do you see any spiorads right now?" Lucía whispers to me.

I shake my head.

"Grace won't see any spirits other than Aradia, and then the one who has chosen to guide Grace, whoever that is, and only if and when that A. C. arrives," says Milagros.

I'm amazed she even heard Lucía's question because I am right next to the girl and barely heard it.

"I cast a protective spell earlier, before we left in the hearse."

"Is *that* why I haven't been seeing spiorads?" I ask.

"Yes, child. The last thing we needed when visiting Mohammad's sister was you seeing ghosts at the strip mall. Now please stop talking, so that we can get down to business.

Dusk is the best time for this, and the longer you talk, the harder it might be."

"Sorry," I say, and I pantomime locking my lips with a key.

Milagros begins to chant in Italian, a language that feels as ancient as time itself, her words weaving a tapestry of sound that seems to echo across the ages. The air grows thick with the scent of sage and cedar, as the smoke from the fire pit curls upwards like tendrils of mist, taking on the shape of a young and quite beautiful woman, with a flowing dark gown and a sparkly long headscarf gathered in a knot at her nape. Her body language and facial expression are sly and knowing, a bit playful and pleased with herself. I know she's not a gypsy—or traveler, as we are supposed to say now—but something about her outfit feels that way to me. Like she's someone who might be pretending to see your future in a crystal ball at the state fair. Maybe it's the big hoop earrings.

As Milagros continues through the ceremony, her voice rises and falls like the rhythm of the tides, each word imbued with a power that feels both ancient and profound. She switches from Italian to English and calls upon the spirits of the earth and sky, the wind and the rain, inviting them to lend their strength to our gathering. Then it's back to Italian, and her voice is low and dusky, and truly sounds like a completely different person.

I close my eyes and allow myself to sink into the rhythm of her words, feeling the energy of the earth pulsing beneath my feet. I can sense the presence of something ... otherworldly, a whisper of many voices that seem to dance on the edge of my consciousness. My eyes pop open when I sense someone right in front of me, so close that I can almost feel the warmth of their presence about to touch my forehead.

And then, as if by magic, she appears before me—a lovely young indigenous American woman dressed in tattered white garments, her large dark eyes filled with a sorrow that cuts straight to the bone. I recognize her instantly. This is without a doubt the ancestral spirit guide Milagros sent Aradia to find for me. And unlike Milagros' spirit guide, who is playful and smiles, mine seems to be the pure embodiment of sadness.

"Who are you?" I whisper, my voice barely more than a breath.

She does not answer, her form shimmering in the fading light. She opens her mouth as though to speak, then bends forward at the waist as though she's been punched, and the most plaintive, mournful wail twists out of her throat. There's something of a wolf's howl to it, something of a witch calling the others to the coven and something of a mother who has just found her children torn to shreds in the rubble of a bombed building. She spreads her arms like wings, and then, with a final wail of sorrow, she shoots into the sky and is gone, leaving me alone with the echoes of her presence.

"Grace?" Lucía is struggling to hold me in her arms as I sink to the cobblestones.

I am weeping, and my legs feel like they're made of sand.

"What's wrong with her?" she asks Milagros.

"Nothing's wrong with her," says Milagros, rushing over to help ease me down.

"Why is she like that?" I ask Milagros. "Why is she so sad?"

Milagros settles herself on the bench and says nothing for a long moment. I see a new expression in her eyes, one I've never seen there before. Awe. She is awestruck.

"What?" I demand. "What is this?"

"Can someone please tell me what's going on?" asks Lucía.

"Did you not see her?" I ask.

"All I've seen is the two of you, and that dog."

"This is really quite something," says Milagros.

"Did you see her?" I ask the old woman.

Her eyes open very wide as she nods slowly. "Oh, yes, indeed I did."

"Why is she so terrifying?" I ask. "Isn't your guardian angel who is looking after you for your whole life supposed to be, I don't know, more freakin' angelic?"

"There is no hard and fast rule about their temperament," says Milagros.

"Did you conjure the wrong thing?" I ask. "Because if that was my guardian angel, I'm straight up doomed."

"No, she was the right spirit," says Milagros. "And believe it or not, Grace, she is quite famous. And you are absolutely lucky to be descended from her. She is spirit-world royalty, practically. Much discussed, but little seen. That she did not stick around is quite telling. She does not like for people to see her. Well, adults, anyway. Usually, she only appears to children."

"What? Why the hell would that thing want to appear to children?"

"To scare them away from harm," says Milagros. "Specifically, to scare them away from ditches and rivers when there are no adults around to supervise."

"Hold up," says Lucía. "It sounds like you're describing La Llorona."

"That's exactly right," says Milagros. "But Aradia tells me that is not her actual name. Her real name is Pakwá-ule."

"What the holy hell," I say. "You can't be serious. My guardian angel is La Llorona, the literal demon who literally drowned her own children?"

"I am not sure that's the most accurate description of her, Grace. We need to learn more about her. But, yes, that's what I'm saying."

"Well, tell her no, thanks. I'd rather not," I say.

"As I mentioned earlier, dear girl, we do not get to choose our Ancestral Spirit Guides. They choose us. And for whatever reason, Pakwá-ule chose you."

"This is extremely metal," says Lucía.

"No," I say, "it's not. You didn't see her. You didn't feel it. She's pure sorrow. No wonder my life sucks so hard."

"Let's go inside," says Milagros. "I'll make us some nice cinnamon tea and find a book or two about La Llorona, or Pakwá-ule, that might help you to understand things better and manage all of the important changes you're going through. Come, come."

She's smiling like there's nothing to worry about, like having one of the most notoriously terrifying ghosts on the planet as your spirit guide is no big deal.

"I knew it," I say. I find myself clinging to Lucía's hand, my mind reeling with the weight of what I have just experienced. "I'm cursed."

"Maybe think about it this way," says Milagros, stopping just short of the door and turning back toward where we still sit. "With her on your side, there won't be many other entities out there that can harm you."

"She's got a point," says Lucía.

I watch the fire crackle and feel Pakwá-ule still around us, though not visible. I realize she has almost always been with me, the weight of her sorrow somehow my inheritance. Maybe it was my mother's, too.

"Let's go inside," says Lucía. "I've never had cinnamon tea, and I really want some."

"Yeah, whatever," I say, slowly rising to my feet again. "I'm terrified because I'm doomed, and you want tea. That's fair."

The shadows of the past loom large around me as we head toward the door and as I come to grips with the reality that my spirit guide is one of the most terrifying mythological ghosts of all time, because of course she is. It's not bad enough that my mother committed suicide, and I got hit by lightning. Now, I see the spirits of the lingering unhappy dead. Nope, there has to be this, too.

Fear grips me like never before as I realize I might actually have been born cursed and horrible, doomed to a life of never-ending sorrow of the type I saw in Pakwá-ule's eyes. The revelation sends shivers down my spine, and a cold sweat breaks out across my forehead. Despite my attempts to convince myself otherwise, I am overcome with the urge to self-cut. Maybe more. I don't want to be here, not like this. Not with a guardian demon. No wonder things have always been so hard for me.

For the first time since my accident, I am utterly, irrevocably afraid, and not just of the spiorads but also of myself.

Chapter Twelve

As Lucía and I step out of the bookshop, my arms heavy with occult books about my demon guardian, the night air wraps around us like a damp and heavy blanket, suffocating and oppressive. Lucía's eyes sparkle with excitement, her cheeks flushed with the thrill of the evening's events. She's loving this. These past ten days, she tells me, are the most exciting of her life. But I can't shake the feeling of unease that gnaws at my insides, like a rat trapped in a maze with no way out. What's theoretical and fun for her is all too real and not at all fun for me.

Jacob's obnoxious red vintage Camaro with the white racing stripes on the hood grumbles and gleams in the glow of the streetlight, a shiny macho symbol of everything I hate about him—arrogance, entitlement and a complete lack of self-awareness. He and his dad work on this car as their shared hobby, and he loves talking about the fortune his very rich father has spent on making the 1967 car "cherry," meaning like new. It's the quintessential muscle car, throaty and loud. He revs the engine by way of a greeting, a smug smirk plastered across his face as he leans back in the driver's seat, all too eager to play the part of the big-shot high school jock.

As we get to the car, I see that he's not alone. He's brought one of his football-player buddies with him, a boisterous sandy-blond-haired dude who's got to be at least six-foot-two. I've met him once before, but his name escapes me at the moment because I don't bother to memorize things I don't care about.

"Do I look okay?" asks Lucía. She pats her hair a little and sucks in her non-existent gut. I have no idea why she finds my stenchbrother attractive and wish she'd stop.

"You're always very pretty," I say, truthfully. "Not sure why you're so worried about what these douchenozzles think, though."

"What? Jacob's not that bad, Grace. I don't get why you hate him. He's actually pretty nice."

"My stepbrother? No."

"And he's hot."

"Also a big no."

"Hotness is subjective," she reminds me.

"Thank God for that," I say.

"Like, you could not pay me to make out with a guy like Blake," she says.

"Nor would I want to," I say. "And we're not talking about him. Remember?"

Jacob's buddy bursts out of the passenger-side door, still in his practice jersey, pants and tennis shoes. His dirty blond hair is cut short, and his biceps are bigger than my thighs.

"Hey, Grace. And … Lucy, right?" he says. He's actually not terrible looking. Okay, he's extremely hot, in a very conventional, chiseled, male-model sort of way.

"Her name's Lucía," I interject, sliding into the backseat with a mix of reluctance and resentment and settling in with the five books on my lap.

Lucía follows suit, her excitement practically palpable.

Jacob's friend settles in the front and turns to face us, his mischievous grin sending a shiver down my spine. His gaze flits between Lucía and me, as though he's trying to decide who's prettier or something stupid like that, and for a moment, I find myself holding my breath, unsure of what he's thinking.

"What?" I finally prompt, breaking the tension that hangs in the air. "Why are you sizing us up like chicken breasts?"

"Can I ask you something?" he shouts over the blaring music, not bothering to wait for my response before firing off another question. "Did Jacob really have to pick you up because you can't drive after getting hit by lightning? Or is my boy here full of it?"

I blink, caught off guard by his blunt inquiry, but before I can respond, Lucía jumps in, leaning forward in her excitement.

"She did! Amazing, am I right?"

The guy turns the music down so he can hear her better. I swallow hard, feeling a surge of discomfort at the way she shares my personal story so easily with a stranger. I love Lucía, but sometimes she doesn't have the best boundaries.

"Can we just go, please?" I plead with Jacob, who seems in no rush to leave the comfort of this parking space. Away from this bookshop. Away from Pakwá-ule.

"Sure," he says, distractedly, as he searches for the next song. He cranks up the music again and revs his dumb engine, drowning out any chance of meaningful conversation. "You ready?"

I force a tight-lipped smile, struggling to suppress the frustration bubbling within me as I click my seatbelt on.

"Could you turn it down a little more, please?" I yell at Jacob.

"Sure thing, *grandma*," says Jacob.

"Loud music hurts because I was hit by lightning," I say. "It's neurology, not decrepitude and joylessness."

It's not true, but this lightning thing is turning out to be a very convenient excuse.

"I can't believe that!" cries Jacob's friend. "Freakin' *lightning!*"

"I'm sorry," I tell him, "who are you?"

"What? Girl, I'm *hurt*. I'm Cameron!" he says, super happy. "You know me. I'm over at your house, like, all the time. We've talked before."

"Sorry. Memory loss is part of the lightning thing, too," I say. This part might be true, because I don't remember talking to him, ever.

"Oh, snap! Yeah, I get that. No worries. I'm not mad. I was just asking if it's true your heart stopped, and you were revived by some nerd."

"It's true!" Lucía answers for me. Ordinarily, I'd have defended Blake from the insult, but I'm not exactly in disagreement at the moment. "He's our friend, so maybe don't call him that, but, yeah, he is actually kind of a nerd."

"Dope! What was that like, when the bolt struck you, Grace? I'm fascinated, I can't lie. I've always had a special affinity for extreme weather. You can ask anyone."

"Cameron wants me to chase tornadoes with him," says Jacob. "He literally does that as a hobby. He's got a van with all these radars in it."

"Cool," I say, and to my own surprise, I kind of mean it.

While I'm definitely not going out looking for lightning anytime soon, I can admire Cameron's unusual, passionate hobby. I'm also ashamed to find that I'm surprised he has this much depth as a person.

"Jacob tells me you're a writer, Grace," says Cameron. "I'm a big reader. Scifi is my jam. Right now, NK Jemison is, like, my guru. So I bet you could, like, describe what it was like to get hit by lightning in crazy detail. Have you written about it?"

"No."

"You should!"

"Maybe."

"I'm dying to read that. I'm so jealous, man. You have no idea. Seriously."

"You saying you want to get hit by lightning and have your heart stop, dude?" Jacob asks him. "That's beyond screwed up."

"Heck yeah! If I knew I'd come back and be fine, like Grace, hell yeah, man! It's got to be such a rush. Right?" Cameron grins at me awaiting an answer.

I am going through my memory of the lightning strike, trying to find a piece of it I can safely tell him, when Lucía intervenes.

"She came back with special powers, too," blurts Lucía.

"Like Spiderman or something?" asks Jacob, laughing. "No way!"

Before I can stop her, Lucía says, "Exactly like that, except Grace can see dead people now."

I can tell she's trying to impress the boys by telling them my secrets, leaning so far forward and over me, she's practically in the front seat with them. Uncool.

"No, I can't see dead people, don't listen to her, she's kidding," I say, because I don't want to deal with their ridicule or with Jacob telling my dad and his mom that I'm seeing spirits. "Lucía's full of crap. Also, a spider bite is very different from a lightning bolt."

"But they can both be deadly," says Jacob.

"Yes, you can, Grace … oh." Lucía starts to correct me but seems to take the hint that I want her to shut up by the way I'm glaring at her. She winces and scoots back. "Sorry. My bad. Grace can't see ghosts."

"Because *no one can*," I say, in a deliberate teacherly way.

As Jacob slows the Camaro to a stop at a red light, I catch a glimpse of something out of the corner of my eye, a shadowy figure darting through the darkness, keeping pace with the car. My heart skips a beat, and I feel a cold chill creep down my spine. Then I see her mournful eyes and her tattered white gown. It's my miserable ancestral spirit guide, running alongside us with her bare feet, holding her skirts up with her hands like she's part of the worst square dance troupe in history.

Cameron has snapped his head back around to watch a couple of cute college-age-looking women crossing the street in front of the car, on their way to a bar. This also occupies Jacob's attention. I lean in close to Lucía, my voice barely more than a whisper.

"She's here," I say, my words trembling with fear.

"Who?"

"Pakwá-ule."

Lucía's eyes widen in alarm and she follows the line of my gaze out the window, searching. Her voice is barely audible over the roar of the engine. "Really?"

I swallow hard, my throat dry and constricted. I can't tell her the truth—not here, not with Jacob and his friend listening in. I turn away, my heart pounding in my chest as we speed through the darkened streets of Austin, the ghostly specter of La Llorona haunting our entire commute. She's always been there, I remind myself. It's just that I can see her now, and she knows I can. It probably changes nothing but my perception of things, the way that finding out someone has been lying to you for years changes nothing but the perception of things.

As we continue on our way, Lucía pulls out her phone, her fingers flying across the screen as she searches for information about Warwick Blackwater, the former high school bully Safia mentioned, who is now the man we suspect of killing Mohammad. I glance over her shoulder, my eyes scanning the search results with growing horror. He's very much alive and still looks like a bodybuilding bully, only now he appears in photos smiling in the insincere, aggressive way of a car salesman.

"Holy shizmonkeys, Grace, he's a state *senator*," Lucía whispers.

My blood runs cold, and I feel a wave of nausea wash over me as we whisper about this monster together. How could someone like Warwick Blackwater, who bullied two Muslim kids so badly that one ended up dead and the other still seems afraid to talk about him, hold such power and influence in our city? And what does that mean for Mohammad's murder ... and for us?

Before we can dwell on the implications of our discovery, Cameron speaks up again, his voice filled with a strange mix of pride and unease.

"You girls talking about Senator Warwick Blackwater?" he asks.

"Maybe," I say, surprised he knows anything about politics. "Why?"

"Yeah, you guys know he's my dad, right?"

Jacob gawks at his friend and holds his hand up to high-five him. "Dude, I did *not* know your dad was a senator! What *what*?"

"Really, Jacob?" says Cameron. "Blackwater's not exactly a common name. How could you not put two and two together?"

"Uh, I don't know," says Jacob, sarcastically and defensively. "Maybe because I don't give a rat's ass about politics and have no idea who our senators even are?"

"Fair enough. Politics is trash, if you ask me, which no one ever does. Also, don't get all excited. It's just for the state. He's not, like, in congress or some nonsense."

"This man's your dad?" asks Lucía, turning her phone screen so Cameron can see the photo.

"That's him."

My heart skips a beat, and I feel the world spinning out of control as the pieces of the puzzle fall into place. Warwick Blackwater, the man we suspect of murdering Mohammad, is not only a powerful state senator, he's also the father of Jacob's best friend, stoned and jolly Cameron.

I exchange a horrified glance with Lucía, our eyes wide with shock and disbelief. What have we gotten ourselves into? And how are we ever going to make it out alive?

"We'd love to meet your dad, Cameron," blurts Lucía. I almost throw up because no, we absolutely would *not*. She really isn't good at assessing danger.

"I'm in student government," she says. "So, like, big fan here."

This is a blatant lie. Lucía is not in student government. Why is she doing this?

"Yeah, sure, no problem," says Cameron. "I don't know if you'd want to do this, but we're having a big political fundraiser at our house tomorrow evening. Cocktails for the adults, pool party for the kids. You could come as my guest and meet my dad. I'm sure he'd love it. He's always excited when anyone under 80 shows any interest in politics."

"We'd love to," says Lucía.

"Plus, you can see Jacob in a swimsuit," Cameron tells Lucía, and I realize just what a good reader of people he is.

Lucía blushes. "It would be an honor to meet your dad," she says. "And swimming is always fun, right, Grace?"

Pakwá-ule runs up right next to the car, presses her hands against the window closest to me, stares me in the eyes and wails, the way she is said to do when she spots children coming too close to a dangerous body of water. Of course, I'm the only one who can hear it.

Chapter Thirteen

When we get home, the kitchen island is covered in the shrapnel of what appears to have been the Great Pizza, Breadstick and Root Beer Rebellion. Before picking us up, Jacob and Cameron had already eaten two large pizzas from Eastside Slice Shack, my favorite New York style pizza place, and the house smells of savory pepperoni and oregano. My stomach growls. Whenever our parents have evening events—which is more often than you might think—they assuage their guilt by letting us order whatever we want for dinner. There are two additional large pizza boxes, unopened, and Jacob tells me those are for us "drama queens, and I mean that as a compliment" as he tosses the car keys into the big wooden bowl of keys in the mudroom. Charlie, my beloved dead dog, stands near the island, tail wagging like crazy to welcome us home. I resist the urge to baby-talk and ghost-cuddle him.

My stenchbrother appears to have been deliberate and thoughtful in what he ordered. For me, it's my absolute favorite, the Supreme, with sausage, pepperoni, mushrooms, extra cheese and jalapeños, whereas the pie for Lucía is the gluten-free vegan option. For what it's worth, Lucía keeps threatening to find another best friend if I can't stop eating meat, but every time I've tried, I feel deeply unwell. I hope she's joking, and I am absolutely a reluctant omnivore.

"*You* ordered this?" I ask him.

I don't mean to sound so surprised. Jacob picks up on my tone. He makes direct eye contact with me, something we rarely do, and I sense a humor and softness to his hazel eyes I've never noticed before. Almost a vulnerability.

"Don't act so shocked, Grace," he says, as he plops down on the soft cream-colored sofa in the adjacent TV area of the open great room—a different area than the living room with the butterscotch leather sofas. He plucks a remote from the basket of remotes and turns the giant flatscreen on, leaning back and manspreading to relax. It should be noted here that he could just go up to his wing and watch TV there. He has a massive flatscreen in his bedroom, too. But he's chosen to stick around. He doesn't usually do that. I wonder if my dad told him to keep an eye on me.

"How sweet!" says Lucía. "Thank you, Jacob."

If I didn't know better, I'd say she was almost moved to tears by the vegan pizza.

Jacob's focused on the screen, and Cameron is now seated next to him, but he mutters a "no problem" to my friend, cutting her a sideways glance that seems almost shy. Is he blushing? *What the actual holy hell.* Jacob calls up a streaming app and selects a popular new series about zombies.

"Oh my God, I love this show!" says Lucía.

If that's true, this is the first I'm hearing of it. Is she twirling her hair flirtatiously? Dear. God. No. She doesn't love this show. She loves Jacob.

"Can I … er, can *we* watch, too?"

Jacob shrugs, but Cameron grins at her and wheels his hand to welcome her. He pats the sofa next to Jacob and scoots over to make room for her.

"Is it okay to eat there?" she asks me. "Your house is like a spotless museum. I feel like no one should ever eat anywhere in here."

"This coffee table is basically one ginormous TV tray," says Jacob. He pushes the button that lifts the top of the fancy custom table on its hydraulics.

"Whoa," she says.

"With all due respect," I tell her, in a whisper, "I've had enough of the undead for a while."

"Oh, crap," says Lucía. "Right. Sorry. Do you not want me to?"

She's already headed toward the guys with her paper plate of pizza and a bottle of root beer. She looks so disappointed, like a kindergartener who thinks she's going to Disneyland only to find out she's going to the city landfill.

"Go ahead," I say. "I need to run upstairs real quick and take care of something, anyway."

"Don't you have bathrooms down here?" she asks, both misunderstanding me and embarrassing me at once.

"Not that," I say. I glance at the guys, then give her a knowing look.

"Ohhh," she says. "Got it. Are you seeing Moham …?"

I motion for her to stop talking in front of the guys, and I don't tell her that, yes, I do see him. He's standing at the bottom of the stairs, watching us from across the living room. He looks wistful and lonely, like he wishes he could eat pizza and watch a zombie series, too. He waves to say hello, and I press my lips into a hard line with a curt nod I hope no one else notices.

"Sorry. Are you okay alone or do you need me to …" says Lucía.

"I'm fine. Watch the show. I'll be right back."

Even though I'm starving, I leave the kitchen and, with Charlie trailing me, pass Mohammad and take the stairs two at a time. I go directly to my room on a mission, and immediately pick up the Lorica paper from the top of my desk. Mohammad is already in my room watching over my shoulder. He looks …

different. Better. And, weirdly, a tiny bit more solid with a bit more color to him. The best comparison I can make is early colorized movies. I can still see through him, but he looks more material, and healthier. He uses both his hands to point out the shirt he's wearing, proud. It's another concert T-shirt, but instead of The Beastie effing Boys, it's Dead Boys, one of my all-time favorite vintage punk bands. In spite of my exhaustion and desire not to deal with spiorads other than Charlie, I laugh a little.

"Did you hear me when I told you to update your playlist?" I ask him.

He grins and shrugs like "Who, me?"

"Clever."

His eyes drop to the spell in my hands, and he frowns.

"Sorry, Mo," I tell him. "It's been a long-ass day. I need … I'm not used to being able to see you or anyone else who's dead, and it would just be really nice if I could have some peace right now. Don't take it personally."

The look in his eyes breaks me. Lonely. He is deeply, terribly lonely, and, it seems, has been waiting for me to come home. It's as though he had hope I'd take him off an island and I've only dashed his head on the rocky shoreline instead.

"I know," I say. "It's not you. Listen, I do like you. This isn't a rejection, okay? It's not that. It's that everyone else down there will think I'm crazy if I can't function in their world the way I used to. It's just temporary. I'll see you tomorrow. We'll talk. Okay? But I did want to tell you, before you go, we talked to your sister today."

Mohammad looks astonished by this news, and he zooms closer. I feel the weight of his wanting to goop me again.

"No," I say. "I don't like that. At all."

Mohammad's shoulders drop, and he almost seems to sigh in disappointed acceptance.

"She told us about a former classmate of yours. Warwick Blackwater," I say. "Do you remember him?"

Mohammad's eyes open wide with what I interpret to be fear and surprise.

"Is he the one who … hurt you?"

Mohammad nods. Then he shakes his head. Yes, then no. Then a shrug.

"Sounds like you have mixed feelings about him," I say.

Mohammad just stares blankly at me.

"Well, that dude sounds like a dick," I say. "That giant insanely attractive kid downstairs, with my stepbrother? That's his son. What are the odds?"

Mohammad's eyes open even wider. Like he can't believe it.

"Careful," I tell him, indicating his eyes. "You don't want those things to pop out again. Well, at least I don't. It was very hard to look at you like that."

Mohammad seems to find this amusing.

"What do you do all day, when I'm not here?" I ask him.

He just looks at me. Unable to communicate directly.

"Yeah, okay," I say. "As much as I'd love to sit here trying to figure everything out, I'm starving right now. And my friend Lucía is downstairs, likely making an ass of herself in front of my stepbrother. I have to get back down there, and, if you don't mind, I need to do this spell. Okay?"

More staring. I realize how far I've come in the past day since I first saw him. Negotiating with him like he's an unreasonable customer at an occult bookshop instead of a dead guy.

"Let me ask you, can you see my spirit guide? She's a demon, by the way. La Llorona. Because that is apparently my karma or something."

Mohammad's forehead screws up like he might not quite understand what I'm asking him.

"Never mind. We'll talk tomorrow, okay? Right now, it's almost nine and I need to eat and sleep."

Mohammad still looks devastated, but he salutes me with two fingers. The gesture reminds me of Blake, who often does this same thing to me. Thinking of him makes my heart start to hurt in a way that I do *not* have energy for, either. He hasn't texted me. And I'm not sure how I'd respond even if he did. People always warn you not to date your friends, in case it doesn't work out and you end up ruining the friendship. I'm worried that's what we've done. I wish there were a spell I could do to erase Blake from my life, too. I put the thought of him into the Big Box of Denial where I keep the thoughts of things I don't want to deal with, along with things like how many carcinogens are in a bowl of Fruit Loops and how unfair it is that men don't get menstrual cramps and also get paid more for doing the same work as women, and I lock it.

I say the incantation and watch as Mohammad and Charlie begin to fade. After they disappear, the bluetooth speaker on my desk turns itself on, and after crackling a little as though it were a radio receiver set to static, a song begins to play. I pull my phone out of my pocket, and, sure enough, Mohammad appears to have been able to control the electronic device somehow.

The song he pulled up as he left is "Ain't It Fun," by Dead Boys.

It's been a while since I listened to this one. I realize he's probably not just trying to be cute; he's trying to communicate. I sit at my desk and listen to the song before going back downstairs to eat my pizza. The lyrics are apropos and not a little bit terrifying. I don't know if they're supposed to be about him or about me.

Toward the end of the song, there's a knock on my door. I assume it's Lucía and yell, "Come in, bi-otch!" We call each other bi-otch with affection, by the way. Well, most of the time, anyway.

But it's not Lucía. It's Cameron, the insanely attractive sporty guy whose dad murdered the dead kid in my room. He looks friendly but a little embarrassed. He's carrying a pizza box with a bunch of paper napkins on top of it, and a bottle of root beer.

"Hey," he says.

"Hi?" I suddenly feel very exposed. How long has he been out there? Did he hear me talking to Mohammad? Is he a murderer like his father?

"I hope I'm not bothering you," he says.

"No, I was actually just headed back down."

"Yeah, well. You might not want to go down there," he says. "That's why I brought this up." Because he's going to kill me with pizza?

"Why?"

"There's kind of some serious making out going on downstairs," he says, wincing.

"What? Ew. No. Really?"

"They seem to, um, really like each other," he says, clearing his throat diplomatically.

I sigh, and he seems to empathize. I invite him in. He sets the pizza on the floor, and we sit across the box from each other. This is when I notice Pakwá-ule materializing in the corner with her knees drawn up to her chest, rocking a little, like a person in the midst of a nervous breakdown. She's very faint, little more than mist, but she's watching us with an alarmingly dark intensity. So I guess one's guardian demon is not cast out by the Lorica, then, because of course it isn't. I try to ignore her, so I can focus on Cameron not finding out I actually see dead people. This juggling act of trying to seem normal while not being normal at all is proving to be very difficult.

"Did they just start swapping spit right in front of you?" I ask him, distractedly.

"Not exactly." He serves me a slice of pizza on a paper plate. "They both got up to get something in the kitchen, and next thing I knew she had him pushed up against the refrigerator, and it sounded like feeding time in the wild boar enclosure."

"Damn," I say. I appreciate his simile, even as it surprises me he'd use one. "Damn, Lucía."

He tells me my stepbrother has been talking about Lucía for months, showing all his friends her Instagram. "He's always bragging about how talented and gorgeous she is, and how he gets to see her all the time because she's his sister's friend."

"He calls me his sister? I'm his stepsister."

"He refers to you as his sister, at school."

"This is all very weird," I say. "Because whenever we're around he always acts like we're not even there."

"Yeah, well, I don't know if you've noticed this or not, but Jacob's not exactly confident."

I laugh. "Oh, please. He's, like, mister popular."

"Is that what he told you?"

"No. I just assumed."

"Well, he's not that popular. He's pretty quiet at school. Seriously! He might seem cool as a cucumber around here, but if you get to know him, he's just another insecure dude worried girls will reject him."

"You're kidding me," I say.

"People aren't always what they seem, Grace," he says, his voice low and intimate. "Like, I bet even *you* have some secrets."

I meet his gaze, feeling a rush of warmth spread through me at the burning intensity in his eyes.

"Maybe," I reply softly, the air between us crackling with unspoken tension.

"Everyone does," he murmurs, leaning in slightly closer.

"Does your dad?" I ask him before I have a chance to censor myself. At least I leave off the "like being a murderer?" part.

Cameron looks taken aback by the question, but also unfazed. "I mean, he's a politician, so I'd say that's a definite yes. Why do you ask?"

I scramble to think of a reply that might make sense. "Just because, you know," I say. "What you said. He's a politician. They always seem to have some scandal they're trying to hide."

"What have you heard?" he asks, suddenly seeming defensive. So, there is a scandal. Of course, there is. What am I even doing? This seems like a very good way to get myself hurt.

"Nothing," I say. "Forget I said it. It … it was dumb. I was deflecting."

"From having to think about your own secrets?"

"Pretty much."

"Tell me one," he says, "and I'll share one of mine."

My heart pounds hard. His cheeks flush a deep shade of red, and I can't help but notice how his gaze lingers on my lips. I can't tell whether he wants to kill me, or kiss me … or maybe both?

"You first," I say.

"Well, when I said it hurt me that you forgot my name, I meant it," he confesses, his voice barely above a whisper. "Because … I'd never forget yours. Like, ever. Meeting you was like … like electricity. Like lightning, maybe."

"Yeah, doubt that," I say.

"You fascinate me, Grace."

His words hang in the air between us, charged with a palpable energy that sends shivers down my spine. Is he hinting at something more? Is there a vulnerability beneath his confident façade?

"Want some?" I offer, gesturing to the pizza, attempting to break the spell of tension that surrounds us. But his playful smirk tells me he's caught on to the double entendre in my words.

"Pizza," I hastily add, feeling a blush rise to my cheeks.

"Relax," he reassures me, his smile softening as he reaches for a slice. "I'm not gonna bite you. Sorry for making things weird."

I shake my head, unable to tear my gaze away from him. "Trust me," I reply, softly. "Things in my life are always weird. There's not much anyone could do or say that would or could make them any weirder."

"Well, I like weird girls," he admits, his eyes sparkling with amusement. "I know they're not for everyone. But they're definitely for me. In fact, the weirder, the better. Which is why I really liked your short film, 'Awkward.'"

It's the name of my freshman independent study project from last year, which I uploaded to apply for the internship at NexaWave. It's nothing but me frowning and glaring at myself in a mirror first thing after rolling out of bed for the entire school year, me in different pajamas with my hair messy in different ways, looking a million kinds of terrible, with the background morphing slightly, but all spliced together over the soundtrack of that old song "Popular" by Nada Surf, each day taking a split-second. It has, like, exactly five views and one Like."

"You *saw* that?"

"Yeah, girl! I subscribed to your YouTube. It was genius."

As my phone vibrates beside me, I'm torn between the urge to check the message, and the desire to stay immersed in the moment with Cameron. His presence does feel electric, in a good way, and I can't help but wonder if he'd be a better match for me than Blake. Cameron is excited about lightning and the supernatural, and Blake is … Blake.

"You okay?" he asks, his concern evident in his voice.

"Yeah." I take a breath and set my phone aside without a second glance. "It's just … it's the guy who saved my life."

"The nerd?" he remarks, a hint of playful jealousy lacing his words.

I nod, a small smile tugging at the corners of my lips.

"Lucky guy," he comments, his gaze lingering on mine. "To have your undying loyalty now, I bet."

"It's complicated," I admit, the weight of my words hanging heavy in the air.

"I should tell you, I like complicated girls, too," he murmurs, his tone filled with sincerity as he reaches for my hand, his touch sending a jolt of electricity through me. "It's my Achilles heel, so to speak. The more complicated, the better. Weird, complicated girls. Never a dull moment."

As Cameron's hand finds mine, a surge of warmth courses through me, sending a tingle down my spine. For a moment, we linger in silence, our eyes locked across the pizza between us. And then, almost instinctively, Cameron leans over the pizza box, coming in closer, his lips hovering just inches from mine.

My heart pounds in my chest as I feel the heat of his breath against my skin, the anticipation building with each passing second. And then, without a word, he closes the distance between us, his lips meeting mine in a tender, clandestine kiss.

Time seems to stand still as we share this stolen moment together. But as quickly as it began, reality comes crashing back as the bluetooth speaker turns itself on again, this time at full blast, and I pull away, my cheeks flushed with guilt and uncertainty. The song that blares out is "I Will Survive," by Gloria Gaynor.

"Um, okay?" says Cameron.

"It does that sometimes," I tell him. "Ever since the lightning."

"Right! I've heard that people can have weird electrical things happen after lightning strikes," he says. "Interesting song choice, though? You like old disco?"

"Not especially," I say. "It's only happened a couple of times, and it's completely random." I turn the song off.

"You," says Cameron, "are fascinating."

"Yeah, I don't know. Look, Cameron, I ... I need to get some homework done before bed," I murmur, my voice barely above a whisper. "You should probably go back downstairs ... and send Lucía up, if you can separate them. My dad and stepmom will be home soon, and they'd freak out if they found them all over each other."

Cameron's expression softens, understanding flickering in his eyes as he nods in silent agreement. "Of course," he replies, his tone gentle and reassuring. "I'll see you later, Grace. You should come with Jacob to my place tomorrow. You and your friend can meet my dad, like I said. We can swim, if you want. I'd like to see you in a bathing suit, not gonna lie."

"Yeah, maybe," I say.

With a final, lingering glance, he leaves. The weight of my guilt because of Blake is heavy on my shoulders as I watch him go.

In her corner, Pakwá-ule watches me with what appears to be curiosity. She's now sitting cross-legged, as though about to begin meditating, and looks peaceful. She seems less sad than before, and this surprises me. I had expected her to judge me harshly, to disapprove of Cameron.

"Wait a second. Do you actually *like* him for me?" I ask her.

Pakwá-ule nods and gives me a thumbs up.

"The son of Mohammad's killer?" I ask.

Pakwá-ule shrugs.

"Did you arrange this, for him to be here, for me to be able to investigate his dad?"

Pakwá-ule smiles, and then I hear her voice. It sounds like a million voices all whispering and twisting together, and somewhere, spinning up from the center of the storm, is the chilling, hissing word, "Yes."

Chapter Fourteen

Lucía spends the night, and we both wake up early the next morning to get ready for school, which for me now includes performing the spiorad-be-gone ritual. I've just about memorized it. She has to borrow clothes, which is fine because I'm only a tiny bit bigger than she is. I fold the paper with the spell on it and shove it into my backpack so that I'll not be caught at school without it this time.

"Do I look okay?" Lucía asks me before we're about to head downstairs.

Our styles are very different, to say the least. I'm Therapy Girl goth, and she's aspiring actress elegance. There wasn't much for her to choose from among my clothes that matched her vibe. She's chosen dark skinny jeggings and a fitted long-sleeved plain black T-shirt.

"Jacob's already gone, don't worry," I tell her. "He has zero-hour weight training with the team most days."

"I admire his discipline," she says. "Speaking of the sporty boys. How are you feeling about Cameron?"

I'd told her about the kiss last night, and we both laughed for a long time about how weird it was that we might have each ended up with sporty boyfriends.

"Confused." I tell her honestly. "Like, I thought I loved Blake, but I honestly can't feel anything for him right now. And

I did not expect Cameron to be ... well, Cameron. And Pakwáule seems to like him for me."

"Girl, that's a good sign."

"I don't know. She is a demon."

At this moment there's a loud thump near my desk, and I see that one of the books Milagros gave me about La Llorona has fallen to the floor and opened to a page.

"Um, okay," I say.

"That's scary as frack," says Lucía. She scrambles to stand behind me, as if she needs protection from a book. "... But also insanely cool. What does it say?"

I pick the book up and skim the pages. It's extremely academic, and I do not have the energy for it right now.

"Read it out loud," she says, but remains backed up close to the door.

I sigh. "It says, 'The folklore narrative of La Llorona is one that has been an essential story in oral traditions of *hispanohablante* (Spanish-speaking) communities for centuries. It has been passed on in many forms, deriving her contexts from regions, communities and participants of the lore. In Mexico City, her story takes the shape of a ghostly woman wandering the streets crying out to warn her people of the coming conquistadors (Perez 16). In other regions of the United States, she is a young *hispana*, *mestiza* or indigenous girl, often of lesser means, who is abandoned by a man of lower nobility for a wealthier Spanish woman and drowns her children in grief (Estés 326). In many narratives from New Mexico, she is a young mestiza or Indian mother whose ranchero partner is unfaithful, and she drowns her children in a vengeful despair, left to haunt *cantinas* and walk along the *acequias* (Lamadrid 123). Each narrative reflects the unique identity of La Llorona and positions her in a variety of social, racial, socioeconomic and political contexts within each region, contributing to the collection of a rich oral tradition of her story.'" I pause to consider this, then close the book. "Basically, it's saying she's a myth, I guess."

"But if she's just a myth, how is she your guardian angel?" asks Lucía.

"I don't know."

"Maybe her real story is in these books," says Lucía. "Maybe that's why she's throwing books down. I don't think she likes you calling her a demon."

"Maybe not. We don't have time to figure any of that out right now. We'll be late for school if we don't leave, like, now."

When we come downstairs, my father and stepmother are sitting at the island drinking coffee with worried looks on their faces.

"Lucía, honey, we're going to ask you to go back to Grace's room for a few minutes," says my stenchmom. "We need to talk to Grace privately."

Once she's out of earshot, my father says, "Sweetheart. We're concerned you might be trying to do too much, too soon after your accident. So we'd like to keep you home from school for the day, see how it goes, give you a chance to rest."

"But I'm fine. I don't need that."

"Janice ... er, Dr. Levinson-Abrams phoned us late last night and told us some things that Blake told her, that concern us," says Candi with an i.

"About?"

"Grace, Blake's mom said that you've been telling him and Lucía that you're having visions of demons and ghosts and monsters since your accident," says my father. "He said you seem to think you're helping spirits cross over to the light or something?"

"I believe the word he used was delusional," says my stenchmother.

Because of course he did. *Effing Blake*. Like it wasn't bad enough to change his mind about believing me, now he's ratting me out to his psychiatrist mother and she's calling my dad and stepmother? What the hell, man?

"He's exaggerating," I say. "He does that. He's overly sensitive. Am I having weird visions? Yes. Which is *normal* after getting hit by lightning. That's what Doctor Kapoor said. You knew this. I don't understand why you're acting like this is news."

"Right. We know," says my dad.

Candi with an i interrupts. "We also spoke to Doctor Kapoor this morning."

"We've scheduled an emergency assessment for you, with Dr. Levinson-Abrams, for tomorrow afternoon," concludes my dad.

"What? I do not need to see Janice, okay? Doctor Kapoor, sure. Fine. Janice? No. She's a *child* psychiatrist. I am fine. And we have sophomore documentaries due soon. I can't miss school."

"Please don't get defensive," says Candi with an i. "If there's nothing going on, she'll be able to assess that, right?"

"This is an invasion of my privacy," I say.

"When your behaviors start to impact your friends," says Candi with an i, "and their parents are calling us in the middle of the night to express their concerns, we have no choice as parents but to step in."

"You ... are not my *parent*. I'd appreciate it if you could try harder to remember that. And if Janice is calling you in the middle of the night to talk trash about me, I'd suggest she has bigger issues than I do."

"Language," says Candi with an i.

"Grace," says my father in a warning tone of voice.

"What? Why is it perfectly fine to say poop but taboo to say shit? They mean literally *exactly the same thing*."

"Benjamin." My stenchmother stares at my father as though he should be doing something about my dirty mouth.

He looks at me and scolds, "Grace."

"What? She is not my mom! My mom's only been dead two years, and it's like you expect me to just move on because you did. How did you do that, by the way? Two years?!"

"Okay, I've had enough of this disrespect," says Candi with an i, turning to my dad in a businesslike way that dismisses me. "I'm going to leave this to the two of you. I'll go talk to Lucía, then I'll drop her off at school."

"So you're just leaving me home alone all day?" I ask, thinking that if they do, I'll take my Mustang, whether they like it or not, and I'll go to the old house and try to make contact with my mother's spirit. I need to ask her why the hell she left me with these two assholes.

"We think it's best if you hang out with me today," says my dad. "You can come with me to work."

"Oh, can I? Does that mean I have a choice?"

"No. You're coming with me."

"What? No. That sounds awful, Dad."

"I'll introduce you to some people who might have influence over the internship. We'll make the best of it, okay?"

"This is all her idea, isn't it? Candi. My normal dad, the way you used to be, would never do this to me. My actual mom would never do this to me."

"Well, your mom's not here."

"No kidding."

Moments later, Lucía comes through the room with my stenchmother. She looks bewildered.

"Are you okay?" she asks me.

"I guess. They won't let me go to school."

"I wish I had parents like that," she jokes.

"No, I assure you, you don't."

I see now that she's holding one of the La Llorona books.
"Doing a little light reading?"

"Oh," she says, noticing that I see the book. "Okay if I take this? I started reading it just now and it's *very* interesting. She would be an amazing character to play."

"Fine. Take it."

Lucía looks respectful of my father and stenchmother but worried for me. "I guess I'll see you later, then?"

"Yeah. I guess." I look at my dad and add a little white lie. "We were invited to Jacob's friend Cameron's house after school today, so Lucía can interview his senator dad for her documentary. He's holding some big fundraiser. Can I go? I'm supposed to be doing camerawork for her."

"We'll see how it goes today," says my dad.

"I'm glad you're finally giving Jacob a chance," says Candi with an i, to me, as though I'm the only reason her dull son and I have not become besties. She looks at my father and says, "He could be a good influence on her. The Blackwaters are an outstanding family. I hear they're looking to sell their home...."

She digs through her fancy purse and pulls out a silver business-card holder. I can't believe she's about to give me a card to give to Cameron's murderer dad.

"Not now," my father tells her in a rare display of actually defending me.

Candi with an i gives my father a light kiss, telling him she'll see us later and wishing him a good day. She refuses to even look at me. She holds the mudroom door open for Lucía, as though Lucía, too, were a penance.

"She's really something," I tell my dad. "Is she ever not trying to make a deal?"

My dad ignores the questions but offers to make me my favorite blueberry pancakes.

"If you're going to force me to go with you to work, the least you can do is let me get *conchas* on the way. And Mexican coffee."

"That actually sounds pretty good," he says, patting me on the back. "We'll make the best of it."

We pick up the box of Mexican pastries and our coffees, then drive to my dad's company in Round Rock, a suburb about 25 minutes north of Austin. On the way, I finally bring myself to look at Blake's texts from last night. I haven't wanted to deal with them because I honestly don't know what I'm doing anymore. In the texts, he tells me he's sorry for how he worded things with me at Rosen's. He says he "wants to believe" me but that he's worried about me and wants me to be safe. I see that he even tried to call me, as in making a phone call, which is not something we do, ever. He's also gone on my YouTube channel and left comments on a couple of posts telling me to read my texts and get back to him. To his credit, he did text that if I didn't reply within an hour that he would text Lucía about his concerns. Technically, this is probably all my fault, for ignoring him. If I'd responded, he might not have talked about me to his mother.

I text Blake back now, to let him know his mother contacted my father and stenchmother and that he has in effect destroyed my life forever. He apologizes and confesses to having told his mom about what was happening because he and his mom are good friends, and she noticed he was too upset to do his homework. He says he had no idea his mom would contact my dad. He says he's going to talk to her and let her know how *not effing okay* that was. Then, he says he has to turn his phone off because he's at school. Before he goes, though, he says he needs to know whether we're okay or not. He's being so sweet now; I feel terrible. Do I tell him about the kiss with Cameron? Why did I even kiss Cameron? I was tired. He was hot. I was confused.

He liked my films. I opt to keep all that to myself and deal with the guilt. I tell Blake to have a nice day, and he again asks if we're okay.

    Blake: I love you.
    Me: Then maybe don't tell your mom everything.
    Blake: So no ♡ ?
    Me: I might need space.

Not three seconds later, I get a good morning text from Cameron. I send back a rising sun emoji and a smiley face. He asks if he'll see me later today at his dad's "shindig," and I say I'm working on it but my dad might not let me.

    Cameron: Want me to break his kneecaps?

This makes me laugh out loud.

"What's so funny?" asks my dad.

"Nothing," I say.

The NexaWave Technology compound where my dad works is a massive U-shaped complex of large six-story gray buildings with two thick stripes of dark glass wrapped around it like belts. The people who work there refer to the buildings as a campus rather than an office, and it has that kind of a feel to it, in some ways, like the bland campus of a massive community college. There are sprawling bright green lawns and courtyards with fountains. The interior of the buildings tries to be young and hip and cool the way tech companies try to be all those things, with ball pits and firehouse poles and kombucha bars and people sitting on balls instead of chairs at their desks and whatever the hell else they think will make people forget they're wasting their lives in an office building. I follow my dad into an elevator and up to the sixth floor, where the legal and executive suites are. I've only been here a couple of times before, and I'm amazed yet again by how fancy it all is compared to the places my dad used to work before my mom's suicide convinced him to become an emotionless Republican. His old office used to be tucked between a nail salon and a dumpster.

"I just have to pop in here a quick sec," he tells me, as we near the open door of a large and elegant corner office. "Come with me. I'll introduce you to the big boss."

"Who?" I ask.

"Smitty," he says. "The guy who founded NexaWave. Could help with your internship application."

I remember now. Smitty, the one-named founder of the city's biggest tech company, is a guy so important he apparently doesn't need two names. Like Bono or Lorde. A guy regarded as being on the same level as Steve Jobs and Jeff Bezos, one of the richest men in the world. I'm suddenly intimidated.

As I reluctantly enter Smitty's office alongside my father, I'm struck by the familiar sight of the famous bald figure awaiting us. Smitty's aura of confidence and authority is disarming. It feels almost like an act to me, designed to impress naïve investors and unsuspecting interns alike, but, then again, my mother cultivated in me distrust of the Uber-rich. As my father goes through the formalities of introducing me, Smitty rises from his seat with a practiced smile plastered on his face. It's almost comical how he tries to seem welcoming, like he's genuinely interested in meeting me.

"Grace, it's a pleasure to finally meet you," Smitty says, extending a large, dry hand in greeting. His handshake is firm and confident. "Your father has told me so much about you."

"He has?"

"Yes, I hear you're quite the young screenwriter," he says. "Believe it or not, we have quite a few screenwriters working here now."

"Cool."

"Grace actually applied for the high school internship in the narrative design incubator," says my dad.

"Did you? That's great!"

Smitty is surrounded by screens displaying intricate graphs and charts that represent the heartbeat of his company. His desk is cluttered with papers and prototypes.

Smitty motions to the little kitchenette across the room, near the sectional sofas. "Grace, why don't you help yourself to a snack or something to drink, and have a seat in the lounge area while your dad and I chat about a business matter for a minute."

My father takes a seat at Smitty's desk. Smitty sits back down across from him, and they quickly become engrossed in work that bores me. I wander to the kitchen area, passing by a long bookcase with many photographs and awards displayed on it. One of these stands out to me, and I stop in my tracks. I have seen this photo before. In fact, I have a copy of it on my phone. It's the same yearbook photo of the Amateur Radio Club from Johnston High School, with Mohammad in it. Milagros' words immediately come back to me: "Once you're in flow with creation, the spiorads will lead you where you are meant to be led."

I run my finger over the photo, and Smitty seems to notice.

"Hey, you guys just moved to East Austin last year, right?" he calls out, in a loud voice. "I grew up around there. I went to Johnston, back before it was rebranded as Eastside Memorial. Isn't that picture great, Grace? That's me with my buddies when I first came up with the concept to move analog cell service to digital. Back in '85, as a fifteen-year-old. It's what kick-started this whole company."

"This is you?" I ask.

"Stephen Smith," he says. "Of course, I had way more hair back then. Smitty is more memorable than Steve Smith."

"Cool," I say. I try not to show the bewilderment I'm feeling.

My dad's boss is the same guy who has his arm around Mohammad in this photo! I try to remember if I've ever been in this office before. I don't think I have. Is it possible that I saw this photo somewhere in the past, and even though I didn't consciously register it, it got recorded in my memory somewhere? Am I actually losing my mind and making all of this up?

My father and Smitty finish up whatever they're doing, and my dad gets up and shakes his hand. They talk like pals, about going golfing soon. My dad never used to play golf. Now he pretends like he's a guy who loves it.

As we're leaving the office, Smitty calls out to me.

"Grace, if you've got a minute, I'd like to chat with you, alone. About the internship."

My dad's face lights up as Smitty winks at him. Dad leans in and says, "Knock 'em dead, kid."

As I sit down across from Smitty at his desk, I can't shake the feeling of unease that washes over me. Smitty's piercing gaze seems to dissect me, analyzing every subtle shift in my demeanor with unnerving precision.

"Grace, is everything all right?" Smitty's voice breaks through the silence, his tone laced with genuine concern. It's disarming, almost convincing, but I can't help but feel there's something a little bit off about this guy.

"Yeah, I'm fine," I reply, forcing a smile that feels more like a grimace. I decide to just lie my ass off. "Just a little nervous to be meeting you, I guess. You are, like, super famous."

Smitty's lips curve into a reassuring smile, his charm oozing from every pore. "There's no reason to be nervous, Grace. I just called up your application. You've got all the qualifications we're looking for. And very good references."

I nod, trying to push aside the nagging sense of dread. But before I can stop myself, the words tumble out in a rush. "Did you know a kid named Mohammad Ahmadi back in high school?"

The question hangs in the air. I watch as Smitty's expression flickers, a brief flash of uncertainty crossing his features before he regains his composure.

"Mohammad Ahmadi?" Smitty repeats, his voice carefully neutral. "Of course, I remember him. We were good friends, actually." He delivers this information with an odd tone of voice. There's almost a palpable tension, a flicker of something dark lurking behind his façade of charm and charisma.

"Seems like he was pretty smart," I say. "I mean, from that photo."

Smitty's smile tightens imperceptibly, his eyes narrowing ever so slightly. "Mohammad was brilliant, no doubt about it. It's a tragedy what happened to him. How, may I ask, did you know that was him in the picture?"

"Oh. The caption."

"Why are you asking about him?"

"I-I know about Mohammad because …," I start, my voice faltering slightly. "Because my house is actually located on the site of the old house where he … where he was found hanged in his garage. My …"

There's a pregnant pause as Smitty absorbs my words, his expression unreadable. But beneath the surface, I detect a flicker of something akin to unease, a subtle shift in his demeanor that sends a chill down my spine.

"How … how did you find out about that?" Smitty asks, his voice tinged with an undercurrent of suspicion.

I swallow hard, my throat dry with apprehension. "It's … it's a long story," I reply, my words barely more than a whisper. Here I decide to boldly lie, because there's something about the way this man is watching me that is making me extremely uncomfortable. "My stepmother, who's a real estate agent, told me about how it was a murder house, that's why we got the land so cheap."

"I was under the impression Mohammad ended his own life," says Smitty. "Are you saying you think he was murdered?"

"No. I mean, that's what real estate agents call houses where a famous tragedy occurred. 'Murder houses.' I guess suicide counts as a kind of murder."

"I see."

"I've been researching the boy who used to live where I lived.... As part of a school project for my history class, we're supposed to try to find out information of the land beneath our homes, as far back as we can go."

"Cool project idea."

"Yeah. And it just seems like a crazy coincidence that there's a photo of him in your office."

"You know what Albert Einstein said about coincidences?" he asks me.

"Can't say I do."

"He said coincidences are God's way of staying anonymous."

"Interesting," I say. "What was he like?"

"God? Or Einstein?"

"Mohammad? What was he like?"

"You want to know this for your school project?" asks Smitty, guardedly.

"Yeah," I lie.

Smitty's gaze softens, a hint of sadness clouding his eyes. "Well, okay. Mohammad was bright, incredibly bright. Like you. But he didn't have it easy, you know? His mother died violently, in front of him. He was a political refugee who lived through war. And he had kind of a hard time fitting in at our school."

"Do you know if he was bullied?" I press on, sensing there's more to the story than Smitty is letting on.

Smitty's expression tightens, a shadow passing over his features. "Yes. Mohammad and his twin sister were unfortunately the victims of bullying at Johnston. His father, too. It wasn't limited to school or just to Mo. They targeted his whole family."

"Why?"

Smitty scoffs. "Because people are ignorant. They called Mo and his family terrorists, you know? Even though they were literally the people who had fled terrorism. It all has to have been extremely difficult. It's almost understandable, that he ended up doing what he did. I wish we'd known more back then about how to help someone in that kind of situation."

"Was his bully's name Warwick Blackwater? I think he was a football player," I ask, trying to hide the urgency in my voice.

Smitty's expression falters for a moment, a fleeting glimpse of unease crossing his features before he regains his composure. "I don't recall exactly who the bullies were. It was a group of boys," he replies carefully. I sense he might be lying. "But now that you mention his name, I wonder if you're aware that Mr. Blackwater is presently a well-known person in our state."

"A senator, right?" I press, watching for any sign of hesitation in his response.

"Yes," Smitty confirms, his tone measured. "We are still friendly and have some business ties. I have only nice things to say about him," he adds smoothly, though there's a subtle undercurrent of tension in his voice, as if he's carefully choosing his words to avoid revealing too much.

"Okay. So let's not name this bully, or set of bullies. What else can you tell me about Mohammad?"

"Mo was a great guy. One of my closest friends, from sixth grade till he died. I miss him a lot."

"I'm sorry. I can't imagine how hard that must have been," I say.

"It wasn't fun. Can we talk about the internship now?" asks Smitty. "As much as I enjoy a trip down memory lane, this one is sort of painful for me. I hope you understand."

"No, yes, of course," I say. "Sorry. I've just been sort of obsessed with this kid's story."

"I understand, completely," says Smitty. "And your single-minded focus is one of the things I think comes across best in your references. In fact, there's one here from an art teacher, Mickey?"

"Oh."

"And it shows in that short, 'Awkward.' I liked that one."

"Thanks."

"If you're agreeable to it, I'd like to offer you the internship."

This surprises me. And to my surprise, I accept.

My father is so pleased to hear about this that he decides he and Candi with an i overreacted this morning.

"I agree with your stepmom," he says. "It probably would be good for you and Lucía to attend the political event at the Blackwater's place. I'll have Jacob pick you up."

Chapter Fifteen

The mid-March afternoon sun casts a gentle warmth over the sprawling riverfront backyard of the Blackwater mansion. It's an absolutely massive home in the Rivercrest neighborhood, with the kind of yard that doesn't just have patios, but pergolas and pavilions and massive outdoor fireplaces and firepits for lavish al fresco parties like this one. The house is two stories tall, all white, with floor-to-ceiling windows, black roof tiles, modern and warmly Mediterranean at the same time, enormous yet impossibly, elegantly understated. It sits on top of a small hill, at the bottom of which is the property's four-boat covered dock on the Colorado River, where it appears they keep a small yacht as well as two other boats and a bunch of jet skis. Though Lucía can't see or hear her, Pakwá-ule is here, too, wandering tragically along the edge of the water, sobbing.

"I don't think I'll ever get used to having a demon for a sidekick," I say.

"Oh. I meant to tell you. She's not a demon at all," says Lucía. "Not according to that book. I couldn't put it down, by the way. I read it in class, at lunch, all day, basically."

"What is she, then?" I ask.

"Best as I can figure, the real La Llorona, the one you see, is a real person. But her life story got all mixed up with a bunch of Aztec and Spanish mythology. In real life, she was an indigenous woman from what used to be New Spain, which could be actually Mexico of today or big parts of the United States, including the Southwest and Texas. She was a Coahuiltecan Indian, Pakawan tribe, a woman who lived in the early 1600s, somewhere in the south Texas, north Mexico area, along what later came to be known as the San Antonio River. Her name is a Pakawan word that means racoon. Before the Spanish arrived and ruined everything, she lived in a semi-nomadic equal society where women had rights. The Spanish didn't like that and imposed patriarchy and Catholicism or death on everyone."

"Rat bastards," I say.

"So, like, even with all of that going on, she still fell in love with this hot young Spanish guy from lower nobility, and he supposedly loved her, too, because she was also hot."

"I mean, she's pretty. That I can confirm."

"See? They had three children together out of wedlock, and the guy was living with the indigenous people. A priest in the area wrote the whole thing down in his journals, that's how we know all this. So ... his family didn't like it, and they came and kidnapped him and forced him to go back to Spain, and they killed two of their children by drowning them in the river in front of her. Within a generation, her entire community was wiped out, but it's said she and one daughter survived and fled to live with the Apaches. Anyway, that's why she wanders the waterways, that's why she's crying, and why she tries to save people."

I look at Pakwá-ule, and she finally makes sense. "Damn, that sucks for her," I say. "But I still don't understand why she chose to be my ancestral spirit guide. Surely, I have happier ancestors in my family tree somewhere."

"Yeah, no idea," says Lucía. "Maybe because you both have a shared mission to save people?"

"You say that like I'm a Jehovah's Witness."

"I mean, we're literally here because you're trying to save Mohammad."

"Mohammad is already dead," I say.

"So were you, and you didn't disappear, right? You're trying to save his soul."

"It sounds so stupid when you put it like that," I say.

"How would you rather I say it?"

She has a point, but all of this is making me very uncomfortable. "I don't know. I just want to find out what happened to him, that's all," I say. "So let's do that."

Lucía and I continue to wander along the winding stone footpaths, that curve from terrace to patio to pergola, and attempt to look natural as we mingle with the hundreds of well-heeled guests. Jacob and Cameron are off talking to Cam's mother and some of her friends, all of them with the same overly polished Stepford-Wife-look to them. I feel incredibly out of place in the only semi-appropriate dress I could find in my closet for the fundraiser's "cocktail attire" dress code. It's black lace with a corset belt and makes me look like the only vampire at the Tinker Bell family reunion. I kind of knew better than to wear this but also kind of didn't give a crap. I wear fishnets and combat boots, and my usual assortment of gunmetal statement rings and various studs and hoops, and yes, people stare, but not for long.

Lucía has pulled herself together more elegantly in a white sweater and beige slacks with pearls and pumps she borrowed from her mom, who apparently told her to try to find a rich husband while she was here, as though any high school sophomore should be looking for any sort of husband at all. Lucía looks like a debutante from a rich family, and she loves being in character, fooling everyone.

Our attention keeps drifting toward the center of the festivities to a spot on the lawn by the gently flowing dark water of the wide river, where Senator Warwick Blackwater holds court over about twenty of what I'm sure he'd call his closest personal friends.

Dressed in his signature tailored suit, Warwick exudes an effortless charm as he navigates the crowd, his magnetic presence drawing admirers like moths to a flame. I catch glimpses of him through the throng of guests, his laughter ringing out above the ambient chatter. He is tall, an older and less thoughtful version of his attractive son, with the same chiseled features and sandy blond hair, though his is peppered with white. Not what central casting might pick for a murderer to look like, but in real life killers look like everyone else.

"Do you see him?" Lucía murmurs, her gaze fixed on Warwick's charismatic figure.

I nod, my curiosity piqued by the air of mystery surrounding the influential senator and likely killer of Mohammad Ahmadi. "He's hard to miss."

To my astonishment, I also see Smitty standing in the group. I tell Lucía who he is.

"These really are the richest of the Texas rich, aren't they?" she says. "They make you guys look poor."

"They all look like they get microdermabrasion," I say.

"They're all preserving themselves to be brought back to life after the apocalypse," she says.

"I'd rather be dead."

"Not funny," she says, slugging me.

"Death was fine," I say.

"Wanna get closer?" says Lucía, softly.

"Not really, but … somebody's gotta do it."

We weave casually through the crowd, discreetly eavesdropping on snippets of conversations. People are talking about their families, their jobs, their vacations, their values, the decline of America, the good old days when slavery made everything better and women didn't try to manage their own bodies, and money, and oil, and steak. Speaking of which, the smell of grilling meat mixes with the scent of fresh-mown grass and the subtle mossy scent of the river. Warwick's smooth demeanor has the people around him laughing in approval. He seems like the kind of guy who's never been insecure a day in his life. The kind of guy who could charm a kid into a noose.

"So," I hear him say, "I tell him, Mister President, that might have worked for you in Massachusetts, but it sure as hell ain't gonna fly here in Texas!" His sycophants nearly cheer for this, laughing knowingly and nodding. "In Texas, I told him, we know the God-given difference between a man and a woman, and we won't have any drag queens coming to school for story time. Not on my watch."

"I wonder what drag queen he's talking about," Lucía muses, her eyes narrowing in speculation. "I hope it's Alyssa Edwards. I would love for Alyssa to read me *Goodnight Moon*."

"He's definitely not talking about the Pope, I bet," I reply, a determined glint in my eye.

"Get. Out." She slaps me lightly on the arm in appreciation of my observations and grins. "You're bad."

"Prove to me the Pope's not wearing a dress," I say. "And never touches women."

"I cannot disprove your hypothesis," she says.

"I rest my case," I say.

Smitty steps forward now and says something to the group, as Warwick Blackwater looks on with the fakest of fake smiles plastered on his face. These people are insufferable.

"The senator and I go way back, so far back that I knew him when he was trying to figure out how to even talk to girls," says Smitty. "But one thing I know for sure about him. He is absolutely committed to preserving old-fashioned, traditional family values."

"That's absolutely right, friend," says Warwick Blackwater. "That's why, friends, a vote for me is a vote for the future and soul of America," he concludes, and everyone seems impressed.

I see Warwick turn his gaze to a young man with slicked-back hair, wearing a suit, standing on one of the many observation decks of the house. The first thought I have is *bodyguard*. I bet there are snipers all over this place. The man gives Warwick a discreet gesture to call him over.

Warwick continues talking as though he hasn't noticed. "I tell you what, friends, if we don't do something about all this cancel culture nonsense, all the left-wing censorship and moral decay, who will? Now, if you'll excuse me for a moment."

He breaks away from the group he's been dazzling and walks with great purpose toward the house, waving in a full-of-crap way to people as he goes. The man from the observation deck ducks through the French doors, into the house.

"Follow that man," I say.

"Ay, ay, captain," says Lucía.

The crowd is thick, and I am too afraid of all these people to get through them on my own. Lucía has no such qualms.

"Excuse me," Lucía murmurs, her tone dripping with faux innocence as she maneuvers through the crowd, pulling me along behind her by the hand. "Pardon us."

We've lost him. How does a man just disappear like that? We quicken our pace, looking everywhere for him.

"Grace, look," Lucía whispers urgently, her eyes widening in excitement.

I follow her gaze, my breath catching in my throat as I catch sight of Warwick, hidden from view of the rest of the party by a tall line of sculpted hedges on the far side of the boat house. He's engaged in a hushed conversation with the man from the deck. The Senator looks focused and patient, but to me it still looks like he might kill this man. The unreadable body language between them is sparking a flicker of intrigue within me. We inch closer, and closer, until we can overhear snippets of their conversation.

"I know this is a bad time, Senator," says the younger man, in a scared and apologetic tone. "But I promise you, on my mother's grave, the breach was not my fault."

"And yet, you let it happen."

"I didn't. I don't know who did. But we'll have to address it with the news. They're already calling. I'll get to the bottom of who was responsible, and we'll manage it. But this is urgent. It demands your immediate attention, Senator. I'm sorry."

"Keep your voice down," snaps Warwick. "Not here. Inside."

As Warwick shoves the younger man toward a side door, looking like he's about to blow a fuse, a sense of urgency grips me. Whatever's going on here, it isn't normal, and it might be just what we need to start to prove this man's violent streak.

Lucía and I follow them into the house, which is so enormous and filled with different sections and staircases and hallways that we soon find ourselves lost within its labyrinth. Just as I'm about to give up, I see Pakwá-ule standing at the end of a corridor, staring at me. I will never get used to the way she just pops up. But I sense, very clearly, that she's done so in order to guide us.

"This way," I tell Lucía.

The corridor leads to a set of stairs, going down into some sort of basement.

"No," says Lucía, but I see Pakwá-ule at the bottom of the stairs.

"It's okay," I say.

"How do you know? There has never been a horror movie where good things happen in the basement."

"It's fine. Trust me."

At the bottom of the stairs we find a vast finished basement, set up to look like a presidential library and office suite in a Swiss chalet or something. All manly leather and brass tacks, and cow-hide rugs. There's a huge, framed painting of Warwick Blackwater and his wife and son hanging over a fireplace. There are dead animal heads mounted and hung up everywhere, humidors with cigars and decanters of whiskey on gold trays. A most cis-het manly man's room.

We hear voices murmuring down a darkened hallway, Warwick's and the other man's. And then, as we inch closer to the room at the end, whose door is cracked open just a little.

The other man cries, "Don't, you're hurting me!" and then the talking ceases and is replaced by a muffled sound.

"Is he killing someone?" I ask. "I think he's killing that guy!"

"Oh, my God," says Lucía.

Lucía whips her phone out of her slacks pocket and sprints off down the hall before I have a chance to stop her. She pushes the door open a tiny bit wider, peers in and snaps some photos, then runs back to me and says, "You won't believe this."

She shoves the phone into my hands. I look at the screen and see the senator passionately kissing the other man. On the lips. Pulling the younger man's head back with his hand gripping the guy's hair.

"What even is happening right now," I say.

"We need to get out of here," she says.

Before we can formulate a plan of action, we hear Cameron calling our names at the top of the stairs. With a sinking feeling in the pit of my stomach, I realize that we've been trapped between a rock and, well, whatever is going on in that back room.

"Pakwá-ule," I whisper. "Help us, please."

Just like that, the ghost appears in front of a closed door across the main lobby area.

"This way," I tell Lucía.

I drag her to the door and, without checking behind it, trusting my guardian demon completely only because there is no other option at the moment, I open it and pull Lucía in.

It's some kind of a storage room. Like a janitorial closet.

"Holy mother of the little baby Jesus," I whisper. "Did I see that right?"

"Love is love," breathes Lucía.

"I told you! It's *always* the family values dudes!"

"Hypocrites gonna hypocrite."

Minutes pass like hours, in cramped, terrified silence, until finally we hear men's murmuring voices and footsteps coming out of the office, going heavily back up the stairs.

We wait another few minutes to be sure we're alone, then get out of the closet—unlike Warwick Blackwater.

We are stunned to see Cameron standing near the fireplace looking at the painting of his family.

"Grace? Lucía? What are you two doing down here?" he demands, his eyes narrowing in suspicion as he takes in our disheveled appearance. "I've been looking everywhere for you!"

Caught off guard, I struggle to find the right words, my mind racing with the implications of our discovery. "We were just … exploring," I stammer, my voice faltering under his penetrating gaze.

Cameron's brow furrows in confusion, his gaze flickering between Lucía and me as he searches for an explanation. "Exploring? In my dad's home office wing? Why?"

I exchange a nervous glance with Lucía, our silent communication conveying the gravity of the situation.

"We were hoping to find your dad, so I could talk to him," says Lucía. "Tell him what a fan I am."

"I just passed my dad's assistant on my way down here," he says, measuring his words carefully. "Did you meet him?"

"No," I say, too quickly. He narrows his eyes in suspicion. "What's going on? Why are you acting so weird?"

"Look, Cameron, we can explain," Lucía begins, her voice tinged with desperation as she searches for the right words.

Pakwá-ule has appeared again, this time standing beside Cameron in a relaxed way that makes me understand he can be trusted.

"It's okay," I tell Lucía. And then, I tell Cameron the truth. Well, part of it. Okay. A version of it. Fine. A lie. I tell Cameron a lie. That we were curious about Warwick and followed him, hoping to work up the courage to talk to him, but instead we found him in what seemed to be a romantic moment with his assistant, so we hid.

"We weren't setting out to trap him in anything. It just happened. We have photos, if you don't believe me," I say.

Cameron almost laughs. "No, I believe you," he says. "And I definitely don't want to see those pictures. Remember our conversation last night, Grace? About secrets? Well, this is my dad's. Our whole family knows."

"Even your mom?" I ask.

"*Especially* my mom," says Cameron. "That's a big part of why she hasn't been sober since 1990."

"I'm sorry," I say. "That's got to be hard."

"It's not," he says. "I mean, it's just don't-ask-don't-tell around here, in everything. We can seem perfect and happy that way."

Suddenly, we hear a man clearing his throat, in the direction of the hallway leading to the room where Warwick had been with his assistant. To our astonishment, Warwick Blackwater is standing at the edge of the hallway, smoothing down his hair, watching us with a calm and eerie expression on his face.

"Oh, hi, Dad," says Cameron. He looks stunned and nervous, but like he's trying to appear normal. "Where did you come from?"

"Hello, son. How about you introduce me to your friends?"

The look in his eyes reminds me of the look in a tiger's eyes when you make eye contact at the zoo. Like it would kill you if it could reach you.

"How much of that did you hear?" asks Cameron.

Warwick Blackwater breaks into one of his trademark dazzling smiles and strolls over to us. "Enough," he says, patting me collegially on the back. "Nice nose ring," he tells me. "Did it hurt?"

"A little."

"Yeah, well, some things in life are worth enduring a little pain, I've found," he says. Then, gesturing to Lucía's phone he says, "May I?"

She hands it to him, terrified. Unable to unlock it, he asks her to please do it for him.

"And if I don't?" she asks.

"I can't imagine why you wouldn't want to," says Warwick, causally, with an unspoken undertone of threat.

Lucía unlocks the phone. He then deletes the photos on the device and from the cloud.

"This the new iPhone?" he asks. "How do you like it? I'm an Android guy myself."

"It's … fine?" says Lucía, bewildered by his casual tone.

"They didn't mean to stumble across … that," says Cameron. "They were just exploring the house."

Warwick Blackwater smiles as though everything were right with the world and says, "No harm done, girls. It's a great big house, easy to lose your way, just like life."

"How do you know these girls, Cam? They don't seem like the girls you usually have over. A bit more …" he looks at my outfit and smiles. "Creative."

"Lucía here, she's in student government, over at Bird Box," says Cameron.

"You know my buddy Jacob, from football?" says Cameron.

"Well, Grace here is his stepsister, and Lucía's her friend."

"I see. You and your stepbrother must be close?" he asks me.

"Not really," I say.

"Lucía wanted to come here today just to meet you," says Cameron. "She's actually a huge fan."

Warwick eyes Lucía like a lizard sizing up a fly.

"Is that right?" he says. "Which of my policies do you like the best, Lucía?"

She's a deer caught in headlights, stammering to come up with a good lie. She comes up with a bad one, instead. "All of them," she says.

"Lucía. What's your last name?"

"Cabra."

"Miss Cabra, let me be the first to teach you something important you won't learn in any political science program or model U.N. exercise." He drapes his arm over her shoulders and leans in close to her ear and says, "First rule of politics? Learn how to make and keep friends and allies. Know who you're talking to and what they stand for. Learn to be discreet. Learn to lie but sound like you're not lying. And whatever you do, don't piss off the wrong people."

"Understood, Senator," says Lucía.

Warwick's face brightens as he removes his arm from Lucía and turns to his son again, cheerful as a scout leader.

"You kids eaten yet?" he says as though nothing strange has taken place. Smooth as glass. "Your mom hired Midnight Ember, the best barbecue catering company in all of Austin. If you girls have never tasted their stuff, you're in for a real treat. I think I read somewhere a reviewer called it a carnivorous conquest." He pauses here and smiles in a disarmingly charming way. "I liked that description. Creative, like you kids. Come on upstairs with your friends, Cam, and grab yourself a bite. Let's go see how your mom's doing. Let's all go and enjoy the party."

Senator Blackwater walks to the stairwell and sweeps an arm toward the steps, while grinning at us, letting us know that we are to go first. It's much the same sort of gesture I've seen parents make with very young children they want to keep an eye on.

Chapter Sixteen

Cameron comes with us when we leave the party. I'd rather he didn't, but he invites himself along. In what I like to think of as a moment of uncharacteristic affability, Jacob shrugs.

Lucía hunches in the back seat next to me as Jacob drives toward our house. She's lost her trademark sparkle for the moment, retreating to what appears to be a dark place, seemingly still shaken up from the creepy confrontation with Warwick Blackwater. I can only guess this is why she's morose. It is also why I'm morose. Well, one of many reasons, I suppose. Her arms are crossed over her chest, and she stares out the window as the city slips past. Actually, all of us except Jacob are in a pretty dark mood now, and he notices.

"Something wrong?" asks Jacob. "What am I missing here?"

Lucía doesn't budge, and I defer to Cameron. His father is absolutely terrifying, and I don't want to do anything to upset him, like accidentally reveal the family secret that could bring down his entire political career. We already know he's probably capable of murder. Cameron handles the situation as I imagine he's handled his entire life with his family ... by pretending Jacob's crazy, and self-medicating.

"Nothing's wrong, bro," he says cheerfully as he holds out a paper box of weed gummies to my stepbrother. "Why would you even say that? Here. Mango. You gotta try 'em."

Jacob pops a gummy in his mouth, and Cameron offers them to us. I decline, but Lucía eats two.

"You comin' to our place, Lucía, or …?" Jacob asks with a hopeful look in his eyes that I see thanks to the rearview mirror.

It is very uncomfortable for me, that these two are a thing.

"No, thanks," she says.

"Mom's making tacos, and I asked her to include a vegan option," he says, dangling the vegan bait like a carrot before, well, a vegan.

"Sounds nice, but I need to get home."

I balk at her, because I know this is a lie. Lucía never has to get home. She has no curfew and essentially lives alone because her mother rarely comes home herself. Also, the Lucía I know would never turn down a free vegan taco dinner. Or maybe it isn't a lie. Her mom certainly isn't going to demand she come home, because she doesn't care where Lucía goes. But maybe Lucía is telling the truth because she herself needs to get home, for her own reasons. Reasons that might involve having been subtly threatened by one of the most powerful men in Texas. I try to make eye contact with her, but she avoids looking at me. She texts her address to Jacob's phone so he can plug it into the GPS, then slouches harder and lower as though she doesn't want anyone to see her. If you know the "look at me" actress personality possessed by Lucía, you'll understand how unusual this is.

I text her, asking if she wants me to go to her house with her. She reads the text and shakes her head almost imperceptibly. I text her again to ask if she's mad at me. She reads it and shakes her head.

Lucía: **Just need time alone. Not you, it's me.**

I text back asking her to please not leave me alone with Jacob and Cameron, and she says I won't be alone because my dad and Candi will be there. I feel panicky. Like I've ruined the only two friendships I have all in the span of a couple of days, and all because I got hit by effing lightning and now I'm acting like an insane person. I text her to please not leave me. She sighs.

Lucía: **Stop being codependent.**

Lucía and her mom live in a rundown rented duplex in the MLK neighborhood, right on busy Commerce Street. There's no yard, just cement, with their unit occupying the bottom half of the ramshackle, somewhat moldy, wooden house. The rickety stairs to the second unit's front door seem to have been tacked onto the front of the building as an afterthought, with no consideration for how they might look like a big scar across the house's face. The wheeled trash barrels are stashed right on the front porch, and they overflow. I can see Jacob and Cameron looking at the house with shock and maybe pity. I felt the same way the first time I saw it. You don't think someone as beautiful, talented, elegant and gifted as Lucía is going to live in a place like this, until you realize what an asshole you were for not realizing before that lots of amazing people live in places like this.

"Bye," she says. She gets out of the car without making eye contact with any of us, her keys already in her fist, and hurries inside.

"Seriously, Grace," says Jacob. "Is she all right? Because she seems pretty upset."

"She's got cramps," I lie. "It's nothing you did. She's just embarrassed about it, and I think her tampon leaked, so she wants to clean up and lay down with a heating pad and take a bunch of freakin' Midol by herself."

"Ah," he says and seems perfectly satisfied with this logic. "Got it. You know, she can talk to me openly about that stuff. It doesn't bother me. It's natural. I'm a feminist."

"I'll let her know you're down for girl-talk about her period," I say, and Jacob misses the sarcasm in my tone.

Cameron shoots me a look that seems to express gratitude. Honestly, all I want is to get away from him, and his dad, and regroup, and figure out what the hell to do. I might have been a bit too naïve in wanting to meet Mohammad's killer. Like, what did I think would happen? That he'd be nice? That we'd conduct a citizen's arrest, and all would be well?

A little later, we arrive at our house, and even though Cameron says he wants to talk to me, I tell him that I, too, have cramps. It's not true. Lucía and I are synched up in our periods, but they're not due for another week.

"Grace, c'mon," he says. "Just five minutes?"

I let him into my room to talk to me in private. The Lorisa spell from this morning has worn off. Mohammad is leaning against the wall, casual as can be, and Charlie is curled up at his feet. They both seem happy to see me, but not sure what to make of Cameron, who, I think, notices me looking at them, because he looks that way, too, as though confused.

I decide to be honest with Cameron, at least to a point, in order to get him to mosey along. "Look. You're a cool guy, Cameron. I like you. It's just that I feel really weird about what happened today with your dad. Okay?" I sneak a look at Mohammad when I say "your dad" to indicate that I am speaking about his bully and murderer.

"I get it," says Cameron. "I feel weird about it, too. I just need to know … not that I'm trying to control you or something, but I need to know you aren't going to, like, out my dad and ruin our family."

"I'm not going to out your dad," I say. "Or anyone else. As a bisexual person, I firmly believe it's up to each individual to come out on their own terms, in their own way."

"You're bi?"

"Yes, but it doesn't matter. I wouldn't out your dad no matter what. There's no way I could, anyway. He deleted the photos."

"Yeah, I know. But ... I'm just saying this for your own good. To protect you. He's aiming for a higher office. Governor, maybe. My dad's extremely ambitious."

Mohammad nods in agreement with this assessment of Warwick Blackwater.

Cameron continues, "He'll be watching you now. I wish it wasn't like that, but it is. He has people. Lots of people. Don't try to become a crusader or something. Others have tried. He shuts them all down. He's very good at that."

"You don't say," I deadpan with an eye roll in Mohammad's direction.

"I didn't pick him, okay?" I see unshed tears glistening in Cameron's eyes. "We don't get to pick our parents. I hate that you're even in this position now. I hate everything about what he's doing. I hate what he's done to my mom. I hate his policies and politics. I honestly hate everything about him. I'm not going to lie. And I am afraid of him."

"So am I," I say.

"Please don't hold him against me," he says.

"Okay," I say. It's a lie, but what else is there to say?

I like Cameron. He's hot as hell. But I'm not willing to die to hang out with him or any guy or girl, and right now I don't want to be anywhere near this particular dude or his powerful murdering family.

Cameron searches my face, just as I see La Llorona enter the room, materializing right behind him with an almost consoling posture. He shivers suddenly and wraps his arms around himself.

"Did you feel that?" he asks, looking around the room, suddenly paranoid and on high alert.

"Um, I don't know. Depends on what you mean by 'that'?"

"Like, this room just got a lot colder, in a split second."

"I didn't notice."

"Man, that's so weird," he says. "I know this sounds crazy, Grace, but I have a sense about haunted houses. Well, haunted places. Ever since I was a little kid, I feel this cold come over me whenever a spirit enters the room."

"You're right," I say, trying not to sound overly interested in this unexpected turn of events. "That *does* sound crazy."

"I know this house is, like, brand new, but I swear it feels off, like there's definitely something—someone—here. I get, like, sad mom energy? Like, a lady from a long time ago?"

The paranoid part of me, which, let's face it, is the biggest part of me right now, wonders whether Cameron found out about me and the spiorads. Like maybe Lucía told Jacob. It is not outside the realm of distinct possibilities. Then I remember, she told him I saw spirits when we were in the car that first night. So he knows that, at least. And there's a stack of books about La Llorona on my desk, in full view. He could be going off that, too. Is he trying to use this to manipulate me somehow? If so, this guy is smooth as glass. As calculating as his killer dad.

"I don't know what you're talking about," I say. "There's no such thing as ghosts."

"Do you really believe that?" he says, inching closer. "Because I noticed you keep looking over there by your desk. I think maybe there's something there. I feel it."

"Goodbye, Cameron." I march to my door and open it. "I'm sure Jacob needs someone to play *Call of Duty* with. Have a great night."

After he leaves, Mohammad zooms up on me with that watery *let's goop it on* look in his eyes. I sigh. He isn't trying to have sex with me, he's trying to communicate with me. He seems even more adamant about this now than he has been yet. He cuts his eyes at the door, then back at me, a couple of times in a way I take to mean the communication he needs to show me is about Cameron. Or his dad.

"Fine," I say. "But let me brush my teeth and get ready for bed first, in case I need to curl up in a fetal position afterwards, and I'm too traumatized by your messed-up life to floss."

Mohammad could not look more delighted. Charlie feeds off this and spins in a little excited circle as though he thinks we might be going for a celestial walk. La Llorona, meanwhile, resumes her usual position in the corner, with her knees drawn up to her chest, rocking lightly.

Once I'm scrubbed and safely tucked into my bed, I give Mohammad the all-clear. He gloms into me in an instant. It feels cold and sticky, like someone has poured slime all over my spine. The images begin immediately.

In the hazy veil of Mohammad's memory, I find myself standing in the bustling hallway of his high school, watching the scene unfold before me like a vivid dream—or like a movie script. Unlike before, when I was actually inhabiting Mohammad's consciousness, he is allowing me, somehow, to merely observe this time. I see him and Steven Smith standing at an open locker, into which Mohammad dumps a bunch of things out of his backpack, replacing them with other things. Passing period. The hall is crowded with other students, and it's noisy.

Mohammad says, "Hey, Steve, have you heard about this new compression technique they're working on? They're calling it Huffman coding."

Steven replies, "Yeah, I've been reading up on it! It's neat stuff. It's all about encoding data in a way that minimizes the amount of space needed to store or transmit it, right?"

Mohammad says, "Exactly! Huffman coding assigns shorter codes to more frequently occurring symbols and longer codes to less frequent ones. It's like a clever way of squeezing out redundancy to make the data more compact. But I have an even better idea, a way to compress it more efficiently. I call it Quantum Entropy Encoding."

"That sounds super cool," says Steve.

As Mohammad and Steven engage in their animated and extremely nerdy discussion, their excitement palpable in the air, the hallway seems to fade away into the background, leaving only the echo of their voices.

Suddenly, the sound of footsteps interrupts their conversation, and the shadow of Warwick Blackwater falls over them like a dark cloud.

Warwick slams the locker shut, "Well, well, well, if it isn't The Prophet Mohammad and his little white nerd making more terrorist plans."

Mohammad's shoulders tense, a flicker of apprehension crossing his face as he braces himself for the inevitable confrontation.

"Leave us alone, Warwick. We're not bothering anyone," says Mohammad

Warwick sneers, "Oh, but you are bothering me, Jihadi Boy. You bother me by existing. You bother me because you should have stayed where you and all the other towelheads belong, having sex with a camel."

As Warwick continues to taunt and belittle Mohammad, his words like barbs piercing through the air, I feel a surge of anger and frustration rising within me. This was a moment of vulnerability for Mohammad, a memory stained by the cruelty of others. But even as Warwick shoves him, Mohammad's resolve remains unbroken, a quiet strength emanating from within him.

Steve says, "What the hell's your problem, Blackwater?"

Mohammad says, "Just ignore him, Steve. He's not worth our time."

With a defiant glare at Warwick, Mohammad turns away, his footsteps echoing down the hallway as he and Steven retreat from the confrontation, leaving behind the lingering echoes of injustice and resilience.

We then cut to a drastic change. I'm in a teen boy's bedroom. Not a very nice one, but tidy. Warwick is there, looking at a couple of trophies on a shelf someone has made out of empty milk crates. He picks one up and dusts it off, turning around and smiling, proudly ... at Mohammad.

"Good job, Mo. I knew you'd win," says Warwick.

Mohammad says, "Did you? Because I sure as hell didn't."

"I wish I could have been there."

"Yeah, no."

"Do you think Steve has a clue?"

"No way."

"I hate 'bullying' you. Is it convincing?"

"Oh, yeah. Very. Even I almost hate you."

"Promise I won't lose you to him one day?"

"Dude, no. What? No. Even if he was interested, I wouldn't be. I have someone I love."

Warwick sets the trophy down and goes to Mohammad, taking the other boy's hands in his. He kisses each of them, gently, and smiles.

"Oh yeah? Who's that?" asks Warwick

Mohammad is beaming with ... love? Wow. Yep. Love. These two are in love. They begin to kiss, and I wish I could look away. In my mind, I beg Mohammad, if he can hear me, to end this scene, because I don't want to see whatever comes next. But the scene keeps going. And it is terrible. But not for the reason I'm expecting, which is watching an intimate moment between two teens in love. Rather, it's awful because someone kicks the door down and comes in, raging and yelling in a language I for some reason know to be Pashto. The boys separate themselves as though they were oil and water, but it's too late.

Mohammad's father has seen what cannot be unseen and begins to violently, brutally beat Mohammad with a belt and its big brass buckle. It has some kind of Arabic lettering on it.

When the goop session ends, I feel thrashed. Every bone, every muscle, every cell is aching and drained. I'm extremely thirsty, but too tired to look for water. I can barely lift my eyes to search for Mohammad. Strangely, he's gone. Charlie is still here, so it isn't that he's been banished somehow. There's a kind of emotional tinge to the air, and the main feelings I get from it are embarrassment and fear. There's a word for this sentiment. Vulnerability. Fearful vulnerability.

"Oh, for God's sake," I say. "I don't care if you were gay, Mohammad. It isn't 1985 anymore."

The emotional density condenses around me, until it forms a snaking smoke trail. This eventually settles into the shape of Mohammad, until he appears almost completely like a living person, perched on the edge of my bed. He looks at me sheepishly and waves a little like maybe he expects to get hit.

"So … was his motive something to do with love, then?" I ask.

Mohammad just stares at me like I'm probably the stupidest person who ever lived and died and lived again.

"Ohhhh," I say, as the entire point of his goop session hits me. "Are you saying you don't think Warwick Blackwater would hurt you?"

Mohammad's face softens, and he smiles in a melancholy kind of way. He touches his chest over where a heart would be.

Per tradition, I suppose, the speaker on my desk crackles on, and Mohammad picks a song to communicate. The song is newer than anything he's picked yet, and I have to hand it to him, he's been putting in the work to update his musical repertoire. This time, the song is from 2024, "No Evil" by SiR. I listen closely to the words, realizing this is the only way he has to speak directly to me.

It hits me that while Warwick Blackwater quite likely broke Mohammad's heart, he did not kill the guy.

Someone else did.

"Your dad?" I whisper, more to myself than to him. I look at Mohammad, and it's harder than staring into the sun. He's staring at me in the darkest, most soul-crushing, plaintive way. It's a look that I take to be a "yes," but a million times more emphatic, a dark effing yes. So, this is the source of that swimming sorrow in the garage.

This new realization absolutely destroys me. For so long, caught up in my own pain, I've been convinced no teen could experience anything worse than a mom who kills herself without leaving much of a suicide note. I never once stopped to consider that there are parents in this world who kill their own teens, for the crime of merely being who they are.

"I can't do this," I say. I feel like I've been punched in the center of my gut.

I curl into a fetal position on my side, as I suspected I might, and pull the covers up over my ear. I'm too tired to perform the Lorica, and I'm surprised to feel the warmth of Charlie cuddling up against my back. After a minute or two, as my eyelids flutter with sleepiness, I'm surprised again, this time because Mohammad has little-spooned himself into me, like a kid who just needs a hug. I feel his presence as a warm, sorrowful glitter across my skin. I don't know how you're supposed to hug a ghost, so I focus my mind and try to glitter my spirit back at him. It feels laughably inadequate as an antidote to the terrors this boy experienced in his life. Inadequate attempts at love, I'm starting to understand, are probably better than not trying at all.

He seems to snuggle in deeper, and a new song comes on, softly, peacefully, almost like a lullaby, with a sound to it that I associate with inspirational pop. I have never heard it before, and I fight the reflex still deep within me to dismiss it cynically. I grope for my phone, pick it up and look at the artist and title. Rita Ora, "Grateful." Not the kind of thing I'd ever listen to on my own. Ever.

I listen to the song, because I know that to the best of his ability from wherever he is stranded, they are Mohammad's words, and only I can hear them.

As the message of the song sinks in, I realize Mohammad is okay. He has been through the worst life had to offer, and he made it. I'm not sure, but I feel like he's telling me he's okay, in spite of it all, and, even more importantly, that I, Grace Martínez, can be, too. If I replace bitterness, rage and a desire for revenge with gratitude and appreciation for the lessons, and for those who truly love me, even if they don't always know how to do it the right way. I don't know if Mohammad means to make me wake up to the gift of friendships and love that I've been busy pushing away, but he did it anyway. I feel the tears start to stream out of my eyes. I realize how much I miss a certain glorious, toe-walking, clueless, considerate, funny, awkward and hopeless yet wonderful effing nerd.

I grope for my phone and text him.

Me: Still can't drive. Give me a ride to school tomorrow? I asked the ghost but he can't drive, either.

He texts back almost immediately a heart, a fried egg and a thumb's up.

I text back a fried egg icon and a question mark.

He texts back the fried egg, an equal sign and the word "Greasy."

I don't want to, but I smile. Why I do it is beyond me. I hate the nickname, as I've mentioned before. But I love the guy who gave it to me. I fire back with the last dregs of my energy and find an inappropriate meme from *Grease*, the movie in which Danny tells Rizzo, "Oh bite the weenie," and she responds, "with relish."

Blake: Not as sexy as you might think.

Me: I missed our banter.

Blake: I missed our everything.

Me: **Lilah tov.**
Blake: **Buenas noches.**

I set down the phone and realize it is possible to smile as you cry.

Chapter Seventeen

The fluorescent lights buzz overhead as the bell rings, signaling the start of another day in Mickey's tenth-grade Documentary Filmmaking class. I shuffle into the room with Blake, our hands tightly intertwined. Lucía is trailing behind us, walking at the same time she reads that same book on La Llorona. She's obsessed. For my part, I know La Llorona is around me, because I'm able more and more to sense her presence. She's not made herself visible to me or anyone else at the moment, for which I'm grateful. Blake, Lucía and I take our usual seats toward the back of the room, settling in for another session of geriatric hippie muckraking cinematic exploration.

I catch a glimpse of Mikaela Hoffmaster as she enters the room. She's the epitome of high school perfection, gliding into the room with Lexi traipsing after her, both with an air of confidence that borders on arrogance. Mikaela's blond hair falls in perfect waves around her shoulders, and her designer clothes cling to her slender frame like they were made just for her. She looks over at me just in time to catch me looking away, which sucks. That's exactly what she probably wanted, to know I was staring. She gets off on being the center of attention and especially in letting me know she's the center of attention. I have no idea why that girl decided I was the kid she was going to torment the most, but she did. I suspect it's got to do with her general hatred of all things gender and sexual that aren't what certain megachurch pastors and politicians say they should be. I wonder how she'd feel about knowing a guy like Warwick Blackwater was into guys. Then I remember that wondering anything at all about Mikaela Hoffmaster is a waste of time and energy.

The teacher, Mickey, adorned in a massive tie-dye garbage bag of a shirt atop his usual black baggy jeans and rainbow Converse, stands at the front of the room with the ugly lights lighting up the part of his head that's bald. That would be the top part. All around the edges grow mangy gray strings that he collects in an anemic low ponytail. He's erasing whatever nonsense he'd scribbled on the whiteboard during the previous class, probably preparing to write almost the exact same nonsense on it all over again. He greets us all with his signature mad-scientist smile, his eyes twinkling with excitement as he prepares to unleash his passion for gotcha filmmaking upon us once again.

"All right, class, settle down," Mickey announces, clapping his hands together once he's silently taken attendance and sent the results off to the office on the desktop computer that always seems to confuse him to the point he asks one of us for help. He does it himself today. Good on Mickey.

"Good to see everyone's here, because today's the day we share our documentary ideas with the group. Remember, you're going to come up to the front of the room and give us the logline, and then the elevator pitch, without reading and without rambling. Imagine you're pitching to a network. Who wants to go first?"

My heart sinks as I realize I still haven't chosen a topic. Between recovering from my accident and dealing with the aftermath of seeing ghosts, being kept out of school and kissing not one but two boys, I've fallen behind on everything. Lucía, always the overachiever, goes first. She announces, to my astonishment, that she has chosen "The legend of La Llorona as a Chicana feminist icon," for her topic.

"My film will detail how La Llorona has been depicted in horror films and contrast that with what is known about the true identity of the real indigenous woman whose tragic story came to be conflated with the demon, which itself was nothing but a Spanish demonization of the Aztec goddess Coatlicue. Viewers will come to know the true nature and circumstances of the life of a woman who once lived and breathed here in Texas, a woman who faced challenges not unlike those many women once again find ourselves confronting here, as many generations of progress are being dismantled."

"Right on," says Mickey. He pumps a fist in the air and keeps it there for a long moment.

Lucía avoids my wide-eyed accusations after she sits back down.

When I poke her arm to try to get her to look at me, she only shushes me.

"Who's next?" asks Mickey. "Blake? Your topic is a little lighter and might make a nice counterweight to Lucía's."

"Huh?" says Blake, who was too busy trying to figure out why I was annoyed with Lucía to pay attention.

"Mister Abrams, when the assistant calls you back for your meeting with the studio executive, will you look up and mumble 'huh'?"

"Um, no?"

"Is that a question?"

"No. I will not mumble huh, and it is not a question."

Mickey gestures to the place in front of the white board where we're all supposed to stand and make our case. "You're up, kid."

Blake takes the spot and tells everyone about his documentary on finding the best latkes and matzoh soup in Austin. "Through the vehicle of this short documentary film, I will lovingly share the fascinating history of the Jewish settlement in the Austin region, and I will feature my own grandmother, who will share her own story as well as judge the dishes we sample."

"Delicious, in every way," says Mickey.

As more and more students begin to volunteer, I feel a wave of anxiety wash over me. What am I going to say when it's my turn? I can't exactly tell them all I haven't picked a topic yet.

Just as my nerves reach a peak, Mikaela Hoffmaster stands up with a smirk on her face.

"I'll go," she announces, flipping her perfectly styled hair over her shoulder. "For my documentary, I'll be exploring the link between lightning strikes and neurological impairments. According to a study from Medlink, 'cognitive symptoms can begin immediately or a few days or weeks after a person is struck by lightning. These neuropsychological and cognitive deficits resemble those of traumatic brain injury, depression and post-traumatic stress disorder. Similar neurobehavioral patterns are often seen in patients with electric injuries.' But don't despair. If you or a loved one are ever hit by lightning, there are therapies to overcome any resulting mental health issues."

Everyone gasps, because they, like I, know exactly what this means and exactly why she's doing it. My stomach churns at the obvious dig she's taking at me. Ever since the accident, rumors have been swirling about my mental state, and Mikaela seems to take pleasure in making me the butt of her jokes.

Mickey seems paralyzed. Stuck. Can't blame the dude. He wants to be a fair and kind teacher, that's his nature. But she's making it difficult.

"Miss Hoffmaster," he says, carefully. "Please stay after class a moment to discuss this topic further."

"Why?" she asks, point-blank. "You didn't ask anyone else to stay."

"It's a sensitive issue right now, and surely you know that," says the teacher.

"Is it?" she asks, feigning innocence. She looks at me, and says, "What do you think, Amazing Grace?"

Instead of sinking to her level, I take a deep breath and summon all the kindness I can muster. "That sounds like a really interesting topic, Mikaela," I say, forcing a smile. "I can't wait to see what you come up with."

Mickey's impressed expression tells me I made the right choice. He nods approvingly before turning his attention back to the class.

"All right, who's next?" he asks, scanning the room. "I think that's just about everyone." He looks right at me, leaving me with no choice but to stand up and face the music.

"I, uh, haven't actually chosen a topic yet," I admit, feeling my cheeks flush with embarrassment.

Mickey's smile never wavers as he looks at me, his eyes twinkling with understanding.

"That's okay, Grace," he says reassuringly. "Sometimes the best ideas come to us when we least expect them."

I slump back into my seat, feeling like a failure. But Mickey isn't done with me yet.

"Actually, Grace, I have an idea for your documentary," he says, leaning forward eagerly. "I heard from Dr. Ramsey that you were offered a summer internship at NexaWave by none other than Smitty himself."

My eyes widen in surprise. How does Mickey know about that? Who told Dr. Ramsey?

"How about you do a documentary about Smitty?" Mickey suggests. "Explore how he feels about being such a huge, global public figure, both loved and loathed, on par with someone like Elon Musk. You have rare access now. Use it."

I chew on my lip, considering his proposal. It might seem like sucking up to do a documentary about the head of NexaWave, but I can't deny that it's an intriguing idea.

"I'll think about it," I say finally, offering Mickey a grateful smile.

"Well, think fast. All topics submitted after today will be considered late."

"Okay, fine," I say, just as the bell rings.

After school, I talk Blake into driving me and Lucía to see Safia again, at her office. I'm not sure exactly what I want to say to her, only that if anyone knows what really happened in their garage the day her brother died by hanging, it's her. As Blake drives, I explain the situation with Mohammad. He and Warwick were actually a couple, but because of the prejudice they both would have faced from their families and the community back then, they chose to not only hide it. They created a ruse that was exactly the opposite—that they hated each other in ways that made both of them fit in better to the culture and family that would have disapproved. I explain how and why I no longer think the killer was Warwick Blackwater, but Mohammad's father, who we already knew was strict and authoritarian and abusive. I'm sitting in the front passenger seat where I have a good view of Blake's face. I can see he's not at all comfortable with what I'm saying. But, to his credit, he's trying to be supportive and does not argue with me or flip out.

Safia is just leaving the mini-mall offices of Unity Haven Refugee Rights Coalition when we arrive, and we bump into her in the parking lot. She's wearing an even more modest outfit than the last time we saw her, with a skirt that drags the asphalt and sleeves that come halfway down her hand. She has her car keys out, and when she sees us, she puts these in front of her as if to use them as a weapon.

"What do you want?" she says.

"I just wanted to ask you a little bit more about your dad," I say.

She narrows her eyes and shakes her head, then keeps walking toward a well-used Toyota sedan with rusted door handles. "I meant what I said before, I have nothing more to say about any of this."

"Mohammad showed me the day your dad found him with Warwick, in his room," I blurt.

Safia stops half opening her car door and seems to freeze.

"The feeling I got from what he showed me is that they were very happy together, but both of them were afraid. He showed me what your dad did to him after he found them together. Your father had a big bronze belt buckle with some kind of Arabic writing on it."

She turns slowly around and stares at me in fear. "How did you know that?"

"I told you, your brother showed me. He can, like, enter my consciousness, if I let him, and show me memories from his life."

"That's not possible," she says.

"I can't explain it," I say.

"It's an Inshallah symbol," she says. She touches her upper arm with the opposite hand. "We both had scars from it. Almost like a brand you'd see on cattle."

"That's horrible," says Blake.

"I agree," says Safia.

"Safia, if your father was responsible for what happened to Mohammad, you need to be honest about it so that justice can be served."

"I have told you before," she says, "I don't know what happened in that garage before I got there."

"But you think it's possible, right?"

"Mohammad had been beaten before he was hanged," she says. "But the police did not think it was unusual for him to have been beaten. The news said it was normal in 'families like ours,' which, by the way, it isn't. It was normal in our family, but not because of our religion. Because of our father."

"He needs to face the consequences," I say. "For what he did to you both. I think that until he does, your brother will be trapped in my house."

"Well, it's too late for that," she says.

"What do you mean?"

"My father had a stroke last night," she says. "He's in the hospital in a coma. The doctors don't think he's going to make it. He suffered a great deal of damage."

"And still, it's not as much as he caused his son, is it?" I say. "And now Mohammad's stuck in the place he died, for the rest of time."

Safia gives me a melancholy, mysterious and maybe even apologetic look, then gets into her car and drives away. As I watch her leave, Blake puts a caring arm around me.

"At least you solved his murder," he says. "That pretty much confirmed it was what you thought it was. And maybe that's enough for Mohammad, just to know that you cared enough to listen, and to believe him."

Lucía joins the group hug.

"I think you might be right," I say.

I feel, for the moment at least, like the luckiest person in the world, that these two amazing human beings care enough to listen to me and believe me. With them on my side, I can finally face someone I have been needing to confront for a while now.

"Where would you like to go next?" he asks.

"My old house," I say.

Chapter Eighteen

It's late afternoon, quickly becoming evening, when Blake's Jeep rolls to a stop across the street from my previous childhood home, a modest ranch house on a tree-lined street nestled near the University of Texas. The house used to be white, but the new inhabitants have painted it dark blue with a white trim. It feels cleaner now. Modern. New. They've also done something different to the yard, but I can't quite place what it is. Flower boxes? New tulip beds? It's been more than a year since I've set foot in this place, and the memories flood back as I stare at the familiar façade.

"What now?" asks Lucía as Blake cuts the engine and the music stops.

"I just want to sit here and see if she shows herself," I say.

My friends glance at each other, seeming worried but saying nothing.

I address Blake in particular, and say, "Please don't go blabbing about my weirdness to your mom this time?"

"I won't. I promise," he says. His hangdog look tells me he's been punishing himself mentally for what his mom did. "I swear to you, I never in a million years would have thought she'd call your ... er, your dad and Candi."

"With an i," adds Lucía, helpfully.

"I know," I say. "It's okay. Honestly, I think you meant well, and I think she meant well, and I think even my dad and Candi probably mean well. But not everyone understands what's best for me right now."

"I get that," he says.

"Thank you."

We all sit for a while, silent, lost in our own thoughts. Suddenly, Lucía breaks the quiet, her voice soft and tentative. "What was your mom like, Grace? You don't talk about her much."

I swallow hard, the lump in my throat threatening to choke me. "She was ... complicated," I begin, searching for the right words to capture the essence of the woman who was both my greatest happiness and my deepest pain.

"She was introverted, you know? But she laughed a lot ... had a very annoying laugh, a snort-laugh. She loved sad-lady music, 'all those droopy damsels,' she called them—Lana del Rey, Banks, Florence and the Machine. She was terrible at staying alive, but she did have a way with words, I guess. That's what people say. People knew her name in certain literary circles, or whatever. But ... she had issues. I mean, clearly. Right? She struggled with depression. She could be moody. And she and my dad ... I remember them fighting. A lot, at the end."

"What did they fight about?" asked Lucía.

"I don't know," I say. "I mean, I do know, but I try not to think about it because it makes me feel awful."

"Sorry," says Lucía. "I don't want to make you feel awful."

"No, it's fine. I should think about it. Toward the end, they argued a lot about money, and kids. I think he wanted more kids, and she didn't. He wanted to go to a different church, and she didn't. His family never liked her. So there was that."

"What about her family?" asks Blake.

"She really didn't have one, that we ever talked about. Not like she was adopted or an orphan or anything, but just that she moved out when she was fifteen and was on her own after that. They were all estranged. Her parents are both dead, and I never knew them."

"Have you read her books?" asks Blake.

I shrug. "Kind of, I guess? It's hard to read them. Not hard like difficult words. Hard like stuff you don't want to know about your mom. Angry eroticism was apparently a thing for her. I mean, I've read a bit of her work, here and there, but honestly it feels like pouring salt in a wound still. Maybe someday."

"I'd probably feel the same way," says Lucía, "if my mom ever wrote anything other than putting her phone number on cocktail napkins."

We laugh, and it lightens the heaviness in the air, a little.

"That's bleak," says Blake.

"Hey, humor is just socialized rage," says Lucía. "You guys know who said that?"

"No," I say.

"Jerry Seinfeld," she says.

"I wish it were possible for me to think about that guy without getting a mental image of early 1990s pants and mullets," says Blake.

"They were not the best years for fashion," I say. "Mohammad still can't seem to bring himself to manifest in anything but acid-washed high-waisted pants from the 80s. But I guess they're better than balloon pants or whatever came next."

"Mohammad, like the dead guy?" asks Blake.

"Yeah." I wince, hoping he's not going to try to convince me I'm nuts.

"He can change his clothes?" asks Blake.

"Yeah. I have no idea how."

"I bet it's thought forms," says Lucía. "Like manifesting your thoughts."

"Any sign of ... her?" asks Blake, as his eyes search the front windows of the house.

I want to hug him hard, for trying so hard to be cool about me and ghosts. I rest a hand on his shoulder and peer at the windows, too. I can't see inside because of the reflection of the yard in the low golden sunlight.

"Nope," I say. "Maybe she didn't stick around. Maybe she met her Carl Sagan and was, like, laters, earth, I'm outta here."

The words hang heavy in the air, a testament to the complexity of a life lived in shades of gray. Lucía reaches out and squeezes my hand, offering silent support.

Summoning all the courage I possess, I open the door and step out onto the familiar sidewalk. Blake and Lucía follow me but keep a respectful distance, letting me lead. I approach the door of the house and raise my hand to knock, nerves and anticipation warring within me.

A young mother answers the door with a sleeping baby nestled in her arms. She looks weary, with dark circles under both eyes, but there's a warmth in her eyes as she takes in the sight of us standing on her doorstep.

"Hello?" she says.

"Hi," I begin, my voice trembling slightly. "This is probably going to sound weird, but I used to live here, a couple of years ago. I'm Grace Martínez. My whole childhood practically was spent here, I mean, until I left. A lot of things happened here. The house has a lot of meaning for me, personally. I was wondering if I could show my friends the inside, just for old times' sake."

The woman regards me warily for a moment before nodding, moving aside to allow us entry.

"I'm Ji-Yoon Kim," she says, seeming grateful for the company now. "This is Henry. He's out cold, as you can see. You don't have to whisper. He's a good sleeper, at the wrong times. He likes to sleep all day and cry all night, lucky me. The place is a little messy but it's not easy keeping up with everything when you have a new baby. Please, come in."

We step inside, the air heavy with memories and the weight of the past. Something about it still smells familiar—maybe the comforting scent of the wood floors? I'm transported instantly back in time. There's the corner of the tiny living room where we built a pillow fort. There's the hallway where I accidentally stepped on a spider with my bare foot one morning and my mother cried, mostly for the spider. There's the wall where my dad threw a full glass of wine at my mother's head one night, and it dripped down like blood. Wow. I'd forgotten about that.

As I wander through the familiar rooms, the woman watches us with a mix of curiosity and apprehension, especially when Blake, upon arriving at a bathroom, asks me if it's the one "where you found her."

"Well, the house only has one bathroom," I say.

Lucía, ever the one to think it's her duty to speak for me, can't resist asking Ji-Yoon the question I can't bring myself to ask.

"Have you ever experienced anything ... strange here?" she ventures, her eyes flickering with interest. "Like supernatural kind of strange."

The young mother's expression shifts, surprised concern passing across her features. "Sometimes, maybe," she admits quietly. "Funny you should ask. I was just talking to my mother about this. Sometimes, after I take a shower, I'll find words written on the bathroom mirror. Like someone wrote them with their fingers a long time ago."

My heart skips a beat at her words, my mind racing with possibilities. Could it be ...?

"What do they say?" I ask.

"They change each time," she replies. "That's what's so weird. They're almost too faint to see and they fade completely as soon as the steam is gone. My husband swears he can't see them at all, but I can. He thinks I'm delirious from being sleep-deprived. They're always ... comforting, in a way. Things like 'You can do this,' when I feel so tired I don't know how I'm going to get through the rest of the day. Or, 'Hold on to hope.' At first I thought it was my husband doing it, because I had a rough pregnancy, and I've been a little post-partumy these past five months, but he denied it. It even happened when he was deployed for several months—he's military—so it couldn't have been him. I'm thinking maybe some kind of a trick mirror? I know this neighborhood is full of professors, so maybe someone invented something?"

I rush to the bathroom, my hands trembling. They've had the big clawfoot tub where she killed herself replaced with a large walk-in shower. I am glad the tub isn't here anymore. I ask her if I can turn the shower on, and she lets me. I let the water run, and wait, watching the mirror. Nothing happens. There are no words there, no messages from the other side.

"It's only sometimes," she says. She looks embarrassed now, like she might be afraid we think she's crazy. I know the feeling.

Disappointment washes over me, but the young mother's next words offer a glimmer of hope.

"I found something in the attic that might interest you," she says, setting the baby down in a crib and disappearing for a moment before returning with a dusty box in her hands. "We've been ripping up the old floor, renovating, hoping to lift the roof a little and make a third bedroom up there. I thought maybe these belonged to the previous owners," she explains, handing me the box. "My real estate agent contacted the man, a Mister Martínez ... I'm guessing that's your father. He said to toss them out. They seemed important, so I kept them. I think they might be meant for you now."

I open the box and my breath catches in my throat as I see what lies within: two leatherbound, hand-written diaries, filled with my mother's words, her hopes and dreams, her fears and struggles laid bare on the page. The shock of this makes me feel sick, like a PTSD thing, like I'm going to throw up.

"Excuse me," I say, shoving the notebooks off on Lucía as I hurry to the bathroom. I slam and lock the door behind me. I stand over the toilet waiting for the heave to come, but it stays lodged somewhere below my spleen. I feel clammy, sweaty and cold. Why am I even here? Back here, in this terrible room? Am I some kind of masochist? I use the opportunity to pee, taking my time getting off the can so that I can gather my thoughts and compose myself before heading back out there.

I go to wash my hands when I've finished, and even though the steam has long since faded from the mirror, I see words there. Very faint, almost as though they are written in steam itself.

LET ME GO

Not "I miss you." Not "I love you." Not "You'll be okay."

Let me go.

I came all the way out here, with the newfound ability to see the dead, and she is clearly here, but she doesn't even have the decency to show herself? And this is the message she has for me? What. The. Eff.

To hell with her. Seriously.

As I return to the rest of the group near the front door, I see Lucía leafing through a diary.

"The writing on the mirror," says Lucía to the homeowner. "Does it look like the writing in these books?"

The young mother lifts her eyebrows as though she had not considered this before. "Now that you mention it, maybe? I'm not sure. I'm sorry, did something happen in this house that I should know about?"

"No," I say, opening the door and storming out. "There's nothing to see here."

Chapter Nineteen

Night has fallen like a heavy velvet curtain. I sit alone in my room, staring at the diaries. They're on the floor next to me. Charlie is on the floor by me, looking worried. There's a loud knocking on my door and the sound of someone trying to open it. It's locked. My father's voice booms through the wall.

"Grace? Dinner."

"Not hungry," I yell.

"Then come sit with us. It's what families do."

I refuse to acknowledge this. Do families also instruct people to throw out the diaries belonging to your daughter's mother, who ended her own life and ruined everything? Does that sound like something a family should do? God, I hate him right now. Him, and his new wife. And my mother.

"Let me go?" Really? Why? So she doesn't have to face the consequences of her actions? So she can just move on to whatever comes next without guilt? Yeah, no. Ain't happening, Mom.

My phone pings. Lucía's texting to see if I'm okay. I asked Blake to drop me off and told them both I needed to be alone. Blake has also been texting with the same inquiry.

Blake: **If you need us, just say the word.**

I do not have the energy for them, or anyone, or anything. I turn off my phone and stuff it in my jeans back pocket, desperate to shut out the world and the pain that threatens to consume me.

Honestly? I kind of hoped Mohammad would be here, so that I could vent to him. He understands pain. He would get it. He might even play a comforting song for me. DJ Mo. I haven't done the Lorica in a while, and Charlie's here, so if Mohammad isn't appearing, it's because he doesn't want to. Did he move on to the light, now that I figured out what happened to him and he basically told me he's forgiven everyone, and it's okay now? I feel like crying and realize I've become somewhat attached to the ghost guy in my house. How messed up is that?

Alone with my thoughts spinning out of control and lying innocently on the floor next to the diaries, I'm drawn to the steak knife in my drawer. The urge is overwhelming. It calls to me, its sharp blade whispering promises of release. I get to the drawer, pick it up and look at it in the light, turning it around and around. I push up my sleeve and press the flat side of the blade into the skin of my inner forearm. Not hard enough to cut. I just want to feel the pressure. I just want to feel something, anything other than emotional pain. I consider it for a moment, the temptation almost too much to bear, but something holds me back. Fear, perhaps, or maybe just a flicker of hope that refuses to die. If Mohammad was able to forgive, to feel gratitude, even after what his dad did to him, then surely I can get my act together and stop hurting myself, so that the pain others have caused me fades into the background, right?

I set the knife down, and Charlie, the loyal ghost dog who has been my constant companion through it all, positions himself over it, as though trying to keep me from picking it up again. He seems to sense the emptiness that fills the air, and his love for me breaks my heart in a whole new way. I never knew a solitary heart could be broken in so many ways.

Suddenly, like the classic specter emerging from the shadows, La Llorona appears in her usual corner, her eyes watching me with a mix of sadness and understanding. She moves toward me, her form almost human now, becoming more material the same way Mohammad did, and she reaches out to gently open the diaries that lie scattered across the floor.

Dumbfounded, I watch as she reads the words written there, her gaze shifting from the page to me and back again. And then, in a moment of unexpected tenderness, she places one of the open diaries in front of me and returns to her corner.

I pick up the diary, my hands shaking as I find the book opened to an entry dated just a week before my mother's death. The words leap off the page, searing themselves into my soul, her voice a haunting echo from beyond the grave.

"I can't believe what's happening to me," she writes. "I was almost three months pregnant. I was so excited to tell Grace about the new baby, to see the look of joy on her face. She's always wanted a sibling. But then ... I miscarried. And it wasn't just a normal miscarriage. It was ... it was horrible. It happened at work, of all places, in the faculty lounge bathroom. I tried to manage it myself, but after a few days of heavy, gloppy bleeding, and a high fever that kept getting higher, it was pretty clear something wasn't normal. I called my obgyn, and she said that it was likely I got an infection because only half of the fetus dislodged. The rest stayed inside and festered. It's called an incomplete miscarriage. She said if I was feverish, I needed to go to the emergency room. But when I went to the hospital for help, with a high temperature and sicker than I've ever been, instead of helping me, they accused me of murder."

Tears blur my vision as I read on, my heart breaking with each word.

Murder. Doctors and nurses, everyone there. They said I killed my own baby, that I had an abortion at an illegal clinic or something. I called my obgyn and asked for her help, and she told me that she was actually packing up her office as we spoke because she was leaving the state due to the new draconian anti-*abortion laws. She said there was nothing she could advise me to do now, other than move away. She said I needed a 'D & C,' which is similar to an abortion procedure but done when there is infected material that must be removed from the uterus to save a woman's life. The hospital staff refused to do it. They told me they don't offer that medical procedure anymore, by law. What is this world coming to? They refused to do the procedure to save my life. A dilation and curettage.*

I had to drive myself to New Mexico to get it done, because Ben refused to participate. When I came back across the Texas border, the police were waiting to arrest me. They were monitoring my mobile phone and emails and texts because of the suspicion of "murder." They arrested me, and they locked me away, like something from The Handmaid's Tale. *It's all coming true, now. They took me from my daughter, in the name of caring about babies! Took me from my husband. Locked me away like some kind of criminal.*

Ben posted my bail but he doesn't believe me. I told him we needed to move away from Texas, but he said that wasn't happening. He said he wasn't sure I didn't go to New Mexico for an abortion. He thinks I didn't want the baby. It was true I didn't think I wanted more children, when we had discussed it before, and it's true that the pregnancy was unplanned and a surprise, but once I was pregnant, I knew I wanted to keep him. I felt it was a little boy, I don't know how. I didn't end the pregnancy, it ended itself, maybe because of my age. I don't know.

Ben doesn't believe me!

> He thinks I aborted the baby and says he'll never forgive me. He said he's met someone new, too, who shares his values, that he's been going to a new church on his own, and she goes there, and he wants a divorce. And, he's going to petition the courts for full custody of Grace. Even if I don't end up in jail for the rest of my life, I'm going to lose my daughter. I'll end up in prison. There is little doubt about that. Now there's going to be a trial, and with my own husband refusing to support and believe me, with the medical establishment and the police and everyone else against me, I don't see any way I can possibly win this. It will be all over the news. All over the world. I don't know what to do. I don't know how to make it stop. I'll spend the rest of my life in prison, because I had an incomplete miscarriage?!
> I can't do this to Grace.
> I could handle prison. But I can't stand thinking of what it's going to do to her life, having a "murderer" for a mother. Having a mother who is all over the news for killing her baby. It will destroy her life. I can't do this to her. It would be better for her to be known as the daughter of the crazy mother who ended her own life than to be the daughter of the murderer mom. I need to save Grace. I know this. She needs to let me go and carry on without me. I'm scared. I'm so scared.

The diary falls from my hands, landing with a soft thud on the floor as I struggle to comprehend the magnitude of what happened, and of my mother's pain. In that moment, I realize that she wasn't just battling her own demons. She was fighting against a world that had turned its back on her, a world that had condemned her for a crime she didn't commit. Why didn't she tell me? I would have been on her side! Why was she convinced there was no way out? We could have moved away, to Mexico or something. I would have gone with her. She didn't have to end her life!

With a choked sob, I bury my face in my hands, the weight of grief and anger pressing down on me like a vice. Then I decide enough is enough. I rise to my feet, unlock the door and open it. Mohammad didn't have the chance to confront his father, but I can sure as hell confront mine.

I descend the stairs two at a time, with the diary clutched in my shaking fist. I find my father, Candi and Jacob seated around the dining table in some sort of polite, hushed conversation. The aroma of meatloaf and mashed potatoes hangs in the air, normal American food for a normal effing American family, right? Yeah, no. Red wine glimmers in the adults' glasses, a stark contrast to the dark and furious storm brewing within me.

They barely have time to look up and notice me before I slam my mom's diary down on the table with a resounding thud. Everyone stops eating, shocked and maybe a little afraid.

I meet my father's gaze, my voice trembling with emotion. "Why did you tell the owner of our old house to throw this away?" I demand, my words dripping with accusation. "What kind of a man does that?"

My father's reaction is immediate, his face contorting with anger as he rises from his seat. If he recognizes the diary, he doesn't let on. He shifts right into turning the whole thing around to make it a *Grace* problem, like everything else.

"Grace, how dare you speak to me like that!" he barks, his tone sharp and unforgiving. "I have no idea what you're talking about right now."

"My mom's diaries!"

"Look, I know you're going through some difficulties since your accident," he says, "but I have to draw the line at disrupting us in this violent way. Go to your room and come back down when you've calmed down and can speak like a civilized person."

I refuse to back down, my resolve solidifying with each passing moment. I pick the diary up and throw it at him, with all my might. "What is wrong with you?!" I scream. "How dare you say I'm violent, after what you did to her!"

"Grace, where is this coming from? What are you talking about?"

"Quit lying!" I shriek.

"That is quite enough, young lady," says my stenchmom. She gets up and goes to stand protectively next to my father. "Lower your voice."

"That's my mother's diary," I scream at her. "My dad told the lady who lives in our old house to throw it away when she said she found it. That's what your husband did, Candi. He ordered someone to destroy my mother's diaries. Is that the kind of husband you want?"

"Grace, that's not true," says my father.

"If he did, it was probably for your own good," says Candi with an i.

"For my own good? Like when he threw a glass just like this at my mom's head?" I retort, my voice cracking with the weight of my accusation.

I pick up Candi's full wine glass and hurl it at the wall. I turn to stare at my father. "You think I don't remember that? You think I wasn't there, watching the whole thing? Oh, I was. I was there for that, and lots of other fights. It's all coming back to me now. Maybe because of the lightning."

The air crackles with tension as my father's expression darkens, his eyes flashing with anger. "You are out of control," he warns, his words a harsh reminder of the walls that divide us. "And if you keep this up, I will call 911 and we will have you hospitalized."

"For what?" I scoff. "For calling you out for your abuse? She had a miscarriage, you monster. She miscarried. And you betrayed her in the worst possible way. You went along with everyone in accusing her of murder. Seriously? I should call 911 to hospitalize you, except they'd probably celebrate you instead. Because that's the disgusting world my mother lived in."

"This is not the time or place for this conversation," he says. "Pull yourself together, Grace. I'm warning you."

"What, Texas? This is exactly the time and place for this conversation, Dad. Because you know what? Even if she did have an abortion, which she did not, that would have been her choice, not yours. Her God-given right to self-determination over her own body. Oh, and you know what else? I know that you cheated on her, with this horrible person right here, while she was going through all of this, and that's probably what drove her over the edge. I will never, ever, ever forgive you!"

My father picks up the diary, as though he plans to hide it from me, and I feel a rage wash over me. I lunge at him and wrestle it away from him.

"It's *mine*," I say. "Don't you put your disgusting hands on it."

"Grace, I swear to you I didn't know anything about this," he says.

"I'll call the police," says Candi with an i. "Unless you get your hands off your father this instant."

"Don't bother," I scream. "I'm done. Okay? You know what? I was just leaving."

"Grace!" yells my dad. "Where are you going?"

I storm away from them, using my free hand to flip them off. I open the front door of this beautiful, sleek, terrible, haunted new house that stands on the ground where Mohammad Ahmadi was killed, and leave.

With tears blurring my vision and streaming down my face, I run toward the banks of the Colorado River. It's only a few blocks away, and once I reach it, I just keep running north and west along the trail that clings to its edge. I run for what feels like an hour, until I'm so out of breath and the cramp in my side is so excruciating that I can't keep running anymore. I sit down in the cool grass by the water's edge, a slight breeze whispering through the tree branches and washing over me like a soothing balm. La Llorona has come with me, and she paces mournfully along the edge of the water, looking down. I guess she always comes with me, being my guardian angel.

Yes, angel.

I let the tears fall freely. I let the sobs shake me to my bones. I let the wail rise from the depths of my soul. I am no longer Grace Martínez who cuts and smokes to numb herself and never cries. I am Grace Martíncz, Texan teen girl, tied to a cultural stake in the new burning times, 18th-great-granddaughter of La Llorona, daughter of wrongly accused poet Eva del Río, sister of a boy who chose, in the end, not to be born. I carry the screams of a thousand generations of women wronged, in the very meat of my cells, and unless and until I set them free, they will consume me from the inside out. And I am done. I am done blaming myself. I did not ask for this. I am done. I am done keeping quiet.

As my rightful inheritance upon this earth, I have earned the right to loudly cry at the edge of this and all the rivers of the world, on this and all the nights throughout time, with this and all the beautiful misunderstood spirits by my side, with the banshees and the sirens, with the crones and the witches, with the wraiths and the ghosts.

With Mohammad.

With my mom.

Chapter Twenty

Once I finish crying, I realize I'm starving. But I can't go back to Candi's house. Not now, probably not ever. I also can't stay here, next to the river, at night, in the middle of the city. I don't have my wallet or backpack to, say, rent a hotel room, even if I could do such a thing at the age of 16. Which I can't.

I pull the phone out of my pocket and am relieved to see there's just enough juice left for me to fire off a text or two. Barely. I text Blake, because he's got a car and Lucía doesn't. Once he gets here, we can text her. What I text him: THE WORD. I don't have to explain to him that this is me, asking for help, responding to his previous text telling me that if I needed anything to "just say the word."

Blake: **At your service. What can I do?**

Me: **Come get me?**

I include a screenshot with a map and a red pin on the exact coordinates where I am.

Blake: **Wait. You're in the river?**

Me: **Next to it.**

Blake: **Oh.**

Me: **I'll explain later.**

As I wait for Blake in the darkness of the riverside park, I wish I'd picked a better-lighted place to run to. I was too busy crying to notice this before, but there are sounds and movements in the trees. It smells like trash. I'm not familiar with this part of the river and hope there's no one in there watching me. No sooner do I have this terrifying thought than I see the darkened silhouette of a man walking toward me. I wish I had my pepper spray. I pull my phone out in case I might need to call for help, but the battery is dead now because of course it is.

"I know jiu-jitsu," I say, loudly.

It is not true and also a fairly stupid thing to say, but for some reason I think saying jiu-jitsu will sound more convincing than the more common "karate."

"No, you don't," says the familiar male voice, laughing.

"Jacob?" I ask, just as my stepbrother steps into the pale orange glow cast by the lone streetlight. "What the hell?"

"I was worried about you," he says. He hands me my backpack, which he's brought with him. "I thought you might need this for school tomorrow, in case you decided to never come back. I wouldn't blame you, by the way … if that's what you decided."

"Did my dad send you to drag me back?"

"What? No. I came on my own."

"To drag me back?"

"What? No, Grace. Would I bring your backpack if I was just planning to take you home?"

"I guess not, no."

"I followed you to make sure you were okay. What your dad did to your mom before, and to you just now, is not okay. I'm sorry about my mom, too. It's messed up they were seeing each other while they were both still married."

"Wait, I thought that was just my dad?"

"Nope. My mom, too."

"Wow."

"Anyway, I just thought you might need … well, a big brother. Right now."

"We're the same age, Jacob."

"I am two months older," he says. "Actually, one month and twenty-six days."

I smile a little. "Okay. Well, I'm fine. So you can go back home now."

"You literally just yelled 'I know jiu-jitsu' into the dark in the most terrified tone of voice I've ever heard," he says. "You're not fine. And I'm not comfortable leaving you here."

"It is a little scary," I admit.

"I'll walk back with you," he says. "Or we could Uber."

Headlights sweep over us, and I see that they belong to Blake's Jeep, which is now parking at the curb. Jacob recognizes the vehicle.

"Ah. The nerd," he says.

"Indeed," I say.

"Think he might give me a ride?" asks Jacob. "You clocked seven miles, Grace. I had no idea you could run that fast. Or at all, no offense."

"Wow."

"But only because you wear really big shoes, boots, most of the time. But also, I don't really want to walk back."

Blake is more than happy to give my stench … stepbrother a ride. Yes, brother. But when Jacob realizes Lucía's in the Jeep, too, and Lucía sees him, he changes plans to stay with us for a bit.

As we drive through the night, the city lights flickering like distant stars, I find solace in the company of my friends. Blake's comforting presence beside me, Lucía's quiet laughter ringing out from the back seat, where she and Jacob seem to be having a happy reunion of sorts. I tell them I'm starving, and Blake says he knows just the place.

Soon, he pulls the Jeep up to the curb, and we find ourselves greeted by the inviting glow of a late-night deli, Brooklyn Bites Delicatessen, its neon sign flickering softly against the darkened cityscape. There are only a few other cars here.

"According to my bubbe, this place has the best matzoh ball soup in Austin," he announces. "And I've found there's no better comfort food in all the world than matzoh ball soup, except maybe *albóndigas* soup."

Stepping inside, the air is thick with the savory aroma of freshly baked bread, coffee and roasting meat. My mouth waters, and my stomach growls loudly enough for Blake to hear it, but he's merciful and doesn't acknowledge it. The middle-aged woman behind the hostess stand comes out to greet him with a warm embrace and asks him how his family is doing. He introduces us to her, saying she's the owner. She grabs a few menus and leads us across the deli. It's a cozy mishmash of worn leather booths and Formica-topped tables, the walls adorned with framed photographs of old New York and faded posters advertising the deli's signature dishes. Above, the ceiling fans spin lazily, their rhythmic hum adding to the comforting ambiance.

We settle into a corner booth, the cracked vinyl seats creaking softly beneath us as we gather around the table. The chatter of other diners fills the air, a lively backdrop to our conversation as Blake makes recommendations and tells us about how he's been coming to this place since he was a little kid.

A waitress approaches a few minutes later, her apron stained with the day's work, a pencil and pad in her hand to take our orders. Soon, large steaming bowls of soup, platters of knishes and frosty milkshakes are placed in front of us, the rich aromas enticing us to dig in.

Once we're done with our meal, I tell them about what I found in the diaries. I tell them about the fight. About my run through the dark. About Mohammad being gone.

"Who's Mohammad, and why would he be in your room?" asks Jacob.

I suddenly realize I haven't told him about my new mediumship, out of fear he'd tell his mother. I decide Candi thinking I see ghosts is the least of my worries now, and fill him in. To my surprise, he not only tells me he believes me, he says there's always been something creepy about our house to him, too.

"Where to now?" asks Blake, once the check arrives.

He takes out a credit card and places it on the tray with the bill. He refuses to let anyone else contribute, saying it's research for his documentary and that his mom and dad gave him a special card to use just for that.

"I can't go back to my house," I say. "Not tonight and probably not ever."

"You can come to my place," says Lucía. "But it's kind of chaotic because the cops are doing a SWAT thing next door, and we don't really have anything to eat right now."

"Are you serious?" asks Jacob.

"It happens a lot," she says.

"Which?" asks Jacob. "The SWAT team or the food?"

"Both." Lucía shrugs as though this is no big deal. "Very annoying. The food thing is more common. There was, like, a shooting next door tonight."

"Are you serious?" I ask.

"You say that like a shooting in Texas is surprising," she says.

"You're all welcome to come to my house," says Blake, tapping on his phone. "I just asked. My folks are fine with it."

"No," I say emphatically. "Your mom wants me committed to a mental hospital. Remember?"

"No, she doesn't," he says. "I think that's really grossly misrepresenting my mother's thoughts."

"She said as much to my dad."

"I'm not going to argue about this. I think if you tell her about what you just told us, about what your mom went through with losing the baby, she'll be more than sympathetic. Believe me."

"How can you be so sure?" I ask.

"Because she's on the board of NARAL, Grace," he says.

I stare at him like I have no idea what that means, because, you know, I don't.

He explains, "It's the National Association for the Repeal of Abortion Laws," he says. "My mom's a big-time feminist. This is a cause that's important to her. To all of us, to my whole family. My dad's a civil rights attorney. It's important to me, too, just so you know."

I feel the tears come like hot lava and put my face in my hands. I feel an overwhelming mix of emotions, so many of them I'm honestly not even sure what they are. Sorrow, anger, relief. Blake pulls me in and just holds me.

"Reproductive freedom is important to me, too," says Lucía.

"Same here," says Jacob.

"Dude, your mom is one of the biggest anti-abortion people ever," I say.

"And?" says Jacob. "I'm not my mom, am I?"

"Happily, no," I say. "You know how I know that? You're not wearing a lady's pantsuit the color of a sherbet flavor."

"As long as you don't mention the ghosts, Grace, I'm sure she'll be cool," says Blake. "So that goes for all of us. No talking about spiorads and spells, or Mohammad, or La Llorona, not around my mom. Okay?"

"Fine," I say.

An hour later, we all sit in the comfortable family room at Blake's house, talking with his mother and father as Blake's two younger sisters work on a jigsaw puzzle at the nearby kitchen table. I would like to mention here that it's hard for me not to say anything about being able to see ghosts, because there's one in the room with us, a portly, happy, kind-faced old man who watches over the family with great pride. He has a pigeon on his lap, presumably also dead. I have no idea who he is, but he feels like someone's grandpa. Not Blake's. Someone else's. Just as I think this, I get a name, almost as an instant download into my mind. Arthur. This old man's name is Arthur. I get the taste of bubblegum in my mouth for a split second, and I know it has something to do with him. I do my best to ignore him and tell Janice and Martin about the diaries, about my dad wanting them destroyed, about my father abusing my mother when I was little and me blocking it out, about how hard things have been and how emotional I've been since the lightning strike.

"It's not safe in this state anymore, for any woman," says Dr. Levinson-Abrams. "I can't even believe this is happening, in this day and age, after how hard we had to fight for women's rights. It's absolutely atrocious."

"People talk about the impending arrival of fascism to the United States," says Mr. Abrams, "but for some of us, it's already here."

"For many marginalized Americans, it always has been," says Dr. Levinson-Abrams.

I feel like hugging her. My mother used to say things like that. She would have said exactly that.

They tell us we can stay with them overnight, as long as we let our parents know where we are. I text my dad, then turn my phone off.

The guest room is decorated like the rest of the house, its soft earth tones and muted hues creating a warm and inviting atmosphere. The plush carpet is soft underfoot. Two twin beds with rustic wooden headboards, adorned with crisp white linens and fluffy pillows, seem tailor-made for me and Lucía. Delicate floral accents on the throw pillows lend a feminine touch to the space. A vintage-inspired bedside table sits beside each bed, adorned with antique lamps and a stack of well-worn books. With a shock, I see that one of them is my mother's.

Blake gestures toward the room with a warm smile, his eyes sparkling with hospitality. "I hope you'll be comfortable here," he says, his voice filled with genuine concern.

"Look," I say. I pluck my mother's book from the shelf and hand it to him. He looks at it without understanding.

"*Echoes of Liberation*," he says, reading the book's title. "A collection of Chicana feminist poetry."

"Look at the author's name," I tell him.

"Evelyn del Río," he says.

"What?" cries Lucía. She grabs the book and stares at it. "That's Grace's mom. You have one of Grace's mom's books in your house."

"Wow," says Blake. "But to be fair, we have a lot of books in this house."

"I feel like it's a sign," says Lucía.

I grab the book and put it back on the shelf.

"I doubt it," I say. "She didn't even let me see her at our old house. I don't think she's leaving me signs here."

Blake looks extremely uncomfortable about the topics of our conversation. Awkward and pink-cheeked. "Is the room okay?" he asks. "Other than the book."

"It's nice," I say.

"That's it," says Lucía, plopping down on one of the beds. "I'm moving in forever. This house is great. I mean, your house is nice, too, Grace, but it doesn't feel like a home. *This* feels like a home."

"That huge sterile box is not my house," I say. "I'm houseless."

"If it's okay, I'm gonna head to my room," Blake says. "I still have a ton of homework to do."

"Crap," says Lucía, sitting up like she's just heard a loud noise in the night. "That's right. The preliminary research list for our documentaries is due tomorrow."

"What's your WiFi code?" I ask, already pulling out my laptop from my backpack, and he tells us.

I get comfortable on "my" bed, put my earbuds in and settle in to start gathering as much string on Smitty as I can. My fingers fly across the keyboard as I navigate through a series of interviews with him, my eyes glued to the screen as he recounts his rise to fame.

I come across a "TEDx Talk" he gave in Silicon Valley, about letting young people's minds run free. He's wearing his usual suit but seems about ten years younger than he is now. He comes across as affable, even kind, and I feel fortunate, at least, that I will have a chance to work for him over the summer.

"Ladies and gentlemen, esteemed guests and fellow explorers of what is possible," he says. "It's an honor to stand before you today and share my thoughts on the limitless potential of young minds. Supporting young thinkers is my passion. As we delve into the depths of innovation and discovery, I invite you to journey back with me to a time when the world was a playground of endless possibilities, and the boundaries of imagination were limitless.

"You see, as a teenager, I was fortunate enough to have the freedom to let my mind roam free, to explore the uncharted territories of thought and idea. It was during this formative period of my life, at the tender young age of seventeen, that I stumbled upon what would become my greatest invention: Quantum Entropy Encoding.

"Imagine, if you will, a world where the very fabric of wireless communication is transformed, where data flows effortlessly through the airwaves, unencumbered by the limitations of traditional encoding methods. This is the world that Quantum Entropy Encoding, known the world over now as QEE, has ushered in. It's a world where information is no longer bound by the analog or even digital constraints of time and space, but instead, moves freely and fluidly, transcending the barriers of the physical realm.

"But let me be clear, this revolutionary breakthrough was not the result of mere chance or happenstance. No, it was the product of countless hours spent tinkering and experimenting alone in my room, of daring to dream the impossible and refusing to accept the status quo. It was the culmination of a relentless pursuit of knowledge and understanding, fueled by a passion for discovery and a belief in the power of young minds to change the world.

"And so, as we gather here today, let us embrace the spirit of curiosity and exploration that lies within each and every one of us. Let us dare to dream big, to push the boundaries of what is possible and to never shy away from the unknown. For it is only by embracing the untapped potential of our youth that we can truly unlock the secrets of the universe and shape the course of history for generations to come."

I pause the video, then rewind it to the part where he talks about his big discovery. It seems like I've heard that phrase before. Quantum Entropy Encoding. But where? And then it hits me. It was in the memory Mohammad shared with me, in the casual conversation he was having with Steven Smith at his locker, before he was bullied. I am almost one-hundred-percent sure Mohammad had told Smitty about it and that Mohammad, not Smitty, invented it.

I open a new window in my browser, and, using Google and ChatGPT, research who invented Quantum Entropy Encoding. Every source credits Steven "Smitty" Smith with inventing it. But I am almost certain he did not. The search engine and AI also characterize the technology as revolutionary and credit it with changing the way the entire world of wireless communications worked. Then I ask AI to tell me how much money Smitty made off this invention of "his," and the number hits me upside the head like a baseball bat full of holy crap.

The figure is $110 billion. With a B.

Excitedly, I summon Blake to the room and gather him and Lucía around my laptop. I make them watch the "TEDx Talk," and Smitty's voice fills the room, boasting about his groundbreaking invention. I tell them about the goop session with Mohammad and show Blake the photo from their high school yearbook, of Mo and Smitty together as sophomores in not one but two nerdy clubs together.

"I can't believe it," I murmur, shaking my head in disbelief. "You guys ... Mohammad talked about this exact thing in that memory he shared with me. Only in the memory, *he* invented it. I'm almost sure of that."

Lucía's jaw drops. "Get out," she says. "Really?"

Blake seems very uncomfortable, and I ask what his problem is.

"Are you sure you're actually communicating with ghosts, Grace?" he asks. "It could just be ..."

I interrupt him. "There's an old bald man in a cardigan in your family room, and his name is Arthur," I tell him.

It shuts him up. He stares at me.

"He wears glasses and he's watching over your family. He's proud of you."

"Arthur?" he asks.

"He's got a pigeon on his lap," I say, "which, given the frequency with which pigeons take dumps, seems unwise."

Blake's face could not be redder. He stutters for a few seconds, then finally chokes out some words. "How could you know about him?"

"Dill weed," says Lucía, smacking Blake not-so-playfully on the arm. "Are you for real right now? She. Sees. Dead. People."

"He hated having his picture taken and never wanted any of us to post him on social media," Blake says. "So there's no way you should know anything about him. He's my mom's grandfather. He came to live with us at the end of his life. I was just a baby and really don't even remember him. People talk about him all the time, because he hid the family jewels and never told anyone where they were."

"Who has family jewels?" asks Lucía.

"Families that run from Hitler," says Blake.

"Oh, jeez, sorry," says Lucía. "Didn't mean to be so glib."

"Thanks," says Blake.

"Were they worth a lot?" she asks him.

"I don't know about money-wise, but they have a lot of sentimental value. But that's not what we're talking about. I think we need to focus on what Grace just revealed, because if it's true, it's really, really bad."

A chill runs down my spine as I make the connection. "Exactly," I whisper. "Mohammad invented QEE, not Smitty. Smitty had no idea what he was talking about. And now look at where Smitty is, one-hundred-and-ten-billion-dollars later, while Mohammad … well, you know."

The weight of the revelation hangs heavy in the air as we exchange incredulous glances. "Grace, you're saying … Smitty could have been involved in Mohammad's death?" Blake asks.

"I'm saying Smitty killed Mohammad," I say.

"But I thought his father killed him," says Blake.

"I mean, maybe he did? But think about it. If Smitty's capable of stealing Mohammad's invention and lying about it to the entire world, who knows what the hell else he's capable of?"

The room falls silent as we contemplate the implications of my discovery. "We need to do something about this," Blake says firmly, breaking the silence. "We can't let Smitty get away with this."

I nod in agreement, my determination renewed.

Not Lucía, she's shaking her head. "I don't know, you guys," she says. "It was pretty scary to confront Warwick Blackwater. I swear to you he has people following me. I don't really want to piss off another rich and powerful asshole. You know?"

At that exact moment, almost as though by divine intervention, my phone pings with yet another text from Tish Adoeoye, the reporter from the *Austin Alternative Times*. The reporter who, I now recall, seemed to think that my father worked for a very unethical company that is run, I'd presume, by an unethical man. In her hands, this could be the scoop of the century. If only we could figure out how to prove something that I learned in a memory shared with me by a dead guy.

"Who else in this world might remember that Mohammad, not Smitty, invented this technology?" asks Blake. "Who else was close to him?"

I look at Lucía and say, "You're not going to like my answer."

"No," she says. "Please, God, no."

"Warwick Blackwater," I say. "I think it's maybe time to pay him another visit."

"As much as I love you, Grace," says Lucía. "And you know I love you, right? You're going to have to do that visit without me."

"I'll go with you," says Blake. "We got this."

Chapter Twenty-One

After school the next day, Blake and I drive, together, to the Blackwater estate. Lucía has an acting workshop after school and would get kicked out of the club if she missed another session. We plan to meet back up with her later on.

The last time I was here, I came with Jacob and Cameron, so there was no problem getting past the security gate. In fact, I don't even recall there having been one, although maybe it was open at that time because of the fundraising party. Anyway, there's a security gate now, and it's blocking us from getting in.

"Now what?" Blake asks as we sit in the idling Jeep in front of the massive locked gate.

There's something that looks like a call box next to the driver's side door. I notice it has a camera on it, and the lens is moving like an eye taking in the entirety of our vehicle. I hear a loud beep come from it and then a voice coming through, crackly.

"They know someone's here. Talk to them, I guess?"

"Dang," says Blake. He powers his window open and calls out, "Hello? Um, hi?"

"Can I help you?"

The voice is male, but thickly accented—maybe a German accent? I can't tell. It's no one I know from the few people I know here.

"Um, hi there!" I call out, across Blake. He's flummoxed. I try to sound breezy and casual. Like I do this all the time. Like I belong here. "I'm a friend of Cameron's? I was here at the fundraiser? Grace Martínez. I think I left something here. I just wanted to come and pick it up?"

There's a long pause, and then a different beeping noise as the gate unlatches and slowly swings open.

"Who's Cameron?" asks Blake.

"I told you," I say. I feel guilty and fake as hell. "He's Jacob's friend. The one who invited us to the fundraiser to meet his dad? His dad is Warwick Blackwater."

"Sorry," he says. "I think I kind of blocked everything out over those couple of days because I thought you hated me."

"Well, I didn't."

"Does this Cameron guy know we're coming?" he asks as we motor slowly up the long, twisty driveway to the house on the hill.

"No. He's on the football team with Jacob. They're at practice right now. He's not going to be here. We can just pretend to be looking for whatever it is I supposedly left here, and maybe accidentally run into his dad and politely ask to talk to him."

"How do you even know his dad is here?" asks Blake. "It's a workday."

"I don't."

"No offense, Grace, but this seems like a very poorly thought-out plan," says Blake. "I'm not sure I would have come if I realized how lame it was."

"Do you have something better up your sleeve?" I ask.

"I do not. But I do think that if we're investigating a murder and the theft of earth-shattering technology, we should probably plan things better than this."

"I'm going on intuition," I tell him. "I know that sounds incredibly lame. But ever since the lightning, my gut feelings about things have been pretty spot on."

"La Lorona?" he asks.

"I think so."

As we round the final corner of driveway that leads to the semi-circle drive in front of the massive house, I am surprised and terrified to see Cameron standing outside the front door at the top of the large stone staircase. His leg's in a cast, and he's held up by two crutches, one jabbed under each of his armpits. He's wearing sweats and looks a little less well put-together than he usually is. But he's still hot as hell.

"Oh, great," I say.

"What?"

"That's him. That's Cameron."

"The guy on the crutches?"

"Yes."

"I thought you said, and I quote, 'Jacob's friend is not attractive at all.'"

"I mean, not to me, he's not," I lie.

"There's no planet anywhere in the known universe where that guy would not be considered extremely attractive."

"Maybe to you. But not to me."

Blake just draws in a sharp, long breath and makes a big production out of sighing, as though nothing has ever made him more exhausted than, well, me.

"I didn't know he'd be here," I say. "I don't see what the big deal is."

"There's a thing called a phone," he says.

"I don't have his number," I lie.

"But Jacob does, right?" he says.

"Stop crying over spilled milk, okay? I'm trying to think of a new plan."

"Won't it contradict the one you already told the very scary-sounding German person at the other end of that intercom? Who was that, by the way?"

"No idea. Just let me do the talking," I say. "Or you could wait here."

Blake shoots me a look that seems half amused and half worried. "What? You see that extremely hot, extremely buff guy and now you want your weakling boyfriend to wait in the car?"

"No, I did not say I wanted you to wait in the car. I said it was an option, if you wanted."

"Uh huh."

"Come on. Let's just go," I say. "No point sitting here discussing this."

We get out, and the weight of what I'm about to do feels heavier with each step closer to the front door. We're here to confront Warwick, but I can't shake the guilt gnawing at me from the inside out, because I'm also about to introduce my boyfriend to the guy I cheated on him with, a guy I haven't technically told I can't see anymore.

"Hey, Grace!" Cameron says cheerfully, his voice tinged with confusion. "What are you doing here?"

"I might ask you the same thing, Mister Man," I say in perhaps the most epic feat of awkwardness ever committed in the history of Texas. "I mean, I just figured you'd be at practice with Jacob."

"Torn hamstring," he says.

"Sorry to hear that," I say.

Cameron nods distractedly, his eyes focused on something behind me. Presumably Blake. "And you are?" asks Cameron. "No, let me guess. You're the brave one … um, *guy* who saved Grace's life after she was hit by lightning? Am I right?"

Blake wipes a hand nervously on his jeans and reaches out to shake. This is the second most awkward feat in the history of Texas, however, because it necessitates Cameron balancing his right crutch without holding onto it, at the perilous top of a staircase. It also means he has to keep all his weight on his one good leg in order to return the polite greeting.

"Cameron," says Cameron.

"Blake," says Blake.

I feel like hiding, but of course I laugh nervously, like an idiot, instead.

"We were just in the area and stopped by because I am pretty sure I left an earring here," I say. I am such a bad liar, it literally makes my teeth hurt. Like really cold water.

"An earring?" asks Cameron.

It should be noted here that I usually wear about ten earrings at once, with a dozen ear holes pierced, and I can tell from his expression that he thinks it odd that a girl with so many earrings would notice if one went missing.

"Yeah, a skull one? Silver. It's my favorite. But it's heavy. I took it off in the bathroom because it was bothering me. When I got home, I realized it was gone."

"And you had to bring your boyfriend here with you for that?" asks Cameron.

"I mean, he's my ride," I say.

"I could have brought it to you," says Cameron with a hurt look in his eyes that I take to mean he's unhappy that I've just confirmed for him that Blake is my boyfriend. He was fishing for that. "Or given it to Jacob, if you just, like, maybe could had returned the four texts I sent that you left on read. Are you mad at me or something?"

Blake looks at me with suspicion now. *Why is this dude texting you when you just told me you don't have his phone number?*

Busted.

I keep laughing nervously.

"But, sure, come on in. Let's find your earring," says Cameron. "I got nothing better to do anyway."

As Blake and I walk behind Cameron into the cool quiet of the mansion, I try to grab Blake's hand to hold it, but he snatches it away. He slows his pace till he's behind me, and we're all weirdly walking in single file.

I swallow hard, feeling Blake's gaze burning into my back.

"Um, Cameron?" I say, in the vast entryway. "I'm sorry. I lied. I'm not here about an earring." I whisper the next part: "We need to talk to your dad."

Cameron turns to look at me, an even more bewildered look on his face. "I'm sorry, did you just say you came here to speak to my father, with your boyfriend?"

"I can explain," I say. "Is there somewhere private we can talk about this?"

Cameron's expression shifts to one of curiosity, and he has us follow him to what appears to be a room for video gaming. He closes the door. As he and Blake eye each other warily and puff out their chests at each other like gorillas, I tell Cameron the truth. The entire truth. His expression changes from insecure and bitter mistrust to fascination, as I detail my ability to see ghosts and the real reason Lucía and I wanted to talk to his father in the first place.

When I finish, he says, "You know, if you'd just told me that earlier, it would have saved all of us a lot of pain and confusion, Grace."

"Pain?" asks Blake, still in puffed-up gorilla mode.

"I don't understand," I tell Cameron.

"I'd have just shown you the letters," says Cameron. "Love letters, between my dad and Mohammad. Like, a big box of them."

"What?" I say. "You have such a thing?"

"Not me, personally, but I know where he keeps them. He doesn't know that I know. And you can't tell him. Please."

"I would never. Is there anything in them about Quantum Entropy Encoding, you know, QEE," I ask.

"I believe there is," says Cameron. "And the only reason I know this is because my dad joked with Mo in those letters that he needed to change the acronym of his invention so it didn't sound so much like 'queef.' I remember thinking, damn, Dad, you're cooler than I thought."

"Oh, my God," I say. I look at Blake, hoping he'll at least crack a grin, but he doesn't find it amusing.

"Can I still look at those letters?"

Cameron seems uncomfortable as he considers this. Like he's weighing doing nothing against doing something that could ruin his life. He looks at his phone, to see the time.

"My dad's coming home in about an hour. I can get you the letters, and you can borrow them. Bring them back as soon as you can, or better yet, let me come get them. There's no time to read them here, and he'd think it was weird if you were here, anyway. I doubt he'll notice they're gone. But you have to promise to give them back, and you can't go public with them, Grace. Promise me that."

"Okay."

"You can, like, use them to confirm your suspicion, or whatever, to help free that ghost .... But if you go public about this, it'll screw everything up for my dad, and for me. 'Cause he'll figure out where the information came from. Keep it anonymous."

"Fine," I say, "I promise." It sounds easy enough to me.

We follow Cameron to the stairs that lead down to the same office complex where Lucía and I got stranded during the fundraiser. There, at the back of the exact same closet where we hid, is a secret door, and beyond that is a temperature-controlled, vast storage room, filled with boxes and boxes of papers.

Something tells me that the teen love letters with Mohammad aren't the only secrets he's keeping hidden down here.

"I know," says Cameron, almost as though reading my mind. "I told you. Politicians, man. Half the stuff in here could probably lead to World War III. He doesn't even know I know about this room."

Cameron finds a large cardboard file box by a back wall, hidden by several rows of similar boxes, and opens it. The letters are all there, organized by date and meticulously color-coded in ways I don't understand.

"My God," I say. "Your dad is kind of anal, isn't he?"

Cameron looks at me like he's trying not to laugh.

"No pun intended."

Blake groans at the terrible joke.

"He's tidy," says Cameron. "Well, if you're going to break lots of laws, it's a very good idea to keep good records no one but you and your equally corrupt attorney ever see. He's also good at decorating." He looks around and finds an empty mail tub made of clear plastic. He takes the letters, in their hanging file folders, out and puts them in the other box. "Just take them in this. He won't notice. I hope this helps."

"Thank you," I say.

Cameron makes brief eye contact with me. His eyes communicate so much to me. Hurt, admiration, jealousy, kindness. Being human is a confusing mess.

He sees us out, and as he holds the massive front door for us to leave, he pats Blake on the back and says, "You're a lucky man, Blake. Be good to her. She's pretty special."

As we're heading down the steps toward the circular drive, with the box of letters securely tucked under my arm, a polished black Bentley pulls up, its engine purring quietly. The car comes to a stop in front of us and the driver's window slides down.

Smiling behind a pair of expensive-looking aviator shades is Warwick Blackwater.

"Grace Martínez," he says with a collegial, professional air. "I thought after our last talk we'd maybe seen the last of you. What a pleasant surprise to know we haven't." He slides the shades down to reveal his ice blue eyes and regards Blake. "And who's your friend?"

His demeanor is friendly, but there's a sharpness in his eyes that sends a shiver down my spine.

"Hi, Senator Blackwater," I say. I try to cover as much of the box as I can with my free hand after using it to wave with spectacular awkwardness.

"Son?" he says to Blake. "I didn't catch your name."

"Blake Abrams, sir," says Blake.

"Well, Grace, Blake, what a surprise," he says, his voice smooth as silk. "What brings you here?"

I force a smile, trying to appear nonchalant despite the sinking feeling in my gut. "Oh, just picking up something I left behind," I reply, hoping he doesn't notice the nervous tremor in my voice.

Warwick's gaze flickers to the box I'm holding, and I see a fleeting expression of interest cross his face before he quickly masks it with a polite smile.

"Ah, I see," he says. "Well, I won't keep you then. Have a pleasant evening."

With that, Warwick drives away, leaving me feeling uneasy. I can't shake the feeling that he knows more than he's letting on, that he's somehow aware of the significance of the letters we now possess. I turn to see Cameron, but he's gone, and the front door is closed.

We drive away from the Blackwater estate in total silence. Blake doesn't speak until we've gotten past the security gate and, in fact, left the entire neighborhood.

"You want to tell me what happened between you and Cameron?" he asks.

"Really?" I say, defensive but also annoyed. "That's what you think is the most important thing to talk about, after what we just went through?"

"I'll take that as a no," he says.

"Do you understand what will happen if the senator realizes what we have in that box?" I ask.

Blake nods, his lips pressed into a thin line. "Doesn't make it any easier to feel like there's something else you aren't telling me."

I wrestle with the conflicting emotions I'm feeling. "It was nothing," I say.

Blake laughs bitterly. "So, there was something, then? What happened?"

"He kissed me, once. And that was it," I say.

Blake's face reddens and he accelerates the Jeep. "Uh huh," he says. "When?"

"The day we went to Rosen's," I say. "You were awful to me."

"I was struggling with a difficult change in you, Grace," he said. "I was not awful to you. I was trying to understand what was happening. We'd been through a lot. You're not the only one this whole thing with the lightning was hard on, okay? I know I didn't die, okay? But it was pretty stinkin' traumatic, and then you turned into this woo-woo person who believes in ghosts. It was a lot. I wasn't trying to be awful to you. I was trying to survive, to understand things, just like you were."

I notice that he's crying now. And so am I.

"I know," I say. "I know. It was hard. We were both awful to each other."

"I was not awful to you," he repeats. "But you went out and kissed some other guy that same day? That, Grace? That right there? That is the epitome of awful."

"He kissed me, I didn't kiss him."

"You didn't consent?"

"I mean, I did," I say.

"I can't believe this," he says.

"I'm sorry," I tell him. "I was confused, and sad, and he brought me pizza."

"Oh, I see. Of course. If a man brings you pizza, you have to kiss him."

"That's not what I'm saying."

"Why was he bringing you pizza?"

"He's my stepbrother's best friend, he was over at the house."

"You do realize this brings me no comfort whatsoever, right?"

"Until that day, I didn't even remember his name, okay? That's how little he meant to me."

"Past tense. I guess he means a lot to you now."

"He's a good person, but he's not my person. You are."

"You have a funny way of showing it."

"I'm sorry. I don't know how to love anyone, Blake. I really don't. But I want to learn. I screwed up. And I'm sorry. I don't know what I'm doing."

We drive in silence for a while and finally arrive at Blake's house. He parks in the driveway and turns off the engine. He turns to look at me, tears still glistening in his eyes.

"It's okay," he says and takes my hands in his.

I see how hard he's working to control his emotions and compose himself, how much strength he has. How forgiving and kind and stable and normal he is.

"I understand. I'm not perfect, either," he says. "I didn't handle things well. I can understand why you were feeling alone. I should have been there for you, and I wasn't. I own that."

"Thank you," I say. "And I should have dealt with my feelings better and not kissed Cameron. For what it's worth, I did tell him I couldn't see him anymore, and I stopped responding to his texts."

"Yeah, I got that from how sad he was you left him on read."

"I did that because I love you," I say.

"I love you, too, Greasy. Let's put this behind us and keep going?"

I throw myself into his arms across the middle console and hold on for dear life. As I'm doing this, I notice a van with dark-tinted windows driving very slowly past us. It pulls to a stop across the street. It's the same van I've seen twice before since first meeting Warwick Blackwater. I consider telling Blake, but I feel like things between us are so tenuous that any new stress might threaten to tear us apart. Not only do I love this guy, but I also happen to be living at his house for the time being. I have nowhere else to go, other than Lucía's, if I mess things up again. Maybe I'm imagining the van. I mean, there is definitely a van, but maybe I've imagined that I keep seeing the same one. There are lots of vans like this one around. People trick them out and live in them or whatever.

"You ready to go inside?" he asks.

"Yeah. I am."

Chapter Twenty-Two

It's Friday evening at Blake's house, after a dinner in which I made a complete fool of myself by saying "challah" like "holler," as in "holla at y'girl," and no one laughed. I'd like to note that all bread should taste like challah, however, as it's the best thing I've ever had, even with baba ganoush on it, and I'm not an eggplant person. Anyway. Now, I'm trying to seem like I belong here at this big oak table in the family room, playing Scrabble with Blake, his parents and sisters. And the Arthur ghost, who sits just behind Blake's mom, watching supportively. They have such an easy way with one another, the members of this family. I'm actually shocked by it. So *this* is where he gets his gift for banter? I cultivated mine in opposition to everyone around me, but his was a family heirloom. The whole family banters. When my mom was alive, we had some nice times, when it was the two of us, but there was never a moment that felt like this, like a cohesive family. Like a safe family. There was always tension and sorrow simmering somewhere beneath the surface of things in my old house. It felt the way it feels when you can't get a tight knot out of something but keep trying. And in the new house I ran away from? Well, I just feel like a guest in Candi's house, living by her authoritarian rules, watching my father contort everything about himself to become the man Candi wants him to be. Blake's family feels like a place where you can tell the truth about almost anything and still be accepted. I'm not sure what to do with that other than feel extremely envious of him. I wish this was my house, my family. But it's not, because someone had to get the weird parents, and it was me.

"Grace, could I have a word with you, please?" asks Blake's mom.

She gets up and takes the herbal iced tea pitcher to the kitchen, gesturing with her head for me to join her. I follow her into the laundry room, out of earshot of everyone else, where she lets me know that she's spoken with my father. He's okay with me staying here for the rest of the weekend as long, as Blake and I are supervised and never left alone together. He wants me home Monday after school. "But I work at the bookstore Monday after school," I say, feeling something in me shut down.

I know this isn't a rejection, exactly, but it sure feels like one. I was hoping the Abrams family would find me so delightful they'd invite me to live with them for the rest of my life.

"Oh yes, I think your dad mentioned that. He said he'll pick you up after work."

"Yeah, fine," I say.

I feel like I'm going to cry in front of her, and I don't want to do that. I just leave. I go to the guest room and lock myself inside. No one knocks on the door or tries to pry me out of my misery, other than Arthur, who seeps through the wall and sits down in the chair by the bookshelf. He is polite and avoids eye contact as he takes a book, opens it and seems to be pretending to read. I get the feeling from him that his only purpose in being here is just that, to be here, so that I know I'm not alone.

I take the box of letters between Mohammad and Warwick out of the closet. I haven't had time to look through them yet, because I got roped into helping with dinner as soon as we got back here. With trembling hands, I open the envelopes and slide the letters out. I unfurl the parchment and settle in to read them, on my bed. Well, their bed. The bed that I get to sleep in for only two more nights before I am cast out again, to live with people who don't like or understand me, because I'm cursed like that.

The letters speak volumes, weaving a narrative of betrayal and deceit. In Mohammad's poignant words, I uncover the undeniable truth. He, not Smitty, is the mastermind behind QEE. He names the technology and even describes it in detail to Warwick. My heart lurches with a mix of vindication and sorrow as I realize the extent of the injustice inflicted upon him. The dead guy in my room is actually the inventor of one of the most kickass life-changing technologies known to humankind.

The revelations do not end there. Mohammad's correspondence with Warwick reveals a darker truth. Mohammad was aware of Smitty's insidious machinations, of his repeated theft of Mohammad's ideas, of the gaslighting when Mohammad tried to call him out. Their teachers seemed all too happy to believe someone like Steven Smith could be capable of such inventions, as opposed to someone like Mohammad. He wrote to Warwick that he was afraid something really bad was going to happen, and that if and when it did, it would probably be because of Steven Smith.

Smitty killed Mohammad.

This would explain why he seemed interested in knowing how I knew about Mohammad. And the feline way he watched me as I lied about it. It would also explain why he might have offered me an internship when I had intentionally submitted an exceedingly weak application in hopes of not getting it. He wanted to keep an eye on me. What I didn't understand, though, is why Warwick Blackwater, knowing that Smitty was a danger to Mohammad, didn't go to the police about it. Could his desire to remain in the closet be that strong? So strong that he chose to look the other way for his own personal gain? If so, he wouldn't be the first person in the world to put bald self-interest ahead of everything else. From what little I know of him and his family, that certainly seems to be the case. The fact that Smitty said they were still friends and business associates is even more troubling. I think back to the conversation I overheard between Smitty and Warwick at the fundraiser, and Smitty's words take on a different meaning now. When he said to the crowd, "The senator and I go way back, so far back that I knew him when he was trying to figure out how to even talk to girls," and they exchanged a strange look, it was more than folksy reminiscing.

It was a threat.

Smitty is probably blackmailing the senator. He probably knew about Mohammad and Warwick and, like so many psychopaths, filed that secret information away to use as a weapon later.

This is too much for me. I am just a doomed girl from Austin, who can't have a normal family or life or, it seems, death. I don't have any power to take all of this to the police. The cops would take one look at me and see someone not worth listening to.

I see a stirring in the corner of the room. La Llorona is steaming herself into view. She points at my phone on the bed beside me the instant it pings, alerting me to a new email from that annoying reporter, Tish Adoeoye of the *Austin Alternative Times*. I see Arthur and La Llorona share a knowing look, and the old dead guy nods like he thinks this is a very good sign.

Tish Adoeoye already thinks NexaWave is corrupt, I know this because she and my dad had that little altercation in the parking garage. and she said so. Tish thinks she's after a simple story about the teen girl who survived a lightning strike, but I think I have something even bigger and better for her. For the first time since she started hounding me with her endless emails, I hit reply.

Late Sunday morning, Blake's Jeep purrs to a stop in the parking lot at Zilker Park, a sprawling green oasis in the heart of Austin. It's a typical Sunday morning here, the sky a soft canvas of overcast gray, the air carrying the promise of warmth to come later. We've come here under the guise of a picnic, but our real mission is a meeting with the reporter who could help unravel, and make public, the proverbial tangled web of deceit surrounding Mohammad's death.

I step out of the vehicle, feeling a mix of nervousness and determination. Blake grabs the picnic basket from the backseat, and we make our way across the park to the designated meeting spot, a large field dotted with families enjoying their weekend together.

We spread out a blanket under a sprawling oak tree, its branches providing a canopy of shade. The sound of children laughing and birds chirping fills the air, blending with the distant hum of city life beyond the park's borders. I perform the Lorica, which I have memorized, to keep at bay the many spiorads that like to hang out in places like this.

As we unpack our makeshift picnic of sandwiches, fruit and a thermos of lemonade, I catch a glimpse of a dark black van parked at the edge of the lot. It looks like the same one I've seen following us a couple of times before. It sends a shiver down my spine, but I push the thought aside and remind myself that these kinds of vans are everywhere in this town. I focus on the task at hand.

Soon, Tish arrives, her presence commanding attention amid the sea of families. She's dressed in professional attire, a notepad and pen in hand, her gaze sharp and inquisitive.

"Grace, Blake," she greets us with a nod and takes a seat on the blanket opposite us.

I'm surprised she knows his name, but I guess she does her due diligence.

"Tish," I respond, my voice steady despite the flutter of nerves in my stomach. I don't know what else to say to her except mirror her recital of first names.

I waste no time in pulling out the evidence—copies of the letters, the yearbook photos, the articles—and laying them out before her. Tish's eyes widen as she takes it all in, her expression shifting from surprise to deep concentration.

"Sandwich?" I say.

She waves this away, too absorbed in what she's reading to think about anything else. I unwrap a tuna fish on rye and start gnawing on it, mostly because I need something to do so that I don't jump out of my skin.

"This ... this is incredible," she murmurs, flipping through the pages. "I had no idea."

"I know it's a lot to take in," I say, my voice tinged with urgency. "We need your help, Tish. Smitty ... Steven Smith ... he's been getting away with murder, quite literally, for decades. And Warwick Blackwater is involved, too. You said you need a scoop, a big break, or you might get laid off."

Tish's gaze meets mine, a mix of determination and apprehension in her eyes. "I'll do what I can, Grace," she says, her voice firm. "This is big ... bigger than anything I've ever covered. But we need to tread carefully."

I nod, feeling a weight lift off my shoulders. With Tish's help, maybe we can finally uncover the truth about Mohammad's death and bring justice to his memory.

As Tish gathers up the evidence, tucking it safely into her bag, Blake reaches out to squeeze my hand, a silent gesture of support. In that moment, I feel a surge of gratitude for the people by my side, for their unwavering belief in me and their willingness to stand with me through it all.

As Tish rises to leave, she offers us a small smile. "I'll be in touch," she promises before making her way through the picknickers to leave the park.

With the weight of our secret shared, Blake and I are left alone on the blanket, the sounds of the park fading into the background. As the warmth of the sun breaks through the clouds, I lean in to press a soft kiss against his lips, grateful for this one small moment of peace in the brewing storm.

Chapter Twenty-Three

Monday's here. I push open the heavy door to the documentary filmmaking classroom, the familiar scent of old books and stale coffee greeting me as I step inside. Or maybe it's old coffee and stale books? Six of one, half dozen of the other. Anyway, the room is cramped with rows of mismatched desks and chairs arranged haphazardly. I swear our school just sends someone to go dumpster diving at all the other schools for furniture. Maybe for teachers, too. Case in point: Mickey, our teacher, who stands at the front of the room, his frizzy gray hair wild and untamed, his tie-dye shirt a riot of colors against the drab backdrop of the classroom. He smiles warmly as I enter, his eyes crinkling behind his round glasses.

"Grace, good to see you," he says, gesturing for me to take a seat.

I nod in acknowledgment, not quite fully awake yet, making my way to my usual spot near the back of the room. Blake and Lucía are already there, their eyes brightening as they catch sight of me. If we were the secret handshake type, this would be our time to perform it. But we're not. We're the slouch together and sigh type. I offer them a small wave before turning my attention to Mickey, who has finished sending attendance to the office and is launching into his usual spiel about the importance of documentary filmmaking as a tool for social change, as though he has zero awareness that most "documentaries" on streaming networks these days are salacious true-crime docudramas about women who've had their teeth whitened yet still do things like make stew out of the guys they meet on Tinder.

As Mickey drones on, I prepare myself to tell him that I'm not going to do the tenth-grade documentary assignment. Despite my cheerless demeanor, I have always prided myself on being a decent student. However, I'm now in a position where in order to stay alive, I am going to have to take an F. I'm planning to tell him that I can't focus because I was hit by lightning. It's not true. I can focus. But I can't tell him the truth, which is that I don't want anything to do with Smitty the Millionaire Murderer. Maybe I'll ask for an extension, because now that I think about it, the story would probably sell to a streamer as a docu-drama: *World's richest man killed his high school best friend and stole his invention in order to become the world's richest man.* I honestly think it'd be safer to do a story about a lady eating her Tinder dates, though. The project is a huge part of the grade in this class, and I really don't want to fail. But I'd much rather fail than ever go anywhere near Smitty again.

Suddenly, the classroom door swings open with a loud creak, and Mikaela Hoffmaster sashays in, followed by her giggly squeaking minion, Lexi. Mikaela's stupid long blond hair is cascading down her back in perfect waves, as usual. She's wearing a designer blouse and tailored pants, her outfit a stark contrast to Mickey's hippie chic aesthetic.

"Sorry I'm late, Mickey," Mikaela says with an arrogant toss of her hair, her voice dripping with false sweetness. "I've been busy making real progress on my documentary." She cuts her dagger eyes at me as she says this.

Mickey smiles indulgently, clearly taken in by Mikaela's charm. "No worries, Mikaela. Take your time."

"Barf," says Lucía softly, and I do not disagree.

Mikaela saunters over to her desk, shooting me a smug glance as she passes. I resist the urge to roll my eyes, knowing that engaging with her will only give her the satisfaction she craves.

Instead, I focus on Mickey, mustering up the courage to speak my truth. "Mickey," I begin, my voice steady despite the butterflies fluttering in my stomach. I fight the urge to raise my hand. He refuses to let students call him Mister anything, so much so that I've forgotten his last name. He also discourages us from raising our hands, because he says that kind of thing is autocratic. "I need to talk to you about the documentary assignment."

Mickey's eyebrows shoot up in surprise. "Of course, Grace. What's on your mind?"

I take a deep breath, steeling myself for what comes next. "I … I don't think I can do the assignment," I admit, my words tumbling out in a rush. "I'm still recovering from my accident, and the thought of that much work right now … it's just not something I think I can manage."

Mickey's expression softens, his gaze filled with understanding. "I see," he says gently. "Take all the time you need, Grace. Your health comes first."

I nod gratefully, relieved that Mickey is so understanding. Turning to Blake and Lucía, I see the concern in their eyes, their silent support giving me the strength to carry on.

As class draws to a close, Mikaela can't resist one final dig, shooting me a triumphant smirk as she packs up her belongings. "You know," she says, "my research tells me some people in your position never recover their full mental capacities. Not that you had many to begin with, but you know what I'm saying. Or maybe you don't?"

She's trying to get me to react. In the past, like a month ago, I totally would have. But now, it's just very clear to me, at a gut level, that she's a damaged and unhappy soul.

"I look forward to seeing your film," I tell her. "Sounds like you're putting a lot of effort into it. Good job."

She scoffs, and her little sycophant, Lexi, snickers along with her.

As I gather my things and head for the door, I see a dark shadow slinking after Mikaela. I have never seen anything like it before, and it spooks me to my core. It looks lupine, like the long shadow of a Doberman pinscher as the sun sets, flowing across the walls and floor like oil. I get a terrible feeling in the center of my gut. I just know—I have no idea how—that something terrible is coming for Mikaela.

"Be careful, Mikaela," I tell her. I mean it kindly.

Mikaela misunderstands and spins around to glare at me. "Is that a threat, Martínez?"

"No, not at all," I say. "What I meant to say was have a good day. Like, 'take care,' but it came out wrong. Lightning on the brain. You know?"

Mercifully, I make it through the rest of the day without her attacking me, and, thanks to the Lorica, without seeing Bobby from the theater. At some point I'm probably going to have to deal with him again, but right now I can only handle one needy spiorad at a time.

Later that afternoon, as I stand behind the counter of the Shadowbound bookstore, lost in working on another script, the arrival of an unexpected visitor jolts me to attention. My father is standing right in front of me, his eyes heavy with sorrow, his shoulders weighed down by the burden of unspoken truths. It looks like he hasn't shaved since the last time I saw him, and his hair is in dire need of a comb. His eyes are rimmed with red, bloodshot and weary.

"Grace," he begins, his voice strained with emotion. He looks around the store and sees that, as usual, it's without customers. "We need to talk."

I nod silently, gesturing for him to take a seat at the small wooden table tucked away in the corner of the store. Milagros, ever the curious companion, hovers nearby with her pug Platero in tow, his milky eyes trained on us with an intensity that belies his geriatric canine nature.

"Grace," he begins, his voice quivering, "I ... I want you to know that I've asked for a separation from Candi."

My father's words spill out like a dam breaking.

I freeze, my heart pounding in my chest as I absorb his words. "What?" I manage to choke out, my throat tight with disbelief.

He nods solemnly, his eyes brimming with unshed tears. "I didn't do it because of you. So please don't feel like this is your fault. It's been a long time coming, sweetheart. Things between us ... they're just not working out. She was ... a mistake. A reaction."

"To what?" I ask.

"To things with your mom. Candi felt like a safe place. But the past few days have made it very clear to me that she wasn't. Especially not for you."

A lump forms in my throat as I struggle to process his confession. "But ... why?" I whisper, my voice scarcely audible above the sudden rush of blood in my ears.

"It was her," he continues, his tone heavy with regret. "Candi's the one who insisted on destroying your mother's diaries. Not me. I need you to understand that."

My breath catches in my throat at his words, the truth hitting me like, well, like a bolt of lightning. "Seriously?"

He nods, his expression pained. "I never even knew the new homeowners tried to reach me," he admits, his voice filled with remorse. "She never told me. I didn't know those dairies existed. She should have told me, but she's ... well, without getting into it too much, I'll just say she's possessive and jealous."

"Jealous of a dead woman?" I ask.

"Sadly, yes. I … I should have been there for you, Grace. I should have protected you. I've been so confused."

Tears prick at the corners of my eyes as his words sink in, the weight of his confession bearing down on me like a leaden weight. "Dad," I whisper, my voice trembling with emotion, "I … I don't know what to say."

He reaches out, his hand shaking a little as he gently squeezes mine. "I'm so sorry, Grace," he murmurs, his eyes brimming with tears. "You were right. I changed to please Candi. I felt like I was failing as a husband and father before, and I tried to be someone else. Someone who'd fit in better with whatever this society is becoming."

"Ew," I say, and he cracks a small smile. "Fitting in is overrated."

"I should have been a better father to you. But after all the drama with your mother … I loved your mother so much, Grace. I have never loved anyone more. But she had a lot of pain. She had so much damage, from what she went through with her upbringing, and things got … complicated, at the end."

"Why did you marry her if she was like that?" I ask.

"I wanted to save her," he says, and his voice sounds smaller than I've ever heard a voice sound. "She was beautiful. And so smart. Talented."

I swallow hard, struggling to find the words to express the whirlwind of emotions coursing through me.

"She miscarried, by the way," I say. "And she said you sided with the police."

"That was her interpretation of it. We were having other problems," he says. "I was confused. I wasn't sure. There were other reasons I was never sure what she was saying was true, but I don't want to get into that right now. I should have believed her. But I didn't. I guess I didn't really understand how dangerous it could get for her, if it had been an abortion, with what's happening in this state ... with the new laws. You don't think, after so many years of having reproductive freedom, that anyone is actually going to enforce something like these new laws?"

"Yeah, well, they do," I say. "And they did. And they are. Plus, you cheated on her."

Tears well in his eyes as he bares his soul and the scars of past mistakes. He blames himself for my mother's suicide and for my own use of drugs ... and the lightning strike. He speaks of the struggles of their marriage, the financial problems, the tumultuous storms that battered their fragile union.

Listening to his words, a sense of clarity washes over me. He's speaking of two imperfect beings navigating a world fraught with challenges, seeking solace in the arms of love, yet stumbling in the darkness of their own shortcomings. If I hold being a screwed-up human against my own father—knowing that even I, who I like to think of as a decent person, kissed Cameron in a moment of confusion and pain despite having committed to Blake the day before—I am a huge hypocrite.

"It's okay," I tell him. "I forgive you."

Milagros comes over and tells me she's going to close the store early, and it's okay if I want to leave fifteen minutes before I'm scheduled to clock out. She promises to pay me for the missed time and pats my father kindly on his shoulder.

Together, my dad and I leave the confines of the bookstore and return to our once-shared home. He tells me that Candi has opted to stay with her parents until the house sells. We can live here until then. Once it sells, he tells me, we'll get a place of our own. Candi's absence looms large, in a good way, unlike my mother's absence, which looms large in a bad way. I feel like I can finally breathe. Jacob, too, is absent, and I wonder what's going to become of him and Lucía. Will he and I remain friends, if that's what we were in the first place?

In the quiet solitude of my room, I am startled to find Mohammad waiting for me. His spectral form leaning against the wall, casual as a summer day.

"Hey," I say, "I thought you'd have been set free when I figured out who killed you. Or is that not how this whole thing works?"

He lifts a brow in curiosity.

"It was Smitty, by the way," I say. "Steven nerdy effing Smith. Your amateur radio club buddy. And chess club buddy. But you kind of knew he had it in him, right?"

Mohammed offers up a half-grin, cynical yet amused, like maybe he knew this all along.

I am deeply confused. "I thought spiorads linger on earth because they have unfinished business here." All he does is shrug as though to say some do, some don't.

"If you aren't lingering to resolve your murder, why are you here?"

He points to my speaker and it screeches on. Loud. The song sounds like something you'd hear in a nightclub on an island off the coast of Greece. I look at my phone to see what the song is. "Technologic," by Daft Punk. I can't help but tap my toe to this one.

"Your taste is improving," I tell him. "You must be hanging around a cool girl or something."

He points at his ear, and again at the speaker.

I understand from this he wants me to shut the hell up and just listen to the lyrics. He starts the song over again.

"I don't get it," I say. "Do you want credit for QEE? Because I'm pretty sure you'll get it. There's a reporter who's about to tell the whole world about what happened to you."

A new song pops on: "I Don't Care," by Fall Out Boy. It keeps skipping over the same lyric: "I don't care what you think."

I still don't understand and tell him so.

He gives me another song, this one for little kids, called "Inventions Everywhere," by some group called The StoryBots.

He looks at me and opens his arms to his sides in a gesture of, "Do you get it now?"

"Are you trying to invent something?" I ask.

He grins hugely.

I take this as a yes. "Okay, so what are you trying to invent?"

A new and very obscure song comes on, by an Irish singer, called "If the Dead Could Speak." I don't need to hear the song to understand what he's trying to say. But he seems adamant about me listening anyway.

This catches me off guard, his true purpose for lingering in this liminal space is a revelation I never anticipated. "Are you trying to invent technology so that the dead can speak to the living?" I ask.

Mohammad grins widely and gives me two thumbs up.

"You can do that?" I ask, in astonishment.

He plays snippets of various songs to spell something out. I write down the letters on a piece of scrap paper on my desk. They are R-O-H-P-O-L. I google this word on my desktop computer, and the only thing that comes up is a link to a server in Bangladesh with the same name and a bunch of articles about the date-rape drug, Rohypnol.

"You really need to work on your skill with naming your inventions, dude," I say.

He gives me a "Yeah, whatever, just get on with it" gesture.

I click on the server link in Bangladesh, follow the prompts that come up and finally get to a page with what appears to be a fledgling new app. There is a download button.

"You want me to get this?" I ask.

He points at my phone. I send myself the link, following Mohammad's guidance as he leads me through the intricate steps of downloading ROHPOL. As the digital interface materializes before me, a sense of wonder washes over me, mingling with a profound sense of disbelief.

In the flickering glow of the screen, I find myself face to face with the impossible: a simple chat box that appears to be a rudimentary bridge between the living and the dead, forged in the crucible of this genius spirit's innovation and ingenuity.

I type: **Hi?**

Three dots appear, as happens when someone texts.

Hi, Grace, comes the answer. **I like your red shirt.**

I am, indeed, wearing a red shirt. I look up at Mohammad, and he cracks the kind of grin mad scientists get when their inventions work.

"How the hell are you doing this?" I ask.

He points to the app. These words appear: **Quantum entanglements, cloud-based consciousness repositories, machine learning, theoretical physics.**

"How do I know it's actually you?"

The chat box fills up. **Who else would know that you dislike the Beastie Boys and told me to update my fucking playlist? Good advice, by the way.**

With each keystroke, each whispered word, I feel the divide between worlds begin to blur, as if reality itself is bending to accommodate our shared existence.

"So, this is why you've stayed? This death app?"

Does it always take you this long to understand obvious things, Grace?

"So, you're the one who's been using my soon-to-be former stenchmom's credit cards, right? Why didn't say anything when she yelled at me for that?"

Sorry. Candi kind of deserved it.

I laugh out loud. "This is amazing! How can I help? Besides suggesting a new name."

RohPol is a bridge between worlds, in Pashto.

"With all due respect, most people in the world won't know that."

It's still got bugs. It glitches out after a few exchanges. I'm working on it. It didn't work at all till I met you. I think your caring about me made it stronger.

"You sound like my hippie teacher, Mickey. He always says love is an energetic force field, and students always shoot spit wads at him for it."

Give hippies a chance.

"This is incredible. Will people be able to reach anyone they want?"

There has to be a mutual desire for communication.

"Damn," I say, thinking my mom, who just wants me to let her go, is still going to be out of reach, even with this technology.

You're the one who taught me the importance of consent, remember?

"Shut up, wiseass," I say.

The whole point of this app is I don't want to shut up.

"Touché," I say.

You love me, though.

The screen starts to glitch out.

"You're right," I tell him. "I do love you. Even if you'd be an old man right now if you had lived."

I love you, too, kid.

After this, the app freezes, then disappears from my phone, which has suddenly gotten too hot to hold. I drop it like the proverbial hot potato.

Mohammad grins, then puts a finger over his lips, as though to tell me not to tell the world about his newest and most groundbreaking invention.

"Your secret's safe with me," I say.

Chapter Twenty-Four

The following day after school, Blake and Lucía come with me to my follow-up neurological appointment with Doctor Kapoor. My father was going to take me, but he texted me to say he has to attend some emergency top-management meeting at NexaWave. I suspect it has something to do with Tish Adoeoye's investigative reporting for the *Austin Alternative Times*. Blake was happy to drive me and Lucía.

As we sit in the sterile waiting room of the hospital, anticipation churns in my stomach like a whirlpool, swirling with equal parts hope and worry. Today marks a milestone in my journey of recovery: a neurology appointment with Doctor Kapoor, the final hurdle standing between me and the freedom to drive again. I've been nervous all day, mostly because of the death app. I can't believe Mohammad invented it. It's the most incredible thing ever created and could change everything for our species and planet. For instance, no one will have to answer for Jesus anymore, when someone asks, "What would Jesus do?" We'll be able to just ask him directly. What will all the millionaire psychopath pastors do once that's possible?

The minutes tick by slowly, each second stretching into an eternity as I wait to be called. When my name finally echoes through the cavernous halls, I rise from my seat with a determination to do well on the tests. I know I shouldn't think of medical tests like school, but I do. I want to excel. Get an A.

Doctor Kapoor's office is a sanctuary of order amid the chaos of the hospital. I'm expecting her to look happy to see me, but she's pretty subdued. Professional, I suppose. I remember now that she's humorless and painfully normal. As she conducts the neurological exam with meticulous precision, I hold my breath, willing my body to cooperate, to prove that I am indeed on the road to recovery.

To my immense relief, the results are better than I could have hoped for. My reflexes are sharp, my cognitive function intact. With a smile of genuine warmth, Doctor Kapoor declares me fit to drive. She writes as much in a note for my father.

Leaving the neurology department, I'm buoyed by the exhilaration of my newfound freedom and impulsively decide to visit the ICU. I want to thank the kind nurse who guided me through the darkest days of my recovery and let him know I'm doing well with my newfound skills. I'm excited for him to meet my friends, and for them to meet him, to know that I'm not the only person other than Milagros who can see spiorads. When I inquire about Kilian, the Irish nurse who once offered me solace in the depths of despair, I'm met with a solemn shake of the head.

"There's no nurse here by that name," says the person behind the counter.

"Are you sure? I was just here like a little more than a week ago, and I'm almost sure he was my overnight nurse."

The receptionist types something and then stares at her computer for a bit before announcing, astoundingly, "Well, there *was* an Irish traveling nurse named Kilian who worked here, but that was ten years ago."

"I'm sure he still works here," I say.

"I don't think so," she says, looking at me with a puzzled expression.

"Can you please check again?" I say.

"Miss, I'm sorry, but the nurse you're asking about passed away ten years ago in a car accident."

Stunned by this revelation, I find myself grappling with the implications. If Kilian wasn't living when he appeared to me, he sure as hell seemed like it. He'd found a way to speak directly to me, something Mohammad hasn't even figured out yet. Something only La Llorona has been able to do.

Then it hits me. Kilian himself told me that one's guardian angel, one's ancestral spirit, will show up for you in the form that you most need to see them in that moment, in order for you to feel safe. Carl Sagan at the gates of the afterlife, to make the materialist former atheist in me feel safe and Kilian, the nurse, in order to help me in the middle of the night in the ICU.

With newfound clarity, I leave the hospital behind, blown away by everything I've learned, and all that I still do not understand. We head to my house, because no one's there and Blake has edibles. Our refrigerator and pantry are full of snacks for when the munchies come on. I perform the Lorica spell so that I can focus on my friends instead of Mohammad and Charlie. Despite this, I get a ping on my phone that I've never heard before. I see with a shock that the ROHPOL app is back, and it has a little icon to indicate I have a message. I pretend this is nothing unusual, getting texts from dead people, and check it.

You can tell them about it. Beta testers.

I text back: **Can you see me right now, even though I did the Lorica?**

I invented QEE and ROHPOL, what do you think?

So, I tell Blake and Lucía about the death bridge app and show it to them. Lucía believes me one-hundred-percent immediately, but Blake, true to form, is going to take some convincing.

"Isn't that the kind of thing you were going to be writing for your internship at NexaWave?" asks Blake. "Chatbots that sound human?"

"But it's *actually literally* Mohammad," I say.

"How do you know it's not just a sophisticated algorithm?" asks Blake.

"Dude, stop being such a jerk," says Lucía.

I like Lucía.

I show them the screen, and as they're looking at it, Mohammad texts: **Hi, Blake. Hi, Lucía. Thanks for being there for Grace. Those cookies look delicious.**

"Um," says Blake. "How did it do that? Is it accessing your camera somehow?"

"No," I say. "Mohammad can see us. The Lorica apparently only prevents me from seeing him and the other spirits, but not the other way around."

"He wants us to test the app out?" says Lucía.

Yes. A new window pops up, and it contains a typical search bar.

"Do we just enter the name of someone we want to reach?" I ask.

Yes.

We all look at each other. I sense they know I want to reach my mother. I mean, why wouldn't they know that? We went to my old house for that purpose.

"No," I say, "I can't deal with her right now."

"How about Bobby?" asks Blake.

Look who finally believes us.

"That's creepy as heck," says Blake as he reads the screen.

"Only creepy if you make it creepy," I say. "How about Arthur? Your great-grandpa with pigeon crap on his slacks."

Blake looks scared.

"You could find out what he did with the family jewels," I suggest.

"Hmm," says Blake.

It helps if the person closest to the deceased enters the name. Full name and death date, if known.

Blake takes my phone and enters his great-grandfather's information in the search bar. A typical rainbow spinning wheel appears as the app conducts the search, a minute or so later we hear a cheerful chime. An icon of a green telephone pops up with the words, "Connection successful!"

Hello? Shalom? Is this thing on?

Blake texts: This is Blake Abrams, Janice Levinson's son. Who's this?

What do you mean who is this? You called me! This is Arthur Isaac Kleinberg.

Can we talk?

What do you mean can we talk? We're not talking? Of course, we can talk, my dear grandson. It's so good to hear from you.

I hope you're well.

Eh. I've been better. But you know how it goes.

Yeah. Sorry to hear that. I was wondering if you could tell me where you hid the family jewels before you passed away.

Ah, the family jewels. Such precious memories they hold. You have a good heart, my boy, seeking to preserve our family's legacy.

Thanks, Grandpa. I just want to make sure they're kept safe.

Wise beyond your years, just like your beautiful mother. The jewels are buried beneath the old oak tree in the backyard of the house in Brooklyn, where we used to play as

children. Your great-aunt Estelle still lives there. Look for the blue rose bush nearby. Dig three paces north of that.
Got it. Thanks, Grandpa.
שלום בני. זכור תמיד. (Shalom, my son. Remember always.)

The app glitches out, then poofs off the screen, and the phone becomes too hot to hold, like it did the first time I used it. Blake sets the phone down and just stares at it for a long time, blinking back tears. I can see that his hands are trembling. He uses his own phone to call his mother and ask for his great-aunt Estelle's number, making up a lie about wanting to ask her about something that he remembered from a visit to her house when he was little. Then he calls Estelle and puts the call on speaker. He asks her if there's a blue rose bush in her backyard. She tells him that there is. He asks her if she can dig under the oak tree next to it. She tells him she's 89 years old and can't dig her stockings out of the drawer in the mornings, but she'll ask his second cousin Joshua to do it when he comes to visit. Blake ends the call and looks like he's ... well ... you know ... Seen a ghost.

"What?" says Lucía. "Did you just not believe Grace until this instant or something?"

"I believed her, theoretically," he says, carefully. "But it's a different thing when one of these spirits is talking directly to you, and they know things about you and your family there should be no way for them to know, unless this is legit."

"Welcome to my world," I say and throw my arms around him and kiss him on the cheek.

He hugs me back, harder than I think he ever has.

Chapter Twenty-Five

It's Wednesday morning, I'm driving myself to school for the first time since my lightning strike, and it's totally normal except that there's a dark van following me.

The dark van.

At first I think I'm just being jumpy, but this is not my imagination. When I swerve, the van swerves. When I turn, it turns. I glance into the rearview mirror, and my heart lurches with a sudden jolt of fear. The dark van is not giving up. It's lurking in the shadows like a jaguar stalking a small soft rabbity thing.

"Stay calm," I tell myself. "Call 9-1-1."

I fumble through my backpack with my right hand while steering with my left, desperately searching with my fingers for my phone. I'm horrified, I don't have it! I remember then. I was messing around with the death app till late last night. The app kept draining all the battery life out of my phone and leaving the device four million degrees hot. So, I left it charging on my desk.

Panic tightens its grip around my chest as I accelerate, weaving through traffic with reckless abandon, desperate to shake off the ominous presence that shadows my every move. I keep taking reckless turns in the style of my father trying to escape from a reporter. Suddenly, I find myself heading down a short and very quiet road that dead-ends in the woods. This is not as unusual as it might seem. Half the streets in Austin do this. I try to turn around, using the K-turn skills I learned in driver's ed, but I'm too slow. The van zooms up to within inches of the front of my car. I open my door and start to run, but with a sickening screech of tires, the van lurches forward, blocking my path with ruthless precision. Before I can react, two masked figures emerge from the side door of the van, their movements swift and predatory as they grab me with chilling intent.

The world spins in a dizzying whirl of chaos as I am dragged, screaming, into the van. The doors close with a quiet whomp that feels soundproof and terrifyingly final. I'm quickly blindfolded, gagged and bound, my pleas for mercy drowned out by the deafening roar of fear that echoes through my mind. Thrown into the back of the van like a sack of potatoes, I'm engulfed by darkness, my world reduced to the suffocating smother of captivity. I feel the van start to move. I curl up in a fetal position and, to my surprise, I start to pray. I pray to God, to Carl Sagan, to Kilian, to La Llorona, to Mohammad, to Arthur, to Charlie, even to Bobby, to anyone and everyone who might be able to help me now. Hours pass in a blur of terror and uncertainty as the van hurtles through the world, its destination unknown.

Finally, with a bone-jarring thud, the van comes to a halt and I hear its doors thrown open with brutal force and I'm dragged out. I smell pine and dirt as I'm dragged through what feels to me like a forest floor, over leaves, twigs and stones. I hear latches and creaking hinges, and then I'm shoved into some sort of shelter. My blindfold and gag are removed, and I start to scream for help but am immediately punched in the face.

"Keep quiet," says a familiar male voice. "Just do what you're told."

The bindings are removed from my wrists and I'm tied up again, this time to a cold metal chair. As my eyes adjust to the thick, mildewed darkness, I see that I'm in some sort of shed.

There are tools neatly arranged, and a woodworking bench. Saws. Hammers. Nails. Wrenches. My mouth is very dry, and I have never been so afraid. The two men leave, and I am alone, locked away in the darkness inside the musty old building, left to grapple with the chilling certainty of my impending doom.

The hours stretch on, and night comes. I'm freezing, trapped, thirsty and utterly alone. I struggle to free myself from the bindings, but they're too tight. Fear overrides sleep, and somewhere before dawn I'm comforted by the vision of La Llorona, who appears in her usual snaking smoking way. She becomes manifest and comes to sit down beside me with a patient, reassuring look on her face. I get the sense that she's concerned about me but not worried.

As the sun comes up, a familiar voice cuts through the silence outside. The sound of it feels like a lifeline in this abyss until I realize whose voice it is. It belongs to Smitty. The door opens, and in he steps, arrogant and cruel, and comes over to stand in front of me, his eyes ablaze with malice as he revels in the agony of my captivity.

"You thought you could outsmart me, Grace," he sneers, his voice dripping with contempt. "You underestimated me. Most people know better than to do that. The ones who do not know better, well, things don't end well for them."

He smiles and brings the screen of his phone up to my face to show me a photograph. It's the reporter, Tish Adoeoye, and she appears to be very badly hurt, maybe even dead.

"She made the mistake of thinking journalism still exists. Silly girl. Her copy editors called my legal team to fact-check a ridiculous article she was putting together about me, and they let me know who she was. So, we had a nice long visit to find out where she got all that information. She sang like a bird for us at the end. I have to say, I wasn't surprised that all the threads led me back to you. As I said to your father, I always knew there was something special about you, Grace."

I'm paralyzed by fear as he looms over me, his presence a palpable menace that threatens to consume me whole. He strolls causally to the tools and selects a screwdriver. A very long, very large screwdriver.

"This'll do nicely," he says. He turns back to me with a terrible smile on his face.

Just as all hope seems lost, I hear the sounds of police car sirens and a police loudspeaker, then of people running outside. Smitty's face falls in annoyance. He returns the screwdriver to its place and opens the door of the shed to look outside.

"God dammit," he says. He closes the front door and hurries through a back one on the opposite side of the structure and, just as quickly as he appeared, he is gone. I consider screaming for help, but I'm not sure what's going on outside. I stay quiet and wait.

My salvation arrives several minutes later in the form of a female police officer who, upon finding me, calls for assistance. Another officer arrives, this one male, and together they remove the bindings.

As I try to catch my breath, the first officer asks me, "Are you all right, sweetheart?" Her gaze softens as she takes in my disheveled appearance.

I nod quickly, my heart still pounding. "I'm fine," I manage to say, even if the words feel hollow to my own ears. "But Smitty got away," I add, the frustration evident in my voice. "The famous tech dude. He's the one who brought me here. It's a whole thing. He's a killer."

Her brow furrows in response as she turns to her colleague.

"He went out the back door," I explain, hoping they can catch him before he disappears.

The second officer nods, determination etched on his face as he rushes to follow Smitty's trail. Meanwhile, Officer Reyna

López, as she introduces herself, offers me a comforting hand. "Come on, let's get you somewhere safe," she says as she gently leads me out of the shed toward a waiting ambulance. Sure enough, we're somewhere in the hill country, in the woods.

As paramedics help me onto a gurney and start IV fluids and give me a bottle of water, relief floods over me. I'm safe. I'm not going to die again—at least, not here and not because of Smitty. Things only get better when I see Lucía running toward me from the passenger side of a police car, one of like 15 of them that are here.

"Grace!" she cries. I can tell she wants to hug me, and I sure as heck want to hug her, but the paramedics keep us apart for the moment.

She meets my eyes with a mixture of worry and relief, her presence a reassuring anchor in the chaos of the moment. The inside of the ambulance smells faintly of stale coffee and fast food, a stark contrast to the tension thick in the air. The sound of police radios crackling with static fills the silence, punctuated by the occasional siren wailing in the distance.

"What the hell are you even doing here?" I ask her.

Lucía lifts a phone and wags it a little. It takes me a moment to realize the phone she's holding belongs to me. I still don't understand how her having my phone would have led to her finding me here, so I crinkle my brow in confusion.

"Death app," she mouths. "La Llorona."

"You're kidding me," I say.

A little while later, when the paramedics clear me to go sit with Lucía in the back of Officer López's police car, Lucía tells me what's going on. "So, the cops found your car abandoned in the middle of the road, and some lady who was walking her dog in the area said she saw a young girl abducted from it. I had been texting you and knew your phone wasn't even turned on, so in the off chance you left it at home, I went to look for it. It was on your desk. I opened the app and put in La Llorona's real name and the general dates of her life and death. And there she was! She knew exactly where you were. Told me the coordinates on a map. I told the police we got an anonymous call, because ..."

"Yeah, I know. No one believes ghost stories."

"Right."

"Thank you so much," I say.

"Don't thank me. Thank Mohammad."

"I will," I say.

I can't believe that Mohammad's invention, La Llorona and my best and most dramatic friend literally just saved my freakin' life.

Chapter Twenty-Six

Several weeks later, the Bird Box auditorium buzzes with anticipation as the lights dim, casting a hush over the eager audience gathered for the evening screening of our documentary film projects. Everyone looks nice, even Mikaela Hoffmaster, who stands near the back of the auditorium in an understated black dress, with her hair in an elegant up-do. To my surprise, she nods a friendly hello to me, and even smiles. I am shocked that her best friend Lexie is not standing with her, as they are pretty much Tweedle Dee and Tweedle Dum. Lexi is sitting alone, scrolling through her phone. I wonder if they had a fight.

None of my business.

Anyway, as it turns out, I *did* end up turning in a documentary. After the police found me in the woods, they were able to arrest Smitty. He was charged with all kinds of crimes, not the least of which was murder. Tish Adoeoye of the *Austin Alternative Times* was found bound and gagged in a neighboring cabin, and she and I worked on the final story together. Tish did the print version, and I did the video. We left out the parts about me seeing ghosts, and I pretended to have learned about Mohammad only because I was interested in knowing more about the people who used to live in the house my soon-to-be-former stepmother had torn down to build her dream house.

We'll all find out tonight how our films did. For what it's worth, I have not performed the Lorica this evening. I had a heart-to-heart talk with little Bobby Chavez through the death app to let him know he needed to be on his best behavior tonight, and he agreed. Discreet as usual, La Llorona has made herself invisible, too, which I now know she prefers to do because, as she told me through the death app, her job is to help me to shine.

Students and their families fill the seats, their faces illuminated by the soft glow of the screen, anticipation palpable in the air. I'm perched on the edge of my seat, feeling a mix of excitement and nerves. Blake and Lucía sit with me, and I wave a little to my dad, who has come with Jacob and Cameron. They smile and wave back. My dad told me that he will always consider Jacob a son, no matter what happens with his mother. Candi with an i has made no such overtures to me, and it's just as well, because I would not want her to. I see Tish Adoeoye sneak into the auditorium, and she goes to stand along the back wall, not too far from Mikaela Hoffmaster. She makes eye contact with me and gives me a supportive thumb's up.

Lucía and I are dressed to impress, each of us donning our own unique style. Lucía wears a flowing skirt adorned with intricate patterns, a nod to her Filippina heritage, paired with a bold red blouse that exudes confidence. I've opted for a vintage-inspired dress, its floral print reminiscent of a bygone era, a leather jacket and combat boots for a touch of my usual Gracian edge. Blake is dressed like Blake would dress for a nice event— in something you might find at J. Crew. I should note, however, that he has a new antique tie pin; it was among the many items found in a metal box in the backyard of his great-aunt Estelle's house in Brookyln, three paces from the blue rose bush. He looks adorable, and I love him.

As the first film begins to play, the room falls into a reverent silence. Each project unfolds like a tapestry of creativity and storytelling, weaving together the diverse perspectives of our class.

It's not until Lucía's documentary takes center stage that the true magic happens. Her film, a poignant exploration of the real historical story of my ancestral spirit guide and the ghost who saved my life, La Llorona, stuns the audience with its raw emotion and unflinching honesty. I watch with bated breath as the screen comes to life, the vivid imagery and haunting soundtrack drawing me in. Lucía stars in the docu-drama, playing La Llorona with heartbreaking excellence.

As the credits roll, the room erupts into applause, the sound echoing off the walls in a symphony of celebration. I turn to Lucía, my eyes shining with pride, and squeeze her hand in silent congratulations as everyone rises to their feet.

Blake's film receives just as powerful a response, but in a comedic and heartwarming way, as he drags his cranky Bubbe all over Austin in search of the most authentic Jewish food, interspersing the quest with a well-documented history of the Jewish community. The best part is whenever his Bubbe bites into a piece of round bread trying to pretend its a bagel, and she says, "You call this a bagel? This isn't a bagel! This is garbage!" He also gets a standing ovation the way Lucía did, and to everyone's delight, his Bubbe is in attendance, along with the rest of Blake's family. Even his great-aunt Esther and his second-cousin Joshua have come. When Blake's Bubbe stands up to wave at everyone, the crowd goes absolutely bat-crud crazy, and I suspect someone is going to eventually make a T-shirt of her frowning, holding a piece of bread with a hole cut in the middle of it, saying, "You call this a bagel?"

Mine is the last film to be screened, and I cringe as it comes on because everyone has already seen Tish's story in the newspaper, as well as the many national and international news stories it spawned. They know what's coming, and I've become something of a local celebrity. Smitty was found, arrested and jailed, and the rights to Mohammad's QEE invention were transferred to his closest living relative, Safia. Warwick Blackwater was unfortunately outed against his will, collateral damage in the much bigger story, which I have mixed feelings about. He's lost most of his conservative fan base and will probably lose the next election, but he told Cameron he feels free now and isn't angry at me.

Until now, no one has heard my version of the story, told in my own words. Honestly, they probably never will, either, because the story I present here leaves out the most important element in all of it, which is to say, the dead people, and the fact that I can see them. I'll let the world know about it eventually, but right now I am pretty sure they're just not ready. Instead, I tell of researching the kid who died in my house, just because, I say, ever since my mother ended her own life I've had a bit of an obsession with suicide. I go on to say that as I started to learn more about Mohammad Ahmadi, I realized that he was the victim of foul play, and that through a series of eerie coincidences, I was able to figure out what actually happened to him. Little did I know that doing so would put my life in danger, but I am happy to have made it out alive.

I, too, get a standing ovation.

The all-star panel of film experts, including the luminous Sandra Bullock, takes the stage to announce the winners. Sandra looks radiant in a sleek black pantsuit, her hair styled in loose waves that cascade over her shoulders.

"Now, I've had the pleasure of watching each of these incredible films," Sandra begins, her voice carrying a warmth and sincerity that immediately captures the audience's attention. "And let me tell you, the talent on display tonight is nothing short of extraordinary."

I listen intently as she speaks, her words a testament to the power of storytelling to inspire change and challenge perceptions. Her speech is equal parts insightful and inspiring, each word imbued with a sense of passion and purpose.

"And now, without further ado," Sandra continues, her eyes twinkling with excitement, "I am thrilled to announce the winner of this year's documentary film competition ..."

The tension in the room is palpable as Sandra pauses for dramatic effect, the anticipation reaching a fever pitch. And then, with a smile that lights up the entire auditorium, she announces my name as the first-place winner.

The room erupts into applause once more, the sound thunderous as I make my way to the stage to accept my medal. Lucía, Blake and my dad watch, the latter with tears in his eyes, overwhelmed with pride for me, even though my documentary and Tish's news story cost him his job. He told me it was for the best, because he misses being a public defender and plans to return to that work, even though it doesn't pay as well.

As the evening wears on, the awards continue to be handed out: Blake's documentary earns him second place, and Lucía's documentary ties with his. Meanwhile, Mikaela Hoffmaster's surprisingly poignant exploration of the neurological effects of being struck by lightning takes third.

As the applause dies down, a sense of unease settles over the crowd when Mikaela fails to show up to collect her medal. I turn to look at her, standing against the back wall, and I motion to her, to come forward. She just stares at me with the saddest look in her eyes, and I realize, terribly, that I can see the wall behind her. Through her. As in, Mikaela Hoffmaster is transparent.

"Do you see Mikaela standing back there, against the wall near the exit?" I ask Blake and Lucía. They both follow the line of my gaze and tell me that, no, they don't see her.

"Oh, God," I say.

"Do you see her?" asks Blake.

I nod, and feel sick, my heart racing as I realize the truth. Mikaela is only visible to me.

"She's not here," calls out Lexi. "I don't know where she is. I've been texting but she doesn't answer."

"Oh, okay," says Sandra. "Well, congratulations to Mikaela anyway! What a heartfelt film she made. Now, moving right along …"

Dread washes over me as I come to terms with the fact that there may be another murder to solve, after all.